Cassocked Savage

The life of Patrick Brontë

Cenarth Fox

Cassocked Savage

First published in 2016 by Fox Plays
www.foxplays.com
www.cenfoxbooks.com

ISBN 978 0 949175 09 9

Cover design by Gerald Hapeman

To
Allen and Bronwyn
for an introduction to books

To
Howell and Margie
for an introduction to Haworth

Chapter 1

'THROW IT OVERBOARD, NOW!' screamed a sailor. The crew member holding the bundle prepared to heave it into the Irish Sea.

'No!' screamed the woman as she raced across the deck. Others ran too; more sailors, the woman's husband and the ship's captain. The woman got there first and grabbed the bundle.

'Get off,' yelled the sailor. 'You're the jinx.' He clutched the bundle with one arm and tried pushing the woman away with the other.

She slipped and fell but shouted, 'Hugh, stop him!'

The captain and the woman's husband grabbed the bundle and wrestled it free. The bundle was a child, alive, terrified and whimpering. Not that you could tell as the filthy youngster was dressed in rags and behaving like some wild animal. Others sailors moved in and secured the human cargo. Hugh helped his wife to stand. Bríghid Brunty was furious.

'I'll report this to the authorities. You were going to murder that child.'

'Please, madam,' said the captain, 'the child is safe and was only being warned about the dangers of being a stowaway.'

'What did he mean about my wife being a jinx?' snapped Hugh.

'Please, sir,' said the captain, 'bring your wife to my cabin.'

'And make sure that child is kept safe,' threatened Mrs Brunty.

The couple sat in the cabin and the captain tried to explain.

'There are still many sailors, madam, who believe a woman on board a ship brings bad luck. And yes, I know it is superstitious nonsense.'

'Forget that,' said Mrs Brunty, 'what about the child?'

'We often find stowaways. Poor, desperate people hide their children on board before we leave Liverpool and hope the child will be rescued and find a better life in Ireland.'

'And will it?' continued Mrs Brunty.

'Once we reach Drogheda, the child will be handed to the harbourmaster, who will send the boy to the Foundling Hospital in Dublin.'

'You don't care,' snorted Mrs Brunty.

'Madam, I run a cargo ship for cattle traders like your husband. This is not a rescue service for abandoned children.'

'Then we will take the child.'

Hugh was shocked. 'My dear, it's thirty miles to Dublin and ...'

Bríghid Brunty swept from the cabin causing her husband to hurry after her. She reached the stowaway and addressed the sailors.

'The captain has given me the responsibility of caring for the child.' The men looked at their captain who nodded. Bríghid took control.

When the ship docked in Drogheda, the Bruntys stood on the quay with Mrs Brunty firmly holding the child's hand.

'Dublin is too far,' said Hugh. 'It'll be dark soon.'

'Then we'll take him home,' said his wife, and she and the child climbed onto the cart for the trip to the Brunty farm. Yet again, Hugh played catch-up.

He assumed his wife would take the child to the local authorities tomorrow or the day after. But until then, there was no way the caring mother would allow the stowaway to roam the streets of Ireland, creating mischief or worse, suffering, even starving to death.

Not surprisingly, the trip to Dublin didn't eventuate. The authorities were never told about the urchin, as the Bruntys bypassed everyone, unofficially adopted the boy, and kept him in their home on their farm by the River Boyne. Overnight, their family grew by one.

The Brunty children, brothers Brendan, Michael and Sean, and sisters Bree and Mary, worried. Apart from looking wretched, the child was swarthy with eyes that threatened, even shouted at you. He trembled, and fear added to his spooky appearance.

He needed a name, and as he only spoke a few words in what Hugh believed was an accent from Wales, the new "son" named himself. 'We'll call him Welsh,' said his "father".

And so, from an appalling childhood, Welsh Brunty, now sporting the first pair of shoes he'd ever owned, literally fell on his feet. In the Emerald Isle, Welsh Brunty was a four-leaf clover kid who became one of the Brunty brood. He changed from a street ragamuffin to a much-loved member of a prosperous Irish farming family.

Now to say Welsh was "much-loved" needs clarification. His parents bestowed kindness and affection upon the lad; his siblings, particularly the boys, did not. They hated him.

They distrusted and disliked the incomer. Bullying was rife. Welsh copped it and often. But not one to take things lying down, Welsh hit back by hiding or breaking things precious to his brothers. Favourite possessions disappeared. The brothers knew who was to blame, but couldn't prove it. Having survived living on the streets, Welsh became an expert at not being caught.

And he was smart. He knew his parents had the power, so made himself as attractive as possible to the adults. They would protect and promote him. When the patriarch came home, Welsh was always the first to greet the head of the family.

The siblings' resentment increased as Welsh grew into the apple of the old man's eye. Welsh took to farming and was more enthusiastic about cattle breeding than his brothers. The bond between Hugh and Welsh grew stronger.

Hugh took Welsh to cattle markets in Ireland, and used the lad to spy on fellow farmers. Had Welsh lived in 19th century London, he would've made an excellent member of The Baker Street Irregulars.

He was small for his age and played the role of a carefree child, happy to be at the fair on a day out with his dad. The locals took no notice. But Hugh trained Welsh to collect vital information.

'Find out what they'll accept for their cattle, m'boy,' said Hugh, and so, pretending to be a child at play, Welsh moved close to the farmers, heard their gossip and plans, and reported back to Hugh HQ.

'The man with the big, black hat said he won't take less than forty, Father.'

'I see,' smiled Hugh. 'And what about old man McGuiness?'

'I think he's in trouble and will take even less.'

'You're a grand boy, Welsh Brunty. I'll see you right, lad.'

And so armed with his customers' secret prices, Hugh pitched his bids under the vendors' lowest price then "reluctantly" raised his offer. The farmers thought they got a good deal and, thanks to son Welsh, Hugh Brunty clinched another sale making even more money.

Their prosperity continued from Ireland to England. Hugh took his new assistant abroad, and in the cattle markets of Liverpool, Welsh perfected his spying techniques. Father and son made a great team and the Brunty bank balance bloomed. Hugh trusted Welsh who graduated from spy to trusted partner. To Hugh, Welsh was indispensable.

The three legitimate brothers grew ever more worried. The interloper positioned himself to pinch their inheritance. If ever anyone had a motive for murder, it was the brothers Brunty.

The years went by and Hugh's success as a farmer and cattle breeder continued. His children were now young adults with Welsh his favourite. The brothers stopped bullying Welsh, turning their naked hatred into plans for revenge. How could they remove the foreigner? An "accident", whereby Welsh drowned in the River Boyne, became the number one murder plan. But how and when might it happen? And did Welsh suspect fratricide was on the agenda?

Hugh aged and knew his time as an active farmer and cattle breeder was coming to an end. He planned a final push, amassed his largest herd of cattle, and shipped them across the Irish Sea. Thanks to Hugh's and Welsh's expertise, the profit made in Liverpool was the greatest ever. Life was never so good.

Sailing home to Drogheda with serious money about his person, Hugh stood on deck with Welsh, watching for the coast of Ireland. Without warning, the older Brunty clutched his chest and collapsed.

'Father,' screamed Welsh and knelt beside the stricken man.

Fellow passengers and crew members rushed to help. They carried Hugh to the captain's cabin and made him comfortable.

Distraught, Welsh begged for help. 'Please, can't you do something?'

'I'm sorry but we have no doctor, sir,' said the captain. 'And I fear that even if we did, it would be too late.'

Hugh suffered a massive heart attack and died with his face frozen, contorted with pain. Welsh held his father's lifeless hand. The captain leaned forward, closed Hugh's eyes, and then placed a hand on Welsh's shoulder.

'We'll be home soon, sir. I'll leave you alone with your father.'

Tears streamed from Welsh's eyes. He was sad but had rat cunning, and no amount of grief could remove his ability to connive. He was a survivor, and when the packet boat tied up, the papers and money once strapped to the dead body of Hugh Brunty, were now strapped to the living body of his adopted son.

The Church of Ireland funeral service was packed. Hugh's widow and children were grieving. Their beloved husband and father had died away from the bosom of his family, and they were not with him at the end.

The day after the funeral, the family gathered to discuss their situation. Welsh was missing, and when he arrived his appearance shocked everyone. Fashionable clothes were never his style and yet here he was, strutting about like some poor man's fop.

When he first appeared at the farm fifteen years ago, he wore hand-me-down rags. From these he graduated to simple, basic garments. Now, with the rest of the family in mourning, Welsh bobbed up dressed as a dandy. The siblings were ropeable. The brothers were sure he'd bought the fine clothes with money he stole from their father. Their shock became anger. Welsh flaunted his crimes and mocked them.

'I have a proposal,' he said.

'Where's the rest of the money my father earned on his last trip to England?' growled Michael, the second oldest son.

'Please, let's not argue,' begged Hugh's widow.

'I showed you the papers from the sale,' said Welsh, maintaining his calm and superior manner.

'You showed us *some* papers from the sale,' snapped third son, Sean.

Welsh shook his head. 'If you won't trust me, I'll leave, and you'll never hear my proposal to save the Brunty farm. And if *I* go, the farm will go, and with it a home for our mother and sisters.'

Silence. The brothers had never hated Welsh more, but this was a crisis. Their late father was the sole reason the farm prospered. Now he was dead and without Welsh, so too was that prosperity.

Thanks to their father, the brothers received a good education and found well-paid jobs, two of them in England. But only Welsh knew how to run the farm and breed cattle. Without him, it was finished.

An absentee Englishman owned the land, and could evict any of his tenants at the drop of a hat. He dropped his hat with gay abandon. If that happened on the Brunty farm, Mrs Brunty and her daughters would be dumped on the road at the end of the drive.

Welsh waited until the hostility subsided then spoke without emotion.

'I propose that I become the new tenant of the Brunty farm.'

You could cut the atmosphere with a knife.

'You conniving, little rat,' spat Brendan, the oldest. He stopped when he saw his mother's pathetic face. Grief overwhelmed her. Losing her beloved husband was devastating, but watching her family fight was too much. Brendan backed off and Welsh continued. He revelled in the moment.

'As the new tenant, I will run the property and breed cattle just as our dear father taught me.'

Nobody spoke. The sound of the ticking clock dominated.

Mrs Brunty spoke first. 'I think Welsh's proposal is good.'

None of her children moved. They knew their mother spoke the truth, but couldn't bring themselves to say so. Welsh continued.

'If I become the tenant, I will make sure our mother and sisters remain in the family home.'

Mrs Brunty nodded and her daughters felt a small sense of relief.

'What else?' asked Michael. 'With you, there's always something else.'

Welsh took a deep breath, opened his box of tricks, and withdrew a serve of fake sincerity.

'It's hard to express my love for this family. You rescued me from a life of poverty and crime. You gave me a future. Everything I have and know today I owe to the Brunty family. And now I want to repay that debt by saving the Brunty farm.'

He stalled and in the silence, nobody guessed his next sentence.

'And as a sign of good faith, I will take dear Mary as my wife.'

The family sat stunned. They took a moment to comprehend Welsh's words. Mary, the youngest of the five siblings, couldn't believe her ears. This was the first she'd even heard of such a union. Then the fury exploded.

'You what?' roared Michael. 'Marry Mary? How dare you even think such a thing?'

'Please, Michael,' begged his mother.

He ignored her plea. All three Brunty brothers hurled abuse. Mary's sister, Bree, comforted her distressed younger sibling, and Mrs Brunty despaired as the men traded insults.

Tempers flared and swearing dominated. Sean swung a fist at Welsh who blocked it and punched his attacker flush on the nose. Just as the brawl began, Mary screamed. It was loud and shrill and everyone stopped and looked at her. Sean forgot his bloodied face. The room was silent as Mary stared at the expectant Welsh. She spoke from the heart.

'I think you are so rude to suggest marriage when our dear Papa is only just in his grave, and when you have never spoken a single word about it. You are disrespectful to my parents and me.' She paused. Her soft words were powerful, her final sentence brutal. 'And I will never agree to marry you.'

Her brothers jeered the shattered Welsh. Inside he fumed. His marriage proposal being rejected was not a part of his plan. But for Welsh, worse was to come.

Brendan spoke for his brothers. 'And we will never allow you to control our family's farm—*never*.' His brothers agreed.

There was no need for violence. The words Welsh heard caused far more pain than any blows. His plan, his scheme was dead. He looked at his family with the eyes they saw when he first arrived years ago—if looks could kill. He moved to the door, turned and spoke in a low, threatening voice.

'You will regret this day, you will lose your farm and income, and be spread far and wide; you fools!'

He left, slamming doors. The family tried to put on a brave front. 'Thank God he's gone,' said Michael.

His brothers nodded and mumbled. The women said nothing and the family sat in silence, listening as Welsh's horse carried their brother away. They felt good having sent packing the sibling they hated, but felt bad knowing he was the best chance, the *only* chance they had of keeping their farm and their home.

It was difficult to know why Welsh was nasty. When you consider the miracle that saw him rescued, loved and educated by the Bruntys, you'd reckon he'd turn out half-decent. Alas, no. Greed and grudge-bearing were stamped upon his soul.

He resorted to Plan B. His goals remained the same—become the tenant of the Brunty farm and marry Mary—but he needed another strategy to achieve success.

To enact his new plan, he called on the local agent, the man responsible for collecting rents from tenant farmers. The agent was all powerful, the local magistrate, the person who controlled the living conditions of so many people. Welsh slipped into his salesman suit.

'Sir, I am ideal to work for you as a sub-agent.' Welsh looked and sounded believable.

'And why would I employ you?' replied the sceptical yet curious agent.

An ambitious and devious individual is always attracted to one of their kind. Just as opposites attract, greedy criminals unite.

'Allow me to explain, sir. I've lived here all my life.' Not true but then Welsh and the truth were never close. 'I know the area and the farmers, and can mix with these men, their families, friends and enemies, and give you valuable information. I assume you want their secrets.'

'You assume well.'

'Then I'm your man, sir. My information will allow you to increase rents at will. Like you, I'm ruthless in business and enjoy the power of the word *eviction*.'

The impressed agent disguised his feelings. He played for time. But with a joker up his sleeve, Welsh was relaxed.

'Interesting,' said the agent. 'What else?'

The two men stared at one another. Neither spoke. Both were excellent card players. Without shifting his gaze, Welsh withdrew a handmade envelope and pushed it towards the magistrate. There was another pause then more silence. The agent blinked first. He picked up the envelope and examined its contents. His face remained blank.

'As it happens,' he said, 'I do need a new sub-agent.' Welsh smiled. The agent joined the grinning club. 'When can you start?'

And so, through baloney, bravado and bribery, Welsh Brunty started a new career as a sub-agent. He was perfect for the job—greedy, sneaky and sans conscience.

At that precise moment, Hugh Brunty turned in his grave. All those spying skills he taught his adopted son were about to be used to harass, rob and evict tenant farmers. Surely Welsh wouldn't turn his attention to the family which once saved and succoured him.

Ah, but that's exactly what he did—and without mercy. Plan B began.

Michael and Sean Brunty worked in England and sent money home to their mother and sisters. Brendan married a local girl, Sheenagh, and moved north to make a start on his own property. Back home, the Brunty farm collapsed. The women decorated the old house, grew their own fruit and vegetables and collected eggs, but life was a constant struggle. The once thriving Brunty farm and cattle business was no more.

Welsh spied on his former home, and told lies about its occupants to the agent, who responded with a rent increase. Welsh's treachery knew no bounds. He hoped the family would quit but, desperate to survive, and with help from the boys, they paid the higher rent.

Welsh thrived in his new role. Thanks to his late father, Welsh knew the drinking habits, farming skills, marital situation and health problems of many local tenant farmers. He plied some with drink, and they revealed gossip and details of their income and those of their neighbours. He told his boss which farmers were making good money, those who were struggling, and any who pretended to struggle but had secret funds. This was priceless information for Welsh's boss and even more so for the absentee landlord. "Pay the new rent or we'll evict you".

Welsh stayed patient. Holding the whip hand, he knew what he wanted. He was a merciless sub-agent, hated as much as any cruel absentee English landlord. Farmers refused to cross him knowing his power might increase their rent or worse—evict them. Mind you, hatred can linger for many years, which Welsh would one day discover.

The sub-agent's agenda still included marrying Mary, and he switched tactics adopting a charm offensive. You don't have to be sincere to flatter, and Welsh used every trick in the book.

In many a tenant-farmer's house, he threatened eviction unless paid a we-can-make-this-go-away bribe. Desperate farmers made offers.

'We have no cash, sir but will you please take my wife's (or daughter's or mother's) bracelet (or ring or necklace) as payment.'

'If you insist,' said the smirking sub-agent.

A charming bracelet made a charming gift for a charming lady. Mary Brunty received gifts from an admirer.

'This one arrived today, Mama,' said Mary showing the bracelet to her mother and Bree.

'It's lovely,' said Mrs Brunty.

'Don't you want to know who sent it?' asked Mary.

Her sister spoke. 'We know who, and we know why.'

Mrs Brunty looked at her daughters. Bree hated Welsh, Mary was confused, and Mrs Brunty wished the matter would go away. Tension crept into the room.

Welsh played the long game. One summery Sunday afternoon, when he knew his mother and sisters would be strolling to the local village, he borrowed a carriage and horses from a wealthy tenant farmer, now in debt, and, with a driver, went riding. Welsh travelled a la royalty.

The carriage came along at a gentle clip and, as it passed the Brunty women, Welsh leant out of the carriage and waved.

'Good afternoon, ladies,' he called, then disappeared inside leaving the women to stare in amazement.

'That's an expensive carriage,' said Bree.

'He didn't stop to offer us a lift,' said Mrs Brunty.

'We wouldn't accept it anyway,' said Mary as she set off for home.

One of the other sub-agents was a woman called Marta. Welsh introduced himself, complimented her, and asked if she could do him a favour.

'I'll pay you,' said a friendly Welsh. 'I'm having trouble courting a young lady, and I need a woman's touch.'

Marta laughed. 'So why isn't she in love with such a fine, young man as y'self?'

Welsh liked Marta. They were alike—ambitious and sincerely insincere—and made a good team. Welsh sent Marta to the Brunty farm to speak to Mary on his behalf. Marta had the gift of the gab.

'Did y'not know, Miss Brunty, Mr Welsh is doin' such a grand job, we're expectin' him to become the agent and magistrate any day now.'

Mary was impressed. Marta leant forward and whispered.

'I happen t'know a secret.' Mary was hooked. 'The poor man's heart is broke because the woman he loves cares not a fig. It's a terrible shame now, Miss, don't you tink?'

When Marta left, Mary told her mother and sister everything.

'Perhaps your brothers were too hasty,' said Mrs Brunty.

'Oh, Mother,' said Bree. 'You and Papa loved the urchin, but your children despised him—*still* despise him.'

Mrs Brunty was dismayed. She and Bree looked at Mary, who said nothing. Was Mary wavering?

Welsh persisted, never losing sight of his goal. He adopted a new tactic meaning Mary received beautiful bunches of flowers.

What a considerate man, thought Mary. Alas, it wasn't a case of no expense being spared but rather, no expense being spent. The so-called generous suitor helped himself to various tenants' garden-beds with the gardeners afraid to say a thing—once a thief, always a thief.

Next, Welsh tried the glorious hero approach. He sent Marta to the Brunty farm where she addressed all three women.

'Ladies, I'm not sure you know dis, but in recent times strong moves have been made to see you ladies evicted.' The Brunty women froze. 'The only reason you good folk are still here is because Mr Welsh moved Heaven an' Earth to save your position.'

Bree was sceptical. Marta produced official documents which had nothing to do with Welsh.

'Here are the documents which show how Mr Welsh intervened to protect his dear family.'

Mrs Brunty and her daughters looked at the papers with limited understanding. Marta's acting skills were first-rate.

Oh no! The man we drove away, the man Mary spurned, is an unsung hero. Why were we so cruel?

Marta left to report to Welsh, and the Brunty women discussed the situation. Had they misjudged the man? Perhaps they should invite him to visit once in a while. They talked about the three boys and their possible reaction. Mrs Brunty closed the discussion.

'What the boys don't know can't hurt them. We'll invite Welsh to tea next Sunday.'

It was a tricky occasion. The last time Welsh stood in the Brunty parlour, threats were uttered, blood spilt and Mary threw Welsh's marriage proposal—if you could call it that—back in his face.

Welsh dressed down for the visit. He remembered how once his outlandish clothes infuriated the Bruntys. This time he brought beautiful flowers and fine homemade jam, all stolen. Mrs Brunty was civil, Mary nervous and Bree fought to control her anger.

'It's lovely to see you again, my boy,' said Mrs Brunty. 'We often speak of you; don't we girls?'

An uncomfortable pause was broken by Mary. 'We do, and thank you for all your kind gifts and flowers over many months.'

'I haven't changed,' said Welsh, coming straight to the point. 'My offer to run the farm still stands.' More silence and a longer pause. 'And it breaks my heart to see how rundown things have become.'

Mrs Brunty spoke. 'Let's have some tea, girls.' The sisters went to the kitchen. Their mother called. 'And bring that lovely jam your brother gave us.'

Alone, Welsh stared at the woman who'd saved his life. They discussed Welsh's job and his brothers until he changed the subject and spoke with a softness Mrs Brunty had never heard.

'I can make this farm like it was when my dear father was alive.' Tears filled Mrs Brunty's eyes. 'I can make you and Mary happy. Tell me it isn't true.'

Welsh said his piece with Mrs Brunty about to burst into tears when her daughters arrived with the tea.

The rest of the visit involved bland conversation in which the weather received an exhaustive workout. Welsh ensured he didn't overstay his welcome. He stood to leave and thanked each of the women in turn. They remembered the last time he stood in this room. The hatred and slamming of doors became smiles, fond good wishes and the softest of departures. Alone, the women discussed their visitor.

'He looks well,' said Mrs Brunty.

'What did he tell you?' asked Bree.

'Perhaps he *has* changed,' said Mary thinking aloud. 'Perhaps he only wants to be a part of our family again.'

Her mother and sister stared at her. What did this mean?

Welsh played it cool. After the visit, he ignored the Bruntys, and kept them guessing. Then, weeks later, a letter arrived for Mary from Marta.

'What does she say?' asked Mrs Brunty.

'Marta has important news and wants to tell me in person.'

Bree snorted. 'More tricks.'

'Marta wants to meet me in the village next Saturday.'

'Whatever can it be?' asked Mrs Brunty.

'Don't go,' said Bree.

Mary was confused.

'I'll come too,' said her mother. 'I'll be your chaperone.'

Mary looked at the others. 'Thank you, Mother, but I'll go alone.' She did and met Marta by the church gate.

'Hello Mary. Tank you for comin'.'

'What is so important that we have to meet here in the village?'

'Ah, come out of dis wind. Dere's a ladies' room in the pub.'

Marta set off and Mary scampered to catch her. They walked down the lane beside the hotel and Marta opened a door. They entered an empty room. Mary felt uneasy.

'What is this place?' she asked.

'Not here,' said Marta moving to a door. 'Dere's a lovely fire in here.'

Marta opened the door and ushered Mary inside. She froze. A fire crackled in the room which also contained a bed and a man. Standing by the window was Welsh Brunty. Mary turned to leave but the door closed and the key on the outside clicked.

'Thank you for coming,' he said.

'You told me you'd changed,' she replied. 'Now you've played a terrible trick and put me in this compromising position.'

'Believe me, I didn't want it this way. It was Marta's idea. She said you'd never accept me even though you loved me.' He paused. 'You do love me, Mary, don't you?'

She paused. All the cards were stacked against her. Her father was dead, her brothers gone and her financial future bleak. So many women endured this awful situation. She decided.

'Will you promise to care for my mother and sister too?'

A shocked Welsh didn't at first twig that Mary had agreed to marry him. 'Of course, of course,' he babbled, then moved to her and kissed her hands. 'Oh Mary, you've made me the happiest man in all Ireland.'

He was happy but not so Mary. She accepted his request for a small, private wedding. She knew if her brothers heard the news there would be murder done. Her mother had mixed feelings, wondering what her late husband would say. Bree expressed her disgust, packed her belongings, and departed for a friend's home in Wexford never to return.

The marriage ceremony was performed by a disgraced and disgraceful clergyman, sober enough to make it to the, "I now pronounce you man and wife" bit.

Welsh was over the moon, Mary was over the honeymoon, and the couple returned to the Brunty farm. Mrs Brunty senior moved to a back bedroom and the newlyweds started life as lord and lady of the manor. Welsh moved to the next item on his agenda.

He sat in the agent's office and explained how he should now be given the tenancy of the Brunty farm. 'I grew up there and know everything about farming. I can fix that place.'

'Well if you do, y'rent'll go up,' said the agent.

Welsh laughed. 'Maybe,' he said. 'But once I breed cattle, paying the rent won't be a problem. First, I need that agreement.'

He got it.

Weeks after their sister's wedding, the Brunty brothers received the news. Their baby sister had wed and the groom, the one they referred to as "that miserable bastard", was the new tenant of the family farm. Blood boiled and the brothers headed home.

Michael and Sean came from England together and arrived before Brendan, who only lived about sixty miles away. His letter went astray. The two younger brothers discussed tactics en route, with the preferred options being a simple killing, or anything involving severe torture. A crude bribe firmed as the rank outsider.

It felt strange knocking on the front door. This had been their home for years and they always entered via the kitchen. The front door opened and their mother's face was a picture.

'My boys,' she cried and hugged and kissed them. She called. 'Mary, come and see who's here.'

Mary entered, wiping her hands on her apron. She too was shocked but delighted her brothers were home. But the happiness disappeared when Michael spoke.

'Where is he?'

'Now Michael,' said his mother, 'you mustn't be angry.'

'I'm not angry, I'm furious.'

'How could you, Mary?' asked Sean.

She despaired. 'Welsh has saved this ruined farm.'

'Not your marriage, the tenancy. Who you marry is your business,' said Michael, 'but *we're* the rightful tenants. Our father and the agent agreed that when we had enough money *we* would take over, not that thieving nobody.'

'So where is he?' snarled Sean.

Mrs Brunty begged them. 'Please, boys, no violence. Promise me.'

This slowed things. The sons had total respect for their mother.

Michael nodded. 'For you, Ma, but God help him if he tries anything.'

The men went looking for the "rat". The women exchanged glances and hugged with a mixture of fear and hope. Welsh was in the barn stacking hay. He heard footsteps and turned.

'Well, well, look what the cat dragged in.'

The brothers approached. The tenant grabbed a pitchfork which had strong, sharp prongs.

Michael was calm. 'We don't care about your marriage to our Mary, only about you stealing our tenancy.'

'*Your* tenancy,' scoffed Welsh. 'I've heard of an absentee landlord, but never an absentee tenant.' Welsh turned nasty and jabbed the pitchfork in their direction. 'Now get off my land!'

The brothers stalled as they knew Welsh wouldn't hesitate to use the weapon. He advanced making them retreat. It was the calm before the storm. The brothers separated and stopped. This created a problem for Welsh. With his opponents no longer side by side, he turned friendly.

'Ah, c'mon lads, I've fixed the farm. It's now like the old man's place.'

That last comment was a red rag to the bullish brothers. As one they raced at Welsh. Sean was faster so the pitchfork swung in his direction. The lethal prongs were about to be thrust into flesh when Michael launched himself and crashed against Welsh causing both men to fall. The pitchfork landed on the ground and Sean joined the fray.

Two to one should prevail but Welsh had street fighting skills. He broke every one of the yet-to-be-invented Marquess of Queensberry's Rules. All three combatants fought with screams and threats until a loud voice interrupted the punch-up.

'That's enough!'

The trio of fighters froze. They looked up and saw Brendan holding the pitchfork, thereby ending the brawl.

Inside, Mary and her mother repaired the wounded "little boys". Without any cuts and bruises, Brendan held court.

'This has got to stop. Welsh is making a go of the farm and providing a home for the ladies. So long as he pays the rent and cares for mother and Mary, then that's it.'

'But he stole our tenancy, yours too,' groaned Michael, as his sister dabbed his bruised face.

The fighters continued complaining before agreeing a fragile truce. The visitors retired to their old bedrooms not knowing Welsh had plans. He hated being beaten, wanted revenge, and called in a favour.

Next morning, the three brothers prepared to leave when a posse of locals arrived. Imagine the brothers' fury when they were dragged before the local magistrate and charged with various crimes.

Mary pleaded with her husband to withdraw his complaint. The senior Mrs Brunty despaired. Reluctantly, Welsh stated that Brendan wasn't involved in the assault. He was released but not so his brothers. Michael and Sean were thrown into a stinking, rat-infested prison and kept there for many months. This was a classic case of how not to unite the family with brotherly love.

And all this only added to the strain on Welsh and Mary's marriage—made in Heaven it wasn't. At least the Brunty farm recovered. Not to its former glory, but sufficient to generate a reasonable income. Would Welsh come good?

The years went by and little changed. Mary was barren and the lack of a son and heir—daughters didn't count—ate away at Welsh, making him ever more bitter. The expert cattle-breeding skills possessed by Hugh Brunty were not easy to grasp. Welsh drank too much. Mrs Brunty senior died, leaving Mary alone with her morose brute of a husband.

It was a late summer's night and Mary lay awake beside her drunken, snoring spouse. She wondered if her life could become even more soul-destroying than it was right now. Alas, it could.

Mary smelt smoke. She sprang out of bed, ran to the kitchen, and opened the door where the heat and flames drove her back. She raced to the bedroom screaming at Welsh. He kept snoring. She punched and slapped him. That got him awake.

'Fire!' she screamed. 'The house is on fire!'

Welsh roused himself and they ran to the kitchen. The house was well alight. They got outside and Welsh yelled at Mary.

'Get help! Get help!'

He grabbed a bucket of water and screamed for the farmhand, but the man lived in the smaller cottage and was oblivious to the catastrophe. His punishment would keep. When an exhausted Mary returned with a neighbour, the house was gone. The dying embers cast an eerie glow.

Welsh spat on the ground near his wife. 'What took you so long?'

Mary couldn't speak. Losing the Brunty home was devastating. Being spoken to like that was beyond belief. The neighbour, who had long despised Welsh, walked up to him, glared and without saying a word, smashed his fist into Welsh's stomach. The neighbour walked away leaving Mary watching her groaning husband rolling in his own vomit.

People have long memories. The house fire was lit by a former tenant farmer who, years ago, was hounded off his smallholding by the pitiless sub-agent, Welsh Brunty. What goes around comes around.

Welsh and Mary moved to the smaller cottage built by Mary's father when times were good. This was a major downsizing. Gormless Gallagher, the farmhand, moved to the barn.

Having lost all their possessions in the fire, Welsh and Mary struggled to make ends meet. It was tough but their troubles had only begun.

The agent and magistrate who first employed Welsh was murdered, and his replacement was devoid of compassion. Welsh lost his job as a sub-agent and the boot was now on the other foot. When the new sub-agent arrived to collect the rent, Welsh couldn't pay.

He begged for mercy but got derision and laughter. It was crunch time. Mary's precious "gifts", the trinkets Welsh stole in his wooing days, had been buried to foil any thieves. The precious items were recovered and sold. Who said crime doesn't pay?

By now, Welsh and Mary were no spring chickens, childless and struggling to make ends meet. One night, as they shivered in their tiny kitchen, Welsh had an idea. 'Let's visit brother Brendan.'

Mary was unmoved. 'Brendan? Why?'

'He likes you. And I got him off those charges many years ago.'

'You got him *on* those charges many years ago.'

'He owes me.'

'But why Brendan?'

'He's family. Families stick together in good times and bad. And he's got a tribe of kids.'

Mary looked at him. In the flickering candle light his eyes gleamed.

'So?' she asked.

He shrugged. 'We could start a family.'

Chapter 2

'HELLO!' cried a waving Welsh, driving his cart into Brendan's yard. Welsh had written to his brother suggesting a visit, but got no reply. Welsh decided to go anyway and the journey took four days.

Brendan's wife, Sheenagh, opposed the visit and didn't mince her words. 'You always said he was trouble. And why would he come after all these years?'

Brendan and Sheenagh had four children—two of each. The youngest was a lad, Hugh, six, named after his grandfather, Welsh's benefactor. The lad was friendly, trusting and a redhead.

Sheenagh's spirits sank when her dreaded brother-in-law arrived. But Brendan was keen to see his sister and wanted to know her news. Released from jail long ago, their brothers returned to England. Mary knew nothing about sister, Bree.

Welsh and Mary fascinated the children. The dark and unusual Uncle Welsh turned on the charm, and the children's reticence disappeared.

Welsh became Mr Jolly. He played games with the children, helped Brendan with his farm work, and complimented Sheenagh to the point of embarrassment. After a week, the kids were delighted, but not so their parents.

When will the house guests leave? And why did they come in the first place? Two weeks rolled by and Sheenagh wanted them gone.

That night, the two men were alone with Brendan under instructions to give Welsh and Mary their marching orders. But before the host could speak, Welsh come up with a stunning suggestion.

'Brendan, I've been thinking. Wouldn't it be just grand for your little Hugh to inherit the tenancy of his grandfather's farm?' Brendan was hooked. 'You named your boy after his grandfather, and think how proud your dad would be to have his grandson milking cows and breeding cattle on the family farm.'

'But how?' queried Brendan.

'Well, if the lad came to live with Mary and me, we'd educate him, give him a grand life, and when he grew older, the farm would be his.'

Welsh paused. The serious suggestion came without warning.

'Welsh, what can I say?'

'Say nothing. Sleep on it and we can chat in the morning. Oh, and another thing. While Mary and I have enjoyed your grand hospitality, it's time we made tracks for home.'

Brendan felt overwhelming relief. Sheenagh would be thrilled the unwanted guests were going. But what would she say about their youngest being adopted?

Brendan crept into bed and told his wife the good news about the departing guests. 'Hallelujah,' she cried, but when Brendan described Welsh's offer, Sheenagh's delight died in a heartbeat.

'You cannot be serious,' she said, frantic and stunned. 'He wants to adopt our Hugh?'

'It's only a suggestion,' replied her defensive husband.

'Which you refused.'

'Not exactly.'

'Brendan!' Her loud voice dropped to a savage whisper because of Brendan's manic shushing. 'How dare you even consider such a monstrous idea.'

'I agreed to talk in the morning. That's all.'

'Hugh goes over my dead body.'

It was a restless night with the couple sleeping so far apart, there was room for a sheep in the middle of the bed.

The next morning, Hugh's adoption wasn't mentioned. Maybe Welsh's wild idea had been forgotten. Not so. What Brendan or Sheenagh didn't know was that ever since their house guests arrived, Welsh had been grooming young Hugh for a new life as his son and heir.

He took the boy for walks, helped him climb trees, and told him tales of life on the farm by the River Boyne. Welsh told Hugh the names—all invented on the spot—of his pigs, chickens and cows, and described the fun you could have picking apples and playing games with the dogs. He spoke of adventures going fishing and swimming, chasing rabbits and riding ponies. Welsh stopped, paused, and looked at the child.

'Do you fancy your own pony, Hugh?'

'Oh, yes please, Uncle Welsh,' beamed the boy, his eyes wide and wild.

'And how about your own dog?'

That was the clincher. Little Hugh loved dogs. He was speechless with expectations of joy.

Now this sneaky grooming was Welsh's secret weapon. When he again raised Hugh's adoption, the greatest supporter of the proposal was the wee boy himself. He wanted to go with his aunt and uncle. Welsh's immaculate planning worked a treat.

Hugh's mother refused point blank. She placed the child on her knee and told him how much she and his Daddy loved him. They wanted to care for him forever. But Sheenagh's heart turned to stone. Her youngest, her darling baby boy, was not interested in his parents; he wanted to be with the wonderful Uncle Welsh and Aunt Mary. The boy's head had been turned. His heart belonged to Welshy.

That night in the dark, Sheenagh lay in bed and wept.

'It's not the end of the world,' said Brendan, moving closer to her.

'I'll never see him again.'

'Nonsense. The farm is not all that far away, and Hugh can come home for Christmas.'

Sheenagh shed more tears.

Brendan tried a new tack. 'Imagine. One day our Hugh will inherit his grandfather's farm.'

'It's wrong, the whole horrid idea is wrong.'

'But think of the boy. He *wants* to go. He'll be upset if Welsh and Mary leave without him.'

Sheenagh cried herself to sleep. In her heart she knew her boy was lost. Had she known the real story, she would have died of sorrow. You see, Brendan and Welsh had agreed a secret deal, meaning Hugh would never see his parents again. If any of his family visited or contacted him, the boy would never inherit the Brunty farm's tenancy. Brendan and Welsh swore an oath and told no-one.

The next day, the visitors took their time packing their belongings and loading their cart. Brendan shook his head in confusion and Sheenagh shook hers in torment. Why the delay?

Welsh rounded up the children and they went for a walk in the woods. Hugh sat on Uncle Welsh's shoulders. He and Mary fussed over their new "son", their special passenger, who was never more excited.

Brendan wondered why they didn't set off first thing. His confusion increased because, after they returned, it was time for lunch delaying the departure again. Brendan couldn't stand it any longer.

'Why have you not left? It'll soon be dark.'

'Best time to travel,' said Welsh. 'The roads are clear and we don't pay for those damn expensive inns.'

Brendan had serious doubts. *Have I done the wrong thing?*

As daylight faded, Welsh announced they were leaving. He helped Mary onto the cart seat. The lad kissed his siblings and father, then ran to Welsh who swept him, squealing with delight, into the air and placing him on the seat beside Mary. Inside, Sheenagh wept. She couldn't bear to watch. Welsh climbed onto the cart and sat beside little Hugh. The lad was snug between his new parents. Welsh waved to Brendan and the siblings and smiled. Then with a shake of the reins and cries of "Goodbye", the new Brunty family set sail.

The gloom and rain swallowed the cart and in the darkness, Hugh snuggled into his Aunt Mary. He was cold and wet but excited about his new adventure, and couldn't stop chatting. He didn't hear Welsh who spoke in a low growl.

'Shut y'gob.'

Hugh went on babbling away but stopped when his aunt pulled him close and whispered in his ear. He looked up and saw a different face. For the first time, a tiny seed of worry took root in his heart.

Mary knew her husband was a man of many moods; charming and kind one minute, cruel and evil the next. She prayed the boy would be safe.

Hugh became quiet as they plodded along in the darkness. The unseen potholes caused problems because when the spring-less cart hit one, the travellers bounced. A large pothole caused a severe jolt. Hugh yelled as he shot in the air and landed, his bottom smacking the hard, wooden seat.

Welsh roared at the boy. 'I told you to shut y'gob!'

This time the child heard every word, and in the blackness his uncle's eyes burned with anger. Hugh's happiness switched to fear. He said what he thought.

'Why are you angry, Uncle?'

Welsh hissed. 'Be quiet.'

The terrified boy spoke the truth.

'I want my Daddy. I want to go home.'

Welsh belted the boy's face with a backhander. It smashed into Hugh's soft face and, after a moment of shock, the pain kicked in and the boy screamed like a victim of torture.

Welsh snapped. With one hand he grabbed the boy's hair and yanked him up and over the back of the seat tossing him onto the tray of the cart. Hugh shrieked in pain and fear, Mary wailed and the child experienced unimaginable terror.

Adults use life's experiences to prepare for unexpected events. They draw on these experiences to deal with accidents, tragedies and death. Being young and innocent, a child lacks life's experiences. Hugh trusted adults and enjoyed their protection.

In an instant, he went from the joyful expectation and excitement of a new adventure, to inexplicable horror, shock and pain. And the suddenness made it worse. His life changed in a heartbeat.

His body throbbed with agony, his mind in turmoil. *Why?* was his first thought. Then *What did I do wrong? Why is my uncle a monster?* Terrified, Hugh howled in anguish.

Mary looked back at the miserable child.

'Leave him,' snarled Welsh.

'He didn't mean no harm.'

'I said "leave him". He'll never learn if you go soft on him.'

Mary shook her head and faced front as the cart bounced over yet another pothole. Hugh's painful cries grew softer becoming a whimper. He opened one eye and saw the backs of the adults. He risked lifting his head. In the darkness he heard his father running and calling. "I'm here, Hugh. Daddy's here".

Hugh raised a hand towards his father, and opened his mouth to call out when his youthful brain told him to stop. The night had played a trick. He was alone and sad beyond belief.

His mother taught her children to pray. As Hugh lay on the wet straw, he remembered a prayer.

Dear God. Please bless Mummy and Daddy and my brother and sisters. And please bless ... He wanted to say *Uncle Welsh and Aunt Mary* but the words wouldn't come.

At least the soft Irish rain was kind. It mingled with his copious tears.

Welsh drove in the darkness for different reasons. If they spent the night at an inn, he would have to pay for everything. Travelling by night, meant they could stop at an inn by day. Welsh paid for food and drink, but they could sleep by a fire for nothing.

And Welsh didn't want to be seen, or the boy to see anything. The further they got from Hugh's family the better, and with no knowledge of signs or landmarks, little Hugh couldn't escape and return home.

Next morning, they stopped in a village where Welsh left the cart at the back of a pub. Mary carried the sleepy, snivelling child inside, and fed him bread and butter and milk. She was his only friend, and Hugh avoided even looking at Welsh.

'What?' snapped Welsh, after the child whispered in Mary's ear.

'He wants the privy.'

'Then take him.' Mary led Hugh and Welsh called. 'And don't let him out of your sight.'

When they returned, Welsh had gone. Mary put Hugh on a bench near the fire. She helped him lie down and covered him with her shawl.

'You sleep, little one. I'll find you some new clothes.'

She left and Hugh fell asleep. The fire warmed him, with sleep his best friend. But not for long.

'Who's this then?' asked an old man with whiskers. Hugh didn't stir so the gent prodded the boy who sat up in fright.

The friendly gentleman wanted to know why a small child occupied his favourite seat. The man's dog moved in to investigate and Hugh pulled back.

'He don't bite, laddie. Go on, give him a pat.'

Hugh loved dogs and for the first time in many hours reached out and touched a friendly creature. The happy dog asked for more.

'So what's your name, young man?'

'Hugh, sir.'

'And where be your parents?'

'At home, sir.'

'At home? Are you on your own?'

'No sir. I've been took by my Uncle Welsh and I'm afraid.'

'Took?'

The pub door opened and Welsh entered. 'What's this? I told you to sit over here.' He grabbed Hugh. The dog growled.

'Sir,' began the old man.

Welsh threatened him with a look and spoke in a low, sinister voice. 'Mind y'own feckin' business.'

Mary arrived with a bundle of clothes. Welsh queried her but she ignored him. She took Hugh's hand and led him back to the fire. The old man smiled but said nothing. His dog wanted to chat. Mary removed Hugh's wet clothes and dressed him in dry, warm ones. The trousers were far too big and made of a strange material called corduroy. Mary hoped her nephew would live long enough to grow into them.

The family stayed in the pub and Hugh slept with his head on his aunt's lap, and the dog by his side. With the daylight fading, the family went outside, mounted the cart and continued their journey. Hugh sat next to his aunt but followed her advice and said nothing. It was difficult to imagine the misery and loneliness endured by the child.

They repeated this travel routine for another three days—sit by fire in pub by day, and take to road by night. The weather was never a factor—if it rained, too bad. On the third night, they placed Hugh on straw under the seat of the cart. Beneath his useless blanket, the constant pothole jarring kept him awake. He looked and felt terrible.

Late in the afternoon of the fourth day they reached the Brunty farm. Through endless rain, Hugh saw nothing of the ponies, pets and promises, and was bundled inside the cottage.

'Show him round and then I'll speak to him,' said Welsh.

He went to check his animals and his farmhand, Gallagher, who'd been in charge during the boss's absence. Gallagher, a nasty sycophant, grinned exposing his black and yellow teeth. He once helped Welsh in his work as a sub-agent, and had a long history of criminal activities.

Mary showed Hugh his bed, the privy, and where not to go—ever. The boy took no notice. Mary thought he was desolate when in fact he was ill. In the kitchen, she made supper. The starving child gobbled the food then, looking at her, spoke.

'Please Aunt, why is Uncle Welsh angry?'

Mary looked at her nephew's pathetic face. 'I don't know, child, but if it's any help, he's angry at everyone.' It wasn't the answer he wanted but it was something.

They heard footsteps and voices and the ogre appeared. He seemed even more evil on his own patch. Welsh grabbed a chair and sat.

'Come here, you.' Mary looked at the boy and nodded. He moved to Welsh who turned him so the lad's back was to the door.

'Now listen, son, and listen good. This is your home now, and me and your Aunt Mary, we is your parents. Your Daddy and Mummy wants you to be a farmer. I can teach you but by Jesus, boy, you'd best be grateful. All right?' Hugh couldn't speak. Welsh shook him and spoke louder. 'All right?'

'He understands,' said Mary.

'You keep out of it.' She did. Welsh continued at Hugh. 'Whatever I say, you do. And if you don't, I'll skin you alive. All right?'

This time Hugh nodded. He thought he'd seen the worst of the madman, but his young brain calculated, in childlike thinking, that he'd only just reached the gates of Hell, and something unimaginable was yet to happen once he entered the furnace proper. Tears welled in his eyes and he cried in silence.

Welsh coughed and, unseen by Hugh, the kitchen door opened. Mary gasped. Welsh held the boy's shoulders in a vice-like grip and issued a warning.

'I'll be watching you, boy, every minute of every day. You try to run away, steal something or get lazy and I'll know. D'ja hear me?'

The terrified child nodded again. But his terror was soon to plumb new depths.

'And when I'm not watching, he will!'

Welsh spun Hugh. Bent low, only inches from Hugh's tear-stained cheeks, was the face of the appalling Gallagher, who couldn't remember his last bath. Baring his terrifying teeth, he grinned at the youngster then ran a hand through the boy's hair, grabbed a fistful and yanked the lad even closer.

'I'll be dis close,' he smirked as most of his free-range spittle found its mark.

Welsh thrust Hugh sideways where he landed in the folds of Mary's skirt. She half-carried the shattered child to the bedroom. In the kitchen, the men laughed.

Hugh's bedroom was the only bedroom. His bed was a box with straw at the foot of Welsh and Mary's bed. It brought him closer to the fire with a shorter trip to the privy. But that's where the benefits stopped.

At night, two roosters and a sow with piglets shared the bedroom. Welsh used the fowls as an alarm clock. They fired up at dawn and guess who let out the feathered creatures and cleaned up when the roosters' bedroom became their shedroom?

The sow was a danger to adults, let alone small children, and clearly the sleeping habits of little Hugh Brunty were unhealthy. Add to the mix his uncle's snoring and farting, and the life of the future Brunty farm tenant did not begin or bode well.

On Hugh's first night in paradise, Welsh fell asleep and snored. Mary crept out of bed and knelt beside her nephew. The fire's dying embers created a half-light, and in this atmospheric setting, and while the piglets squealed and the roosters flapped, Mary kissed her nephew.

'Goodnight, little Hugh,' she said.

He tried to say "Goodnight," but his silent sobbing choked the word.

Next morning before dawn, Mary put out the roosters and the sow and her litter. Hugh was asleep so Mary left him there. She went to the kitchen and started her breakfast routine.

After a few minutes, she returned to the bedroom and knelt beside Hugh's box. She turned his face to her and gasped. He looked strange, like death. He was awake but not moving. She touched his hot face, panicked and raced to Welsh.

'Welsh, wake up, the boy is poorly. *Welsh!*'

He grumbled and turned his back to her. Mary slapped his head. He spun around, furious. 'What?' he roared with memories of a house fire.

'Come and see the boy. He's dying!'

Complaining, Welsh fell out of bed, bent over Hugh and made a cursory inspection.

'He's shaming.'

'No he's not. Feel his face. He's got a fever. Look at him.'

Welsh fumed. He'd gone to no end of trouble to capture the damn kid who now looked like dying. What a waste of time and money.

'He needs a doctor,' said Mary. Welsh hesitated. 'Go! Send Gallagher.'

Welsh staggered out to find the farmhand. Mary struggled to lift Hugh out of his box and place him on the bed. She covered him with bedclothes putting her shawl on top. She lit a fire as Welsh came in with Gallagher.

'Not in here,' snapped Mary. 'Fetch the doctor.'

Welsh knew the boy was ailing. He turned on Gallagher. 'If the kid dies, I'll tell the magistrate about you and Marta and your black market baby business.'

Looking scared, Gallagher turned and ran. Welsh yelled. 'And hurry.'

It took more than an hour for the doctor to arrive. Mary tried to give Hugh some warm milk but he struggled to swallow and seemed delirious. Welsh suggested a drop of whisky.

The doctor took only seconds to decide. 'The child has a fever, a bad one.'

'Will he die?' asked a desperate Mary. Welsh too wanted the answer although for another reason.

'He may. Has he been ill long?'

'He hasn't been ill,' said a frustrated Welsh. 'Yesterday he was as fit as a fiddle.'

The doctor didn't believe Welsh. He gave medicine to Mary with instructions to keep the child in bed and warm.

Mary stayed with Hugh. She bathed his head, spoon-fed his medicine, and prayed with a passion. Welsh went farming and popped in once.

'Any change?' he asked.

'He's worse.'

'Well I can't afford the doctor no more.'

'What can I tell Brendan and Sheenagh?'

'Tell 'im nothing. He'll never want to know.'

'What?' Mary was in shock. 'Why won't he want to know? What have you done?'

Welsh pointed at his wife. 'Just get him better.' Welsh left.

That night, Hugh slept beside Mary with Welsh grumbling before falling asleep. Mary kept waking up and speaking to Hugh. She needed sleep but dreaded nodding off thinking that, when she woke, she'd be beside a dead child. Hugh showed no signs of recovery. From time to time he coughed giving Mary some comfort. *At least he's still alive*, she thought.

Next morning, Hugh was much the same. Mary kept thinking about what had happened, about the scheme her husband hatched with her brother. She blamed herself. *Why didn't I oppose this?* The boy's fever was so unnecessary; all those nights travelling in the cold and rain. No wonder the child was dying.

Hugh looked terrible. Late the next day, he swallowed the last of the medicine. Mary sat on the bed weeping. Welsh stopped calling in for reports. Mary stopped praying. Any death can be heartbreaking, but when it's an innocent child, the pain is pure torture.

She needed the privy. She kissed Hugh, went outside, and was walking back when the family dogs came up to her in the hope of food—any food. They liked her but feared the men.

Welsh and Gallagher abused the animals, which were banned from the cottage. Mary looked but couldn't see her husband. 'Come on,' she said and the dogs didn't need a second invitation.

She found some rabbit scraps and the canines devoured the food with relish. 'Out you go,' she said, 'and don't tell your master.' She opened the door, heard Hugh coughing, and so headed for the bedroom. Hoping for more food elsewhere in the cottage, the dogs trotted after her.

Mary didn't notice them. She sat beside Hugh and stroked his forehead. The dogs jumped on the bed giving Mary a fright. She was about to order them outside but stopped.

The patient fascinated the dogs. *Who is this? He's new*. They sniffed and stared. Soldier, the brave one, pawed Hugh's covered body. Keeper took courage from his comrade's behaviour, and moved closer to the child. The dog inched forward and licked Hugh's face.

Mary raised a hand and the dogs moved back. They knew she was gentle, unlike Welsh and Gallagher, and just as Mary decided it was better for the dogs to be put outside, Hugh shifted a smidgeon. Beneath the bedclothes, he moved. Mary leant closer.

'Hugh, are you all right?'

He looked at Mary and then the dogs. Hugh extracted an arm and offered his hand to the canines. They were gentlemen and responded in kind.

Hugh's two excited new friends licked his hand and the smile on the boy's face made his aunt weep for joy. The sound of the kitchen door being opened changed everything. The dogs became scared. Mary patted them and told them to stay.

In the kitchen she spoke to Welsh.

He replied with a crescendo. 'What? Inside? On my bed?'

Mary stood up to her bullying husband and, thanks to her bravery, tamed the brute who came to the bedroom door sans bluster, and saw an amazing sight.

Hugh was sitting up in bed with a tail-wagging dog either side, each being patted by the boy with a much reduced fever.

The good news was that Hugh recovered. The bad news was that his life as a slave began. It took days for the patient to be ready for hard labour and, once he was able, Hugh's first tasks were to let out any animals in the house, clean the fireplaces and set the fires, fetch wood, fetch water, feed the chickens and collect their eggs. Throughout the day he followed his uncle, and needed to be ready to jump when ordered.

If Hugh made a mistake or was too slow, he was yelled at or struck or both. Soon the lad understood the moods of his master. Hugh was a quick learner and taught himself not to cry.

But he didn't learn the evil ways of the gruesome Gallagher. The man was a sociopath who delighted in the suffering of others, and would do anything, especially lying, to inflict pain on Master Brunty. Gallagher reported to Welsh.

'He spilt milk in the barn.'

'He never closed the gate.'

'He broke an egg.'

'He give the dogs food.'

The list was endless. Depending on his mood and alcohol intake, Welsh would slap or beat the child, send him to bed without supper or worse; threaten the most evil of punishments.

'Do that again, boy, and I'll lock you in the barn with Gallagher.'

The farmhand shuddered with delight and Hugh and Mary shuddered with fear.

When Gallagher's lies didn't produce enough misery for the child, the evil labourer damaged tools, spoilt food and even maimed cattle, before blaming it on that "lazy feckin' urchin". Hugh survived the vicious punishment; it was the injustice which stung.

For the next decade, Hugh Brunty endured bullying and beatings. He was an unpaid farm worker on the property once run by his grandfather, another Hugh Brunty.

When he first arrived, little Hugh watched for visitors, looking at anyone passing the farm and wondering, *Are you my father coming to take me home?* But no-one came for Hugh. His misery was exquisite and only two things kept him alive and sane—his aunt and his dogs.

Mary befriended and cared for her nephew. She told him stirring stories about his grandfather.

As for the dogs, well, they adopted and adored him. They slept outside but come the dawn, there they were, awaiting their loving master. When Hugh set out to herd cattle, pick potatoes or pen sheep, his best friends ran in circles around the boy, barking their pleasure.

The years rolled by and Hugh grew from a child to a boy to a young man; tall for his age, strong and good looking. And as he got bigger and stronger, Welsh and Gallagher got older and slower. Both became less aggressive bullies. They knew one day the lad might stand and fight. The bullies weren't stupid.

The dogs too got older; Soldier in particular. He tried to keep up with Hugh, but the dog's liver and eyesight were shot, and arthritis made the once active dog lame. Hugh's heart ached as he tried in vain to hide, feed and care for his dying and much-loved friend.

The day Welsh saw the limping animal and went for some rope, Hugh made no protest. He knew it was right but that didn't stop his tears.

'Not here,' pleaded Hugh. 'Not in front of Keeper.'

Welsh had no sentiment and killed the dog in an instant. 'Feed it to t'pigs,' he snorted and Gallagher laughed.

Hugh agreed, but that night, he carried Soldier across the darkened fields where, beneath a gnarled tree by the useless bog, Hugh dug a grave and laid his companion to rest. Keeper sat staring, panting, thinking. Reluctant to leave, he wanted to stay with his mate.

And Hugh wanted to be with Keeper. Now aged 15, Hugh thought about running away. He faced many problems, the toughest being what to do with Keeper. He owed the dog his life.

One day, as Welsh and Gallagher repaired a fence out on the farm, Hugh chopped wood in the yard and Mary called to him.

'Will you come into the house, Hugh?'

He slammed the axe into a block of wood, and joined his aunt in the kitchen. She looked ill.

'Are you poorly, Aunt Mary?'

'I must tell you something.' She hesitated. Hugh sensed her distress as she took a deep breath.

'Is it Uncle Welsh?'

She blurted out her news. 'I'm having a baby.'

Mary worried her nephew wouldn't understand. He'd never been to school, was illiterate and had little contact with anyone who might explain the facts of life. Welsh couldn't care less about educating the boy.

'Oh,' said a surprised Hugh.

'Perhaps I should explain how babies are born and then ...'

'Thank you, Aunt, but I know already.'

'You do?' said an astonished Mary.

'Gallagher told me.'

'Gallagher!' gasped Mary.

'He explained because I didn't understand when he told me about my mother.'

Mary was in total shock. 'Your mother?'

'Gallagher said I was stupid, like my mother, because she once slept in the same bed as Gallagher.'

Mary screamed so loud it frightened Hugh and Keeper pawed the kitchen door.

'No! That man is evil, *evil!*' she cried. 'What he says is not true; never true. Your mother's a fine, Christian women, a wonderful mother and loyal to your dear father. Do not believe that awful, awful man.'

There was a long pause before Hugh spoke.

'I must tell you something, too.' They looked at one another. 'I want to leave.'

Hugh expected his aunt to be shocked and angry, but instead she quietly spoke the truth.

'I'm surprised you haven't gone already.'

'I can't. You know I have no money or clothes, and I only stay because of Keeper and you.'

'Me? You must not stay because of me.'

'But you have cared for me and now I am older, I must care for you.'

Mary wanted to cry. Despite the years of abuse her nephew suffered, he rarely expressed any feelings of revenge; in fact he had a kind and loving nature he always showed to his aunt. Silence dominated, and neither wanted to speak until Mary could keep quiet no longer.

'I have a secret to share with you. I've wanted to say this for years. Your Uncle Welsh is not a Brunty.' This shocked Hugh. 'It's true your father is my brother, but he and I are not blood relatives of your Uncle Welsh. Do you know what blood relatives are?'

Hugh nodded. 'I think so.' Mary continued.

'My parents, your grandparents, adopted Welsh when he was a little boy; about your age when you came here.'

'So I'm a Brunty but he's not?'

Mary nodded and explained. 'Your grandfather Hugh called the little boy Welsh because of the way he looked and spoke. When your grandfather died, Uncle Welsh tricked your father and his brothers, and took over this farm.'

'Just like he tricked my parents into letting me come to live here.'

A stunned Mary whispered. 'How long have you known?'

'And now you are having a baby, I will lose my inheritance. A second Brunty will lose this farm.'

They stared at one another. Mary opened her arms, Hugh moved to her and they embraced. She wept. He'd trained himself not to cry.

The mood changed when they heard yelling. It was Gallagher.

'Help! Somebody help! Help!'

Hugh raced into the yard. Keeper barked with excitement. In the far field, Gallagher waved and called. Hugh and the dog ran towards him and reached an exhausted Gallagher. With torn clothes and a bloodied face, he pointed and gasped. 'Your uncle—he's fighting with Kelly.'

Hugh and Keeper took off with Gallagher limping after them. Hugh reached the boundary fence and saw Welsh and his neighbour, Kelly, in a no-holds-barred brawl. Swearing was compulsory with both men bruised and bleeding. Welsh wanted to quit; one of his talents.

Gallagher caught up with Hugh. 'Help him. He's gunna be killed.'

Hugh looked at the coward Gallagher then at his uncle. Hugh jumped the fence and waded into the flooded bog. Keeper followed. Kelly prepared to deliver the coup de grâce. Hugh and a bounding Keeper got closer. Kelly saw them and hesitated. Hugh stopped.

Kelly was the neighbour who ran to the burning Brunty farmhouse many years ago. There was no love lost between Welsh and Kelly. Despite its peat being long removed, the two men had disputed ownership of this useless bog for years.

Kelly knew about the abuse Hugh suffered, and the cruelty inflicted by Welsh the sub-agent. Kelly hated Welsh and this dispute over worthless land was as much about child abuse and theft.

The combatants glared at one another and, without speaking, called it quits. Hugh collected Welsh and helped his uncle home with little help from Gallagher. Mary became doctor, nurse and psychologist, and the patient was quiet—for weeks.

Hugh went to visit Mr Kelly and they chatted. The old man remembered Hugh's grandfather and knew the story of Welsh's trickery.

'I know you was treated bad, son,' said Kelly. 'At least when that bastard dies you'll have the farm to y'self.'

'Perhaps not,' replied Hugh, and told Kelly about Mary and her baby.

'My God, boy, you've got to escape. Leave now while you can.'

Hugh agreed but kept thinking about Keeper and Mary.

'One day,' said Hugh, 'and if I go, sir, will you help me? Please?'

Kelly nodded. Hugh half-smiled, and whistled for his dog.

Mary had a son and Hugh knew his so-called inheritance was lost. Welsh recovered from his war wounds and took a perverse pride in becoming a father. Mary and the baby did well.

Hugh's bond with his aunt and dog was never stronger, and this made his wish to escape difficult. He had to go but couldn't abandon his friends. He cared not for the inheritance, but greatly for those he loved.

That night, Hugh slept in his part of the barn with Keeper by his side. Moonlight kept them company as the barn door opened. Keeper's ears pricked but Hugh snored. Soft footsteps got closer and the dog growled. The intruder drew near the sleeping boy. Then Keeper exploded.

Huge awoke in an instant, looked at Keeper, and then turned to see a large figure looming above him holding a raised pitchfork. Hugh dived towards the dog as the prongs plunged into his bedding.

In the soft moonlight, the shadowy humans played a deadly game, with one armed and the other not. But the other had a friend who leapt into the fray. The first human sound was the screaming from Mr Pitchfork as the canine sank its teeth into flesh.

Hugh called off the dog. The wounded man howled. Hugh recognised the pathetic sounds and shape of Gallagher.

'Get him off!' bleated the bully turned coward.

Hugh was furious but called Keeper who returned to his master. 'Stab a man in the back—what a surprise!'

'I'm bleeding. That feckin' dog bit me.'

'You're lucky it wasn't your throat.'

Gallagher crawled away from the enemy. 'It's not my fault.'

'It never is. You're a coward; always will be.'

'Your uncle made me do it.'

Hugh baulked. Gallagher lied for a living. But could it be true? Hugh picked up the pitchfork and Gallagher prepared to die.

'No,' he said. 'Please don't. I'll leave. I'll leave now. Please.'

'Too late,' said Hugh and raised the pitchfork like a javelin thrower. Gallagher cowered in the fetal position. Hugh hurled the pitchfork, plunging it into the timber inches above Gallagher's body. The pitchfork wobbled for ages. Gallagher was alive but never in more need of a bath.

Hugh went straight to the cottage. He didn't knock but entered with Keeper at his heels. Mary nursed the baby. Welsh dozed by the fire, and Hugh mimed an apology to Mary before slamming his fist on the table.

Welsh woke up and saw the intruders.

'Hey! Get that feckin' animal out of ...'

He stopped when Keeper growled. Hugh didn't bother with small talk.

'Did you tell Gallagher to kill me?' A terrified Mary cradled her crying son. Hugh yelled. 'Did you?'

Welsh fought back. 'Don't you dare come in here making filthy accusations. Now get out!' The baby cried louder.

Hugh boiled with rage. 'You've cheated me out of my family, my inheritance, and now you've tried to murder me.'

'No!' shrieked Mary. This fight promised bloodshed. She begged. 'Stop, Hugh, please.'

Hugh hated distressing his aunt and her son. Welsh didn't give a fig. He grabbed a kitchen knife and threatened the lad. Keeper barked.

Mary screamed. 'No Welsh!'

'Feckin' bastard,' roared Welsh. 'I should've drowned you when I had the chance. We fed an' clothed you f'years, you ungrateful bit of shite.' He raised the knife. Hugh stood tall. This defiance inflamed Welsh even more. He started towards the teenager and drew back the knife. Mary screamed. Keeper barked with fury, and as Welsh lunged at Hugh with the knife, the boy kicked his uncle's kneecap. It sounded like a whip crack, and Welsh's scream was louder and longer. He lay on the floor, writhing in agony.

Hugh grabbed the fallen knife and stood over his wailing tormentor. Keeper kept barking. Right now Hugh wanted revenge for the years of abuse he'd endured from this evil man. Mary wept and Welsh howled. His dramatic performance drowned out the baby's cries.

Hugh looked at him, raised the knife to stab Welsh, then shook his head and hurled the knife against the wall. He moved to his aunt, kissed her and the baby, and walked out of the house. Keeper followed.

Back at the barn, Gallagher had vanished. Hugh jammed a piece of wood against the door, lay down and tried to sleep. He must escape.

Early next morning, he crept into the cottage and took some bread. He headed across the fields towards the river. As Keeper bounded along beside him, Hugh broke his rule of never crying.

He reached the bathing spot by the river, stripped off his old, tattered clothes and shivered in the chill morning air. He removed the last piece of bread from his trousers before folding his garments and placing them in a neat pile. His tears flowed as he pointed to the clothes and said, 'Sit'.

Keeper did as he so often did. He loved pleasing his master. The dog sat on the clothes, guarding them for when his leader returned.

Hugh's heart broke as he gave the bread to the dog, stroked its head and fondled its ears before slipping into the Boyne. He swam downstream and rounded a bend. He drifted out of sight. Keeper waited as he always did. He waited in vain.

Farmer Kelly sat eating his breakfast when his dogs started barking. The old man wasn't surprised to find a naked young man in his yard.

'You won't get far in that outfit,' said the farmer. 'Come inside.'

Kelly wanted to help Hugh. The second-hand clothes and boots he gave him didn't fit, they smelt and needed repairs. Hugh loved them.

'I can't thank you enough, Mr Kelly. You've saved my life.'

'I've put food in y'pockets and here's a coin or two.' There were three.

Overwhelmed, Hugh choked and struggled to speak.

'Mr Kelly, I have one more favour to beg of you.'

'I can't spare a horse, lad. You'll have to walk.'

'It's my dog. I'm afraid my uncle will hurt him or ...'

'Where is he?'

Hugh explained and Kelly said he would go to the bridge and fetch Keeper straightaway. Again Hugh ignored his rule about not crying, and with tears streaming down his cheeks, Mr Hugh Brunty shook Mr Joseph Kelly's hand for a long time before starting this long-awaited journey.

Where Hugh was going, how he'd get there and what he'd do when he arrived, was all in the lap of the gods.

Chapter 3

THE ADVENTURE BEGAN. With no possessions and little food and money, Hugh set off. His immediate goal was to avoid Uncle Welsh. After that it was "take it one day at a time". He'd not seen his family for a decade and had no idea where they lived. He had no friends but, having heard tales of Derry and the north, it was there he planned to go.

Walking was second nature to Hugh, and he was no stranger to hunger. He drank from streams and kept moving. He'd been walking for hours when a cart came up behind him. Hugh stood to one side. The driver reined in the horse. Hugh was afraid. *Do they know Uncle Welsh? Am I a wanted man?*

A young woman sat beside the driver. 'Father, he's but a boy.'

Hugh relaxed and removed his cap. The driver spoke. 'Where are you going, young man?'

A relieved Hugh replied, 'To Derry, sir.'

The woman laughed. 'Well if you intend walking, you might get there for Christmas.'

The man took pity on the traveller. 'In the back,' said the driver. 'We'll take you a mile.'

And so it was that Hugh Brunty, former kidnapped and abused child, and now runaway farmhand, got his first break. The gentle speed of the horse and cart was like a majestic carriage to Hugh. His adventure was off and trotting although not for long.

The cart stopped. 'We turn here,' said the driver.

Hugh alighted and bowed. 'Thank you for your kindness, sir,' he said.

'Good luck in Derry,' said the woman.

The cart turned onto another road just as the heavens opened and Hugh stood there getting soaked. He looked at the moving cart. It stopped, the woman waved and the man called. It took Hugh a few moments to understand, before he ran through the rain—not towards Derry but back to the cart.

He spent the night in a barn having enjoyed hot broth, bread and cheese. The man and his friendly dog came to say goodnight. Patting the pooch and fondling its ears was the highlight of the brilliant first day of the rest of Hugh Brunty's life.

Next morning, the determined young man set off armed with bread and directions. Life was tough. He found fruit, chopped wood for a meal, and spoke with several dogs and the odd human. He slept in haystacks, under a bridge and once in the vestry of a Catholic church. Surely assuring the priest of his strong Catholic faith couldn't possibly be a mortal sin for a Protestant in Catholic Ireland!

A week after Hugh began his escape, he came to a busy town. The locals were out shopping, and many farmers and tradesmen were there on business. The reason for such activity was the nearby lime-kiln. Agriculture and construction were big consumers of lime, and Hugh followed some carts, arriving at the office of the company. Business was brisk with workers being run off their feet. Many carts meant many customers, complaining and demanding.

'You want lime, young man?' asked the harassed foreman.

'No sir,' replied Hugh. 'I'd like a job.'

The foreman stopped, looked at Hugh then pointed. 'See them barrels of lime over there.' Hugh nodded. 'Load 'em on this gentleman's cart.' Hugh hesitated. 'Well,' said the foreman, 'do you want a job or not?'

'I do indeed,' said Hugh and followed the farmer into the yard.

The hard and smelly work made it easy to decorate your clothes, face and hands with lime. Hugh placed the last barrel on the cart and a voice made him turn.

'Is that how you always work?' Hugh smiled at the foreman.

'Yes sir, it is.'

'Dermot McNeill,' said the foreman, 'and you, young man, have got y'self a job.'

They shook hands and Hugh's throat went lumpy. It was part relief, part pride and part distress from the smell of the lime. With money in his pocket and directions from the foreman, Hugh knocked on the door of a Mrs Ryan's cottage. She was a local widow who took lodgers, and that night the newly employed Hugh Brunty enjoyed a deep sleep in a proper bed for the first time in ten years.

The months rolled by and Hugh was never so happy. Tired, yes, smelly, definitely, but delighted with his job and the respect shown to him by his fellow workers and many customers. With his hard-earned wages, he bought "proper" clothes and Mr Brunty made a name for himself.

Mrs Ryan's cooking was a joy, and his only disappointment when boarding with the widow, was her fondness for cats.

'But Mrs Ryan, I can't take the cats for a walk through the fields. If you had a dog, I'd care for it day and night—even two dogs.'

'Two!' The widow laughed. She was fond of Hugh Brunty and enjoyed his company. He was the ideal son she'd never had. She worried that Hugh didn't attend Mass or speak of his family. She sensed his troubled childhood but whenever she made polite enquiries, her boarder changed the subject.

One day at work, Dermot interrupted Hugh and asked if they might have a word. The teenager worried. *Is my work unsatisfactory? Has a customer complained?*

'How long have you been here, Hugh? Must be eighteen months?'

'It'll be two years next month, Mr McNeill. And I've loved every minute.'

'Two years!'

'Aye.'

Dermot paused. Hugh held his breath. Dermot smiled.

'And we've enjoyed having you. Now listen, lad, I've spoken to the shareholders and they agree. We want to offer you a promotion.'

Hugh was silent. He thought he understood but wasn't sure. Dermot sensed his star employee's confusion.

'It's good news, Hugh. You'll have more responsibility and earn more money—but only if you want it.'

A grin spread across Hugh's face. 'I do, and thank you, sir.'

The men shook hands and tears welled in Hugh's eyes.

'Only I wouldn't tell Mrs Ryan just yet. She'll increase your board quicker than look at you.'

They laughed. Hugh's life had changed in ways he'd never imagined, but then his happiness was interrupted by a customer.

'Any chance of some service around here?' The speaker was a young, red-headed man, Patrick McClory, a regular customer at the kiln, and he and Hugh had become friends.

'Good day to you, Mr McClory, I'll leave you in the capable hands of our new overseer,' said Dermot and departed.

'New overseer?' said an impressed Pat. 'Congratulations, good sir.'

Hugh laughed at Pat's teasing, felt proud and took Pat's order. His barrels of lime were loaded on the cart.

'Seriously, Hugh, I'm pleased about your promotion.'

'I reckon I'm more surprised than pleased,' said Hugh.

'I suppose I'll be tuggin' m'forelock now you're the boss.'

Pat doffed his hat and climbed onto his cart.

'Don't you dare,' warned Hugh and they laughed at their nonsense. Pat looked down from his cart.

'Tell me, Hugh, what will you do for Christmas; go home to y'family?'

Sad memories sprang into Hugh's mind. He sometimes wondered about his mother and father and siblings, and felt ashamed to relate his life story. He didn't know where his real family lived or if they lived at all. His thoughts were many. *Do they miss me? Do they look for me? Are they still alive?*

Hugh grimaced. 'Not me, Pat. I'll be having a quiet luncheon with my landlady.'

'Never,' replied Pat. 'Come and enjoy Christmas with me and my family.' Hugh was shocked. 'It's nothing grand mind, but we'd be delighted to have you join us.'

'That's kind but I don't think I ...'

'Good, that's settled; any time after Mass on Christmas Day. Good day to you—Mr Overseer.'

And with his Irish eyes a'smilin', Pat McClory nudged his horse and drove out of the yard. Hugh wondered about his landlady. *Will Mrs Ryan be upset?*

In fact she was delighted with Hugh's new friends. At breakfast on Christmas morning she wished her lodger "Happy Christmas". For some unknown reason, Hugh felt nervous.

After breakfast, Mrs Ryan put on her best hat. 'Now, Mr Brunty, on this special day, I believe you should come with me to Mass.'

Hugh struggled. 'I'm sorry, Mrs Ryan, I can't remember if I've ever been to church.'

Mrs Ryan gasped. 'Never been to church!'

'And I'm sure I'm not a Catholic.'

'My goodness. And here I am making small talk with a Protestant.'

'Some relatives adopted me as a little child, and they were never religious folk.'

Mrs Ryan smiled. 'Well, I'll say a prayer for you.' She handed Hugh a present. 'Here, I've put a jar of my plum jam in this bag. When you go to your luncheon, you might like to give it to the lady of the house.'

Hugh was lost for words. He still found it difficult when people showed him kindness.

Mrs Ryan continued. 'And I hope you have a lovely Christmas lunch.' With even more gratitude from Hugh, he opened the door for his landlady who left for church.

Hugh washed and shaved again, combed his hair, and put on his best suit—his only suit. He cleaned his boots and wished he'd bought a better pair. It was a cold but sunny day, and he walked some two miles to the McClory home, stepping from one side of the road to the other to avoid the mud and puddles.

His heart beat faster the closer he got to Pat's house. His thoughts raced. *Will they like me? Will I know what to say? Will I make a fool of myself?* Of social graces had he few.

The cottage loomed small. It was modest, white and plain. Such a humble dwelling helped ease Hugh's tension. *At least Pat isn't the lord of the manor. But there will be people inside, strangers. I'm not used to people and parties.* Clutching his hat and homemade gift, Hugh stood at the front door.

He'd rehearsed his lines. "Hello, I'm Hugh, Pat's friend." He knocked. The seconds ticked by and Hugh's anxiety kept growing.

The door opened and the tongue-tied Hugh stalled. He knew what he wanted and needed to say, but the person standing in front of him was ... well he couldn't even think, let alone speak.

'Hello,' she said. 'I'm Alice and you must be Hugh.' Still only silence from the visitor. 'Come away in. You're more than welcome.'

Hugh ducked his head and entered the cottage. His eyes locked on Alice. He didn't think she was the most beautiful woman he'd ever seen, but rather the most beautiful woman *anyone'd* ever seen. Her blond hair in bobbing ringlets, her gorgeous hazel eyes and flawless skin, turned Hugh into a star-struck admirer. If only Hugh had read the book *How to Charm a Woman*. If only the book existed. If only Hugh could read.

Inside his head, a voice screamed. *"Help!"*

'Let me take your hat,' said Alice and Hugh's frozen limbs began to thaw. 'Pat has gone to collect our Uncle Kevin and his family, so we'll all be having a grand time.'

At last Hugh found his voice and went all garrulous. 'Thank you,' he said with a flawless, deadpan delivery.

'Please sit down, Hugh—over there.'

Hugh remembered his manners, and stood by a chair waiting for Alice to sit. She sat and Hugh did the same. Alice was pleased to see her brother's friend had the best of manners. She was pleased too with Hugh's appearance. Pat had described Hugh as a handsome and kind young man. Alice agreed.

Hugh stood and surprised Alice. He blurted out his first full sentence. 'I've brought something for the lady of the house,' and handed her the gift.

'Oh how kind,' said Alice and inspected the contents. 'Plum jam will be perfect with our Christmas lunch. And please, do sit.'

For Hugh, the next few minutes he spent alone with Alice were a mixture of terror and ecstasy. He wanted them to end and to never end. He wanted to run away and to never leave. Her smile lit up the room. She was natural and witty and funny and … gorgeous.

Hugh rarely saw, let alone met young, attractive females, and when his first such encounter was with the most beautiful of Irish beauties, his life changed forever. Hugh flew to Heaven, and when Pat arrived with Uncle Kevin and his family, Hugh was sad his special time alone with the stunning Miss McClory ended.

Pat was the life of the party and treated Hugh as a member of the family. Pat's uncle was borderline rude, and his behaviour triggered thoughts of one, Uncle Welsh, the monster from Hugh's past.

The food and drink were basic but the love and laughter were first class, as the family celebrated the true spirit of Christmas in style. But would the goodwill endure?

Uncle Kevin, having consumed more than enough strong drink, decided it was time to examine the guest. Pat and Alice were nervous but respected their uncle. He didn't respect them or their guest.

'Right then, Mr Overseer, let's be hearin' y'speech.'

Hugh choked. *My speech?*

The tipsy uncle continued. 'And we'll be wantin' to hear you make the toast.'

Hugh grabbed some bewilderment. *What toast?*

Several family members applauded and chanted, 'Speech, speech, speech, speech …'

The chant faded when Hugh stood. As a non-drinker, for which he was unmercifully teased by Uncle Kevin, his mind was clear. He looked at Pat and Alice. Both were smiling. Hugh determined to do the right thing. He cleared his throat.

'Speak up,' cried Uncle Kevin and his family repeated the cry.

Then a hush settled and Hugh began. 'I wish to thank Pat for inviting me to your wonderful Christmas feast.' Some diners murmured their approval. Good start, Hugh. 'As a stranger to the area and having no family, I have found your kindness and generosity … more than I can say.'

What an excellent beginning, nigh on perfect. Hugh's confidence grew. He spoke from the heart. Undecided family members warmed to the stranger. He continued.

'Pat has long been a loyal customer at the kiln and I'm proud to say, is now my friend.' Hugh's sincerity and kind words hit the spot giving Pat and Alice a thrill. Even the tipsy family members liked the stranger. Hugh's confidence soared, perhaps too far. He tried to be funny. He tried to add a respectful but personal observation. Risky. It might cause trouble. Perhaps *might* is wrong. Hugh dived in.

'But had I known Pat had such a beautiful sister, I would have been calling much sooner.' He grinned; he grinned alone.

The temperature in the room plummeted. Pity, because Hugh was sincere and spoke the truth. Too shy to tell Alice in private she was the first angel he'd ever met, he took courage in being able to say so in public. Alas, his compliment backfired. It impressed Alice but Uncle Kevin was furious and shouted.

'Hey! Who da hell do you tink you are?'

Hugh's tongue wouldn't move.

'Now Uncle,' said Pat. 'Hugh meant no harm, did you, lad?'

'No, of course not,' stammered a now rattled Hugh.

Uncle Alcohol was having none of it. 'Let me tell you sometin' for nuttin', *Mr Overseer*. My niece is a good Catholic girl, and no jumped-up Protestant foreigner from the bogs down south is ever goin' to court our Alice. Now is dat clear enough for you?'

'It is and I apologise for any offence I may have caused. And that especially goes for Alice.'

She smiled and the tension in the room eased a smidgeon. Hugh felt both relief and exhilaration. On the best day of his life, he was going to woo this girl if it was the last thing he did. As it turned out, it nearly *was* the last thing he did.

Uncle Catholic made a new demand. 'Just give us the damn toast.'

Thank goodness, thought Hugh. *I'll get this right and everything will be fine.*

Hugh raised his glass and his fellow diners followed suit. Hugh saw expectant faces. Alice smiled. Now, smitten by the lady of the house, Hugh spoke with confidence. 'My friends, on this fine Christmas Day, the toast is ... the King.'

A pregnant pause became a time-bomb-ticking silence. You could smell the anger before you heard or saw it. The room erupted.

Now to be fair, Hugh was ignorant on several fronts. He had no experience in wooing a woman. He could talk for ages about the banks of the Boyne, but not a word about the Battle of the Boyne. Orange was not his favourite colour, and his only religious education came from Uncle Welsh's blasphemy.

He had no knowledge of politics or religion. The fact that the English and its monarch were hated beyond measure by vast swathes of the Catholic population of Ireland, was never prominent in Hugh's thinking. He knew nothing of the unfair English-inspired laws designed to weaken Catholic Ireland. He knew nothing of the starvation and brutal living conditions so many Irish Catholics endured, thanks to the invading Sassenachs. Had Hugh made a toast and said, "Feck the Pope," he might have got a stronger reaction—but only just.

So proposing a toast to the health of His Royal Madness, William the Third, King of Great Britain and Ireland, was not so much asking for trouble, but rather demanding it. And trouble is what he got.

Pat couldn't believe Hugh had said those words. Alice was afraid for the new man in her life. *Outraged* would best describe the drunken Uncle Kevin and his entourage. Kevin lurched to his feet, swearing and heading for Hugh with malice aforethought.

Two of Kevin's daughters threw fruit at Hugh, which struck first a cousin and then a maiden aunt, who both returned fire. Pat grappled with his uncle to save Hugh from a beating. Alice screamed. Uncle Kevin's wife accused Alice of sleeping with a Protestant dog, and the noise level increased exponentially. Some might call it a traditional Irish Christmas.

Hugh panicked as an object headed his way. He ducked meaning Mrs Ryan's plum jam slid down a wall. The living-room became an unofficial war zone. Punches and punch bowls set sail in Hugh's direction. Someone kicked his shin. He bent in pain and copped a fist in the face from a child— a child! With his sleeve being tugged, he was half-dragged outside, ducking and weaving to avoid the barrage of enemy fire. Only outside did he see his saviour was the girl with the golden tresses which danced upon her shoulders.

'My God, Alice, what have I done?'

'Don't give it another thought,' she said, brushing breadcrumbs from his jacket.

'I've repaid your hospitality by insulting you and your family.'

'Nonsense.'

'Please forgive me.'

'It's all my fault.'

'*Your* fault!'

'I should have warned you about my fanatical anti-Protestant Uncle.'

'I can never forgive myself for behaving so badly to you and your brother.' He paused; they looked at one another. Two hours ago, Hugh couldn't speak a single syllable. Now he turned loquacious. 'But I want you to know I meant every word I said in there about you being so beautiful and lovely and kind and wonderful and ...'

'Shhhh,' she said, and placed a finger on Hugh's lips. They tingled.

The raucous sounds inside the cottage continued but, for Hugh, they didn't exist. His eyes, mind, heart and soul were captivated by the divine Miss M.

Alice removed her finger and Hugh dived in again.

'I suppose I'm a Protestant, although I can't ever remember going to church.'

'Lucky you,' smiled Alice, and Hugh's heart beat even faster.

'Would you ... will you ... I mean ... is it possible you might one day ... walk out with me?'

Alice remained calm. 'As you've seen, my family are good Catholics, and I'm certain they wouldn't approve.' Hugh's heart sank. Alice paused, smiled then spoke. 'But I won't tell them if you don't.'

Hugh's heart was recharged. Looking deep into Alice's eyes, he took her hand and kissed it. Her heartbeat matched his.

It accelerated when a roar came from inside the cottage. 'Where is dat feckin' Protestant bastard?'

Alice broke free and ordered Hugh to leave. She moved back to the cottage, but stopped at the door and called to him. 'I'll send a message with Pat.' She blew a kiss and disappeared.

It's true to say that in going home, Hugh skipped most of the way.

Chapter 4

HUGH WAS A NEW MAN. Every waking moment he thought about Alice. At work he had a spring in his step. Mrs Ryan knew something was afoot and guessed right. Love was in the County Down air. All Hugh had to do was convince Alice's family he was a decent man, and wanted only the best for their girl. But alas, the Great Wall of Ireland stood tall, and he was on the other side, the Protestant side.

Getting messages to Alice was tricky. Hugh had rudimentary literacy skills, and when the messenger failed to show, Hugh despaired. Pat, the go-between, hadn't been to the lime kiln for a fortnight. Why? *Did Alice not mean what she said? Was Pat like his Uncle Kevin and against the possible romance?* The not-knowing haunted Hugh.

Then Dermot called Hugh into his office. The last time Hugh and his boss had a private conversation it was good news and a promotion. Was another new job on the cards?

'Have a seat, Hugh,' said Dermot.

A worried Hugh sat.

'I hope there's not been a complaint with my work, Mr McNeill.'

'Not your work, Hugh. You're the best worker we've ever had. But I'm afraid I've got bad news—*very* bad news.'

Hugh couldn't speak.

'I'm sorry to say I have to dismiss you.'

'You mean I'm to get the sack?' said a stunned Hugh.

McNeill nodded. 'It's nothing to do with your work but everything to do with your religion.'

Hugh struggled to understand this new information. 'But I have no religion. I can't remember when I last went to church, if ever.'

'Some Catholic farmers complained about your behaviour.'

'My behaviour?' asked a nonplussed Hugh. 'You said my work was satisfactory.'

'Several of my best customers say they'll travel miles to get their lime elsewhere rather than do business here, unless you leave.'

'But why?' Hugh was close to tears.

'I have to say, Hugh, that making a toast to the English monarch in front of a group of Irish Catholics was either very brave or sheer bloody lunacy.'

It all came flooding back. News of Hugh's speech at the McClory Christmas luncheon had hit the local grapevine, and the consequences for Hugh were dire. The chief gossip-monger had to be Uncle Kevin.

Tears filled Hugh's eyes as he shook hands with Dermot McNeill.

'I've put a little extra in your pay packet,' said Dermot. 'I wish you well, Hugh Brunty. For a Protestant, you're a damn fine Irishman.'

Hugh's world collapsed. The two things which gave him hope and life itself were snatched from him. His labour and lover were gone.

For ten years he'd suffered sadistic abuse from his wretched Uncle Welsh, only to recover and discover the joys of living. First it was honest work and then true love. Now he was out of a job and unable to court Alice. Mrs Ryan sat in shock.

'Good heavens, Hugh. You never toasted the English king?'

Hugh nodded. 'I can't work hereabouts Mrs Ryan. I must leave your beautiful cottage and wonderful company.'

Silence and sadness crept into the Ryan kitchen.

'If only I had a dog,' said Mrs Ryan. She looked at Hugh and, despite the bleak mood, they both smiled.

Hugh packed his meagre belongings, spent most of his savings on a good horse, and rode away from the town and area he loved.

He needed to travel a fair way to escape his new reputation as an anti-Catholic, but he wanted to remain close to Alice as his love for her grew stronger every day. He'd lost his job but would fight damn hard for the hand of his girl.

On the first day of his travels, he came upon a couple with a cart needing repairs. Hugh offered to help and got their vehicle moving again.

'You are a gentleman, sir, and I shall not forget your kindness,' said the old man.

'Give him something for his trouble,' said his wife.

Hugh interrupted. 'Thank you, there's no need. I'm happy to help. But I'd be glad of advice.'

'Certainly,' chorused the couple.

'Is there any work I might find hereabouts?'

The couple couldn't suggest anything. Hugh thanked them, climbed back on his horse and was about to ride away when the woman spoke.

'What about the Harshaws? They employ servants and farm hands.'

'Oh yes,' added the man. 'Go along this road for half a mile and take the first turn on your left. It's a large house set back behind a line of trees.'

Hugh doffed his hat and rode to the Harshaw house. He trotted up the long drive, dismounted, and a servant appeared and held his horse. Hugh was impressed.

'I wish to see the master of the house,' said Hugh.

'Will the mistress suffice?' A woman spoke from the garden.

Hugh removed his hat and walked to the woman.

'Good day to you, Ma'am. My name is Hugh Brunty, and I believe the Harshaw household employs farmhands and workers. I hope you might allow me to offer my services.'

'My husband is in charge. He's out in the west field.' She pointed. 'I suggest you ride out and ask him.'

Hugh bowed. 'I'm most grateful, Ma'am.'

Hugh remounted his horse, and cantered off in search of his would-be employer, who was easy to find if only because of the squeals from his young children, all having a grand old time.

Hugh dismounted a distance away and led his horse towards two men and three children.

'Can I help you?' called Mr Harshaw as Hugh approached.

'I hope so, sir,' replied Hugh. 'But if I may, you'll never inspect that cow holding it as you are.' Hugh paused. 'May I?'

Harshaw nodded and Hugh moved to the cow. The children fell silent as the stranger approached the beast and stroked and calmed it, allowing the farmhand to check its bulging abdomen with the animal standing still.

'I'm impressed, sir,' said Harshaw. 'You wouldn't be looking for a job by any chance?'

Hugh found new employment. Mr Harshaw gave him duties around the farm and as Uncle Welsh, despite his vile behaviour, had taught his nephew well, Hugh's worth to the family proved a wonderful asset.

But finding work, getting on well with his employer, and enjoying doing things he was good at, didn't stop Hugh from thinking about Alice McClory. A lovesick pain throbbed in his chest. He missed her and was sure she felt the same. She'd agreed to walk out with him.

But how can I contact her?

One night, in his quarters, Hugh got talking with a servant, Michael O'Leary, a quiet man who'd worked for the Harshaws for many years. One of his tasks was to travel to town and place orders for various items. Hugh got an idea.

'Michael, could you deliver a letter for me to a girl I'm courting?'

'Oh, it's a matchmaker I am, is it now?'

'I'll pay you.'

'That you will. So who's the Colleen and where does she live?'

'Her name is Alice McClory from Ballynaskeagh and ...'

'Oh no, she wouldn't be related to Kevin McClory?'

Hugh paused. He nodded. 'Do you know Miss McClory?'

'I know the uncle and good luck there. So, where's that letter?'

'Ah.'

The two men looked at one another. Michael spoke first.

'You haven't written it or you can't write?'

'Bit of both,' said Hugh.

Sometime later, Hugh signed his name to a letter which he composed and Michael wrote. The message stated that on Sundays around noon, Hugh would be riding by the old mill on the River Bann.

It was a week before Michael O'Leary went into town with Hugh anxious for his return.

'Well?' pleaded Hugh.

Michael paused then smiled. 'I passed by their cottage and gave it to the lady herself.'

Overjoyed, Hugh hugged his fellow worker just as Mrs Harshaw appeared. She surprised the men who were embarrassed.

'Something to celebrate?' she asked.

Hugh explained that their rejoicing was due to O'Leary having brought good news about one of Hugh's friends. Mrs Harshaw smiled, and asked Hugh if he would come to the main house after supper. Hugh's mind buzzed. *What is that all about?*

She left and the men made faces at one another.

After supper, Hugh knocked on the kitchen door. The housekeeper told him Mrs Harshaw was expecting him in the sitting-room. Once there, he was invited to sit, and did so with a rapid heartbeat.

'Mr Harshaw and I are delighted with your work, Mr Brunty, but believe you might be better suited to another task.' Hugh was hooked. 'We'd like you to spend more time with the children.'

This was unexpected. Hugh was unsure what to say. The Harshaws waited so Hugh took his cue.

'Thank you, Mrs Harshaw. But I've spent my life working outdoors. I'm not a teacher of children.'

'The children have asked for you,' said the lady of the house.

'Oh,' became the standard Brunty reply.

'Why don't you think about it and we can talk again tomorrow.'

Hugh got the message, stood, nodded and made as dignified an exit as possible. Life seemed full of little surprises.

Since Christmas, Alice had spent most waking moments thinking about the young man who captured her heart. It was devastating to learn of his sacking and forced departure from the area. Uncle Kevin took great delight in delivering the news.

She asked her brother for advice and, although keen to help both his sister and his friend, Pat had no idea where Hugh had gone with no way of knowing. Sadness dominated Alice's thoughts.

But her misery instantly became joy when Hugh's letter arrived. Alice's reading skills were not much better than Hugh's, but she understood he was suggesting a rendezvous time and place. Next Sunday she would go riding. Oh roll on the Sabbath.

That evening, as she prepared supper for her brother, she was tempted to tell him her good news. But he got in first and destroyed her happiness.

'Uncle Kevin's coming tonight and bringing Joe Burns.'

Alice stopped stirring the soup and banged the stick against the pot.

'No!' she cried. 'You promised you'd put an end to that.'

'I'm sorry, girl. You know he means well.'

'But you're not the one being forced into marriage, and to a man I can't abide!'

Joe Burns was 37, single, Catholic, owner of a smallholding with livestock, and who might be described as eligible, with *might* being the key word.

Joe lived with his mother. He drank with Kevin, and Alice's uncle decided his niece should be wed to a local "lad" with land, and a soul attached to Holy Rome. Alice had several reasons to disagree with her uncle's selection.

Joe was twice Alice's age, half a rung above ugly, wore farm smells as cologne, and had less charm than a privy. In short, and he *was* short, he was unattractive. And if that wasn't enough, an alternative to Burns was available in one Hugh Brunty, the most gentle, charming and beautiful of men she had ever set eyes on. There was no contest.

Uncle Kevin and Joe Burns arrived bearing drinks. They were in good spirits with Pat and Alice much less so.

'Glasses me boy,' said Kevin placing bottles on the table. Pat fetched the glasses and Kevin poured the drinks. He raised his glass and proposed a toast. 'To da happy couple.'

Joe was keen, Patrick reluctant and Alice motionless.

The mood darkened. The men stared at Alice. She paused then spoke.

'I'm sorry, Uncle, but I don't feel ready for marriage just yet.'

'Of course you're ready.'

Patrick stood up for his sister. 'She is quite young, Uncle.'

'Now don't you start,' snapped Kevin. 'I've set the date and told Father Murphy, and Joe's even bought a new suit.'

'Secondhand like,' grinned the unworldly suitor.

'So enough of dis nonsense. You're gonna be wed, me girl and dat's final.'

There was a pause. The silence dominated. Alice turned away as Kevin spoke in a quiet but menacing voice.

'An' don't you tink for one feckin' moment you an' dat bog-Irish Protestant will ever be wed.'

Alice spun round and faced her uncle. Pat was shocked and Joe reckoned grinning was the correct social response.

Kevin played his trump card. 'An' don't tink I don't know da bastard's been sendin' you letters. I know and da whole feckin' family knows.'

Alice burst into tears and ran from the room.

Pat spoke first. 'I didn't know about any letters.'

'Dat's your problem, Paddy. You know feckin' nuttin'.' Kevin picked up the bottles and started for the door. 'Come on, Joe. We'll finish dese at your place.'

Next Sunday, a worried but determined Alice saddled her horse and rode away. She set off in the opposite direction to the River Bann. If Uncle Kevin knew about the letter, he might follow her, and if he knew the contents of the letter, he might be waiting at the rendezvous.

Out of sight, Alice turned, taking a long route to the mill. She so wanted to meet Hugh, and had a mixture of excitement and fear, being terrified of her violent uncle and what he might do.

Close to the river, she stopped amongst some trees. The sounds of nature dominated and then a horse whinnied. Alice saw Hugh in the distance. She rode into the clearing and he spotted her. She alighted but became frightened as he urged his horse to gallop towards her.

His reckless riding seemed scary, so keen was he to reach his girl. He leapt from his horse and didn't bother to tether the animal as he took Alice in his arms. They said nothing and couldn't, so strong were their kisses.

They stopped kissing and stared at one another. Both were crying.

'I can't tell you how much I've missed you,' said Hugh.

They kissed then hugged although the passion was suspended as Hugh fetched his wandering horse. They tethered the animals then spoke.

'I was afraid I would never see you again,' said Alice.

'I would do anything to see you again, my darling girl.'

The expression on Alice's face changed and, being sensitive, Hugh knew something was wrong. She explained.

'My Uncle Kevin knows about your letter.'

A stunned Hugh exploded. 'What! That damn O'Leary betrayed us.'

'But there's more, I'm afraid.' Alice paused. Hugh felt a knot in his stomach. 'I'm supposed to be getting married next month.'

'Married! But Alice, surely you care for me.'

'I don't *care* for you, Hugh Brunty, I *love* you with all my heart.'

They hugged, kissed and hugged again with both now openly crying. It was difficult for Alice to speak, and being upset, she buried her face in Hugh's chest. She recovered, lifted her face and looked into his eyes.

'The only person I want to marry is you.'

Hugh released his embrace and stepped back. 'Miss McClory, I do believe you're puttin' the cart in front of the horse.' She looked at him, confused. Hugh hesitated, dropped to one knee and looked up at her.

'Alice McClory, do you consent to be my wife?'

Alice didn't hesitate. 'Yes, a thousand times yes,' she cried, and Hugh stood and the kissing resumed. Even the horses nodded their approval.

Then reality arrived. How can they overcome Uncle Kevin, Father Murphy and whatever or whoever else stood in their way?

They sat and discussed tactics. A Catholic wedding was out because Uncle Kevin would forbid the priest from marrying them. To Kevin, Hugh was a dreaded enemy. So it had to be a Protestant wedding with none of her family invited; not even Pat. Everything must be done in secret.

It must be soon. The arranged marriage was due in a few weeks. They could no longer exchange letters because of the traitor at Harshaws. They needed to set the date here and now, agree a plan and stick to it.

They did, and boy was it exciting.

Back at the Harshaws, Hugh found O'Leary. 'I'd like a word with you, Mr O'Leary,' said Hugh.

O'Leary had no idea what Hugh was talking about, and Hugh was glad he didn't accuse Michael of treachery. The traitor was another servant who overheard Hugh and Michael discussing the letter. A good Catholic, the other servant got word to Kevin regarding the "evil" Protestant's plans.

Hugh agreed to a change of role at the Harshaws, and spent two hours every day "teaching" the three children. The two girls and a boy loved every moment of their time with the tall, red-headed man who made them laugh, fixed anything and could even talk to the animals.

By accident, they discovered Hugh was not a university graduate, and so began a wonderful exchange of information. Hugh would tell stories about dogs, bogs, wicked farmers and adventures, and the children would teach him to read—well, almost. It was extraordinary and no-one knew who enjoyed the lessons more.

Hugh's storytelling blossomed, and the children formed a team to teach and test Hugh's literacy skills. If only the outside world had discovered these wonderful events in the Harshaw's library, County Down.

Back at the McClory mansion, Alice's wedding drew nigh and the pressure kept building. The sympathetic priest urged her to do the right thing. She tried on her beautiful wedding dress. She entertained all who called to wish her well. Food and drink kept arriving. The cottage was whitewashed and cleaned. And all this, *everything* was a lie. Alice had no intention of marrying Joe Burns. But could she maintain the deceit?

Hugh delayed going to see Mrs Harshaw. If he won her approval, Mr Harshaw would agree. Finally, Hugh stood before the lady of the house.

'I was wondering, Mrs Harshaw, if you might allow me to take two days off next week,' said Hugh.

'I see. Is there something important you plan to do?' She realised it might be serious. 'It's not a death in your family, I trust.'

'Not quite, Ma'am. It's just that on Sunday I'm getting married.'

Talk about a conversation stopper.

'You are a remarkable man, Mr Brunty. You tell amazing stories to my enchanted children. My husband says you know more about farming and animals than he does. And now, without a hint of a possible romantic attachment, you tell me you're going to be married on the weekend.'

'I'm afraid it's a matter of necessity, Ma'am.'

The lady of the house paused. She wasn't smiling. 'Perhaps such a statement should remain private, Mr Brunty.'

Hugh realised the misunderstanding. 'Oh no. My bride is being forced into a marriage with an older man for whom she has no affection. But we're very much in love and plan on being a runaway couple.'

'For only two days?'

Hugh considered his response. 'Tis a short honeymoon, Mrs Harshaw, but a lifelong marriage.'

She smiled. 'Then congratulations and go with my blessing.' Hugh nodded. 'But I'm afraid there is no accommodation for married couples here on the estate.'

'I know that, Ma'am. My wife will return to the cottage she shares with her brother, and I will return here to serve out my duties as promised.'

Mrs Harshaw raised her eyebrows. 'I said you were remarkable, Mr Brunty. I believe I should add *surprising* and *unique*. Goodbye and good luck.' Hugh smiled, thanked the lady of the house and started to depart. He stopped when she spoke. 'Oh Mr Brunty, I believe every honeymoon should last at least three days. We'll expect you on Thursday.'

The day of the wedding was sunny. Pat worried his sister gave in too easily, agreeing to marry Joe Burns. Pat tried to discuss things with Alice but she muttered something about her parents wanting her to wed.

After the church service, the wedding breakfast was to be at the McClory cottage, and with the weather fine, they set up tables in the yard with no expense spared. Uncle Kevin arrived early to check everything was in order. He hugged his niece, and told her there was no need to thank him for having found her a wealthy and perfect Catholic husband.

Which was the more appalling—Kevin's hug or the lies he told?

As soon as her uncle left, Alice told her brother she wanted to go for one last ride as a single woman. Pat laughed. His sister would never put up with being ordered around by any man, least of all the vacuous Joe Burns.

She gave her brother a strong kiss which surprised him. He assumed it was an emotional day for any woman soon to wed. She galloped away into the hills with a disguised wedding dress draped across the animal.

Meanwhile, Hugh meticulously cleaned his clothes and boots. He'd shaved twice, changed his underwear thrice, and used a week's supply of soap. Nervous, he dressed, then led his horse to the front of the house and mounted. He heard shouting. From an upstairs window, the three Harshaw children waved.

'Good luck Mr Groom,' they yelled, and laughed at his surprise. He smiled, waved his hat, and then galloped away to his wedding.

Back at the McClory cottage, Uncle Kevin returned dressed to the eights. He planned to escort the bride to the church in case she got cold feet. Pat gave him the news about her final gallop, and Kevin fumed.

'Final gallop! She's gettin' wed f'Chrissake.'

Kevin's anger moved closer to apoplexy as the minutes ticked by and Alice failed to appear. Where was the girl? His thinking was clear. *If she's had a fall, that's okay. We can patch her up and get her to the church on time. But if she's run away, my God, what a feckin' disaster.*

Locals called to wish the family well, and news of the missing bride spread like wildfire. Others came to help or enjoy the spectacle. One guest arrived to say he'd seen Alice riding away from her home. Panic stations.

With only an hour before the church service, Kevin told the guests, and anyone else in the vicinity, to spread out and find the missing bride. Kevin's wife rolled her eyes. *If only I'd disappeared on* my *wedding day.*

And so, on the day she was to marry Joseph Burns, Eleanor Alice McClory went riding and disappeared, meaning half the parish combed the roads, woods and fields calling her name. Even Father Murphy joined the search party. Where's Alice? Ah, Alice was in wonderland.

The search was fruitless, and the searchers returned in dribs and drabs, to sit in the McClory yard, kitchen or parlour. Talk about no show without Punch; no Alice, no bride, no wedding.

Then a child arrived, panting and bearing important news. Kevin's hopes lifted before being dashed as the young boy delivered his lines.

'I'm to say that Alice McClory and Hugh Brunty have been married in the Protestant church at Magherally.' Cue a massive reaction. When calm returned, the messenger delivered the punchline. 'Miss McClory wants to thank you all f'comin' to her weddin' and hopes you enjoy t'breakfast.'

Kevin threw a bottle at the child but with his fury dissipated, Uncle's aim was like his attempt at an arranged marriage—a damp squib.

Now spare a thought for the jilted groom. Joe Burns was all dressed up with nowhere to go, and his ageing mother turned purple with rage. Her washing and cooking days were set to continue.

It was a predictable honeymoon. Passion was the first item on the agenda—and the second and third as well—and while both participants were beginners in the lovemaking stakes, they got away to a good start, ran well on a heavy track and finished the course with all whips cracking.

Being young and virile helped, and falling pregnant would not prove difficult for Alice Brunty nee McClory. In fact, in union with her husband, she would produce ten little 'uns with a sense of proportion resulting in five of each sex—boys to begin with girls to follow. She named her third son Hugh and her fifth daughter Alice.

Did the young married couple imagine they would create ten children? Surely they didn't imagine their first born and his family would have a profound impact on the world for hundreds of years.

Chapter 5

FEW NEWLYWEDS SEPARATE straight after their honeymoon, but Alice returned to her brother in the McClory cottage, and Hugh went back to the Harshaws.

When Hugh had a half-day off, the couple met where proceedings began with a traditional and enthusiastic romantic greeting. Then came the "what-have-you-been-up-to" bit, after which sensible chatting ensued. At one such meeting, Hugh produced a bible.

'There's no need to impress me, Hugh Brunty, I'm already your wife.'

'I've been driving the Harshaws to church, and even sitting in their pew for the services.'

'Well done, Mr Protestant. But what use is the holy book to you?'

'I'm learning to read,' he said with a wide grin.

'Really?' Alice was intrigued. '*Really?*'

Hugh nodded with pride. 'And you'll never guess the names of my teachers.'

'Teachers? How many are there?'

When Hugh told Alice about the Harshaw children and their lessons, she shrieked with laughter. She loved him and was proud of him.

But Hugh's education ended when he left the Harshaws and moved in with his wife. They rented a tiny cottage in Emdale. *Tiny* was right. You slept in one room and did everything else in the other. Well, perhaps not everything. The rent was sixpence a week.

Soon after they settled in their rented abode, Hugh came home from his farm labouring work and his wife asked him to sit.

'I have news, sir,' she said smiling.

'You're finally becoming a Protestant.'

'No, you're finally becoming a father.'

Hugh embraced Alice and they hugged for ages. Then he fussed.

'Come and sit, my girl. You must rest. Put your feet here.'

Alice shook her head. 'No, I want no fuss. I've got the supper to make and spinning to do. The baby can wait.'

It did, but when it arrived, Alice had limited family support. Her mother was in the ground and, unbeknown to Hugh, so too was his mother.

Talk about a humble beginning. In the front room of their Emdale "mansion", the baby, a healthy male, was born. So what to name the little chap?

'We don't have a choice, Mrs Brunty,' said Hugh.

'He's got your red hair,' said Alice. 'We'll call him, Hugh.'

'Are you mad, woman? Tell me the date.'

'Oh, my goodness,' laughed Alice. 'It's Saint Patrick's Day.'

It was March the 17th, and every Irish man, woman and child, Protestant or Catholic, knows the birthday of Ireland's patron saint.

So Patrick Brunty he became but later, Patrick something else.

Money was never plentiful. The Bruntys managed because of Hugh's farm-labouring skills and Alice's knitting. She got wool from her brother's sheep, spun it on her spinning-wheel in the cottage, and knitted clothes for her children. Decades later, Patrick Brunty still wore his mother's homemade garments.

Their basic diet had plenty of potatoes and buttermilk. But their marriage wasn't basic; it was rich getting richer and deeper, a match made in Heaven, and they adored their darling Patrick.

Hugh's newfound interest in education meant he stocked the Brunty "library" with three tomes—the bible, poetry by Rabbie Burns, and *The Pilgrim's Progress* by John Bunyan. These were not just the first books young Patrick read, but the first books he saw.

One night, four-year-old Patrick was excited.

'Is it tonight, Papa, is it?' He pestered his father.

'Yes, it's tonight, but you can only stay up if you behave.'

'What's the story, Papa? Will it be about ghosts? Or the dogs that saved the town, or the mountain that disappeared or ...? Tell me, please.'

Hugh was a natural and brilliant storyteller. So many locals crowded into the Emdale cottage to hear Hugh's tales, you couldn't move. Alice spun her yarn and Hugh spun his. Entranced, young Patrick sat at his father's feet. What tales and what storytelling skills his father possessed.

When Hugh whispered stories to his children, sometimes they begged him to stop because the tension he created was so dramatic.

Alice was constantly pregnant, and with a fourth son on the way, the family moved to a larger home. One night after supper, a growing Patrick sat on his father's knee as Hugh did his best to read to his son. The boy stared at the pages.

'Read more, Papa,' said the young boy. 'And what's that word?'

'Please.'

'Please, Papa.'

Hugh took his time. His enthusiasm for reading didn't match his expertise. 'Ah, I think that's ....'

'I know,' cried Patrick. 'It's *sal-va-tion*.'

Hugh and his knitting wife exchanged glances.

'Right young man, time for bed,' said Hugh.

Patrick grumbled, kissed his parents and went to bed pronouncing *salvation* as his new word for the day, with no idea what it meant.

'I'm not sure if you're teaching Patrick or he's teaching you,' said Alice without dropping a stitch.

'The sooner he starts at the school, the better,' replied Hugh. 'I'll see the schoolmaster.'

Patrick was a natural student. He started at the local school with a strong grasp of reading and writing and counting skills. His parents didn't have time to spoil the firstborn—his brothers, then sisters kept arriving at regular intervals.

One night, by a flickering candle, Patrick, now 12, sat reading the poetry of Robert Burns. Hugh joined his son.

'I'm pleased you love reading, Pat. I only wish I'd been a reader when I was your age.'

'Why did you not read, Papa? You never speak of your school days.'

Hugh grimaced. He seldom spoke of his childhood.

'Because I never went to school.' Patrick stared at his father.

'Never?'

Patrick wanted to ask more but his father changed the subject. 'So is this poetry you're reading?'

'It is, and Mr Burns has a wonderful way with words. It's something I'd like to do.'

'What? Write words?'

'Yes, write poetry; my favourite type of writing.'

'But how will you earn your living? You can't pay the bills writing poetry.'

That got Patrick thinking. 'What did you want to do when you were my age?'

'Survive,' said Hugh.

'Survive? What do you mean?'

'When I was young, my life was hard. No school, no church, just hard work on the farm.' Patrick was intrigued. 'But your life is different, Pat, and it's time you started looking for work.'

'I'll always help with the harvest, Father.'

'I know, lad.'

'And the firewood and feeding the animals and walking the dogs.'

'Yes, yes, but now you're growing, you'll need a proper job to earn proper money. And with a proper job, you could buy your own books.'

Patrick liked that idea. 'Money would be nice. But what type of work?'

'I spoke to Mr Flynn, the blacksmith. He can train a lad.'

Doubts appeared. 'A blacksmith?'

'It's a good honest trade, and the forge is just over the road from where you was born. Go and talk to Mr Flynn.'

Alice listened as she stood by the fire, potstick in hand, preparing supper. Hugh went to his wife and placed a hand on her swollen belly.

'How long, my love?' asked Hugh.

'Soon,' said Alice as the baby gave another strong kick.

'I was asking about the supper.'

Her eyes sparkled as she gave her husband a playful slap.

Patrick Brunty left school and trained as a blacksmith. He found the work boring. Once he mastered the basics, the blacksmith left him to get on with simple tasks. One day, Mr Flynn came running in, yelling.

'The fire, Patrick, the fire!'

It was almost out so Patrick stirred the coals and pumped the bellows. The angry blacksmith took charge.

'Oh, for pity's sake, lad, how many times have I told you?'

'I'm sorry, Mr Flynn.'

'And is that a book on the ground?'

Patrick looked sheepish. He'd been caught reading "on the job" and came home ashamed. Here, everything was normal. His mother was pregnant, spinning, nursing and watching the supper. Her middle name wasn't Lazy.

'Why the long face, young man? You look like your mouth has broke your nose.'

Patrick sat but didn't look at his mother. 'I got the sack.'

'Well good for you.' Surprised, Patrick looked at his mother. She wasn't angry. She didn't condemn. 'Be a kind boy and pass me that wool.'

He did, then went outside to play with the dogs and his brothers. He dreaded telling his father but need not have worried. Hugh understood.

'You're keeping up the family tradition, m'boy.' This confused Patrick. 'I once got the sack when I fell in love with y'mother.'

Alice laughed and Patrick was even more confused.

'It's true,' she said. 'So when you fall off the horse, Patrick, you've got to climb back on again, quick smart.'

'Find something else,' said Hugh. 'Have you found any jobs writing poetry?'

Patrick enjoyed being teased. 'I might try weaving,' he said.

'Excellent trade,' said Hugh.

'You could work from home,' said Alice.

'And read a book while you work,' added a smiling Hugh.

Patrick joined the grins and soon became a weaver. At first he worked for others in their homes but as he improved, he set up a loom in his parent's home producing top-quality material. Living at home meant he saved money.

At night he wrote poetry but thought it childish. *Will I ever have my poetry published?*

He couldn't discuss his ambition. Where he lived, poetry was a foreign language. Most people couldn't even read. He devoured the family library and longed for more books. One day, he told his mother he was off to Belfast.

'Patrick, are you sure?'

'Mama, Belfast is the only place to find a good bookshop.'

'No, I mean are you sure you want to spend your money on books?'

Patrick looked at his mother. *What kind of a question is that?* He kissed her, speaking as he left. 'I'll be home for supper.'

'Take care,' she called but his long legs were already in motion.

Belfast was by far the biggest town Patrick had ever seen. He looked in shop windows. The clothes were far superior to his humble, home-made garments. The food made his mouth water. And the bookshops, well, talk about Heaven right here on Earth.

The bell rang as he pushed open the door. Patrick had never been so excited. He remembered his father telling the story of a cat and a bowl of cream. Patrick knew how that feline felt.

'Yes?' A man wearing a suit of superiority addressed Patrick.

'Oh, good morning. I'm looking for books on poetry, please.'

'Poetry?' The missing words were, "What in God's name would you know about poetry?"

Patrick took a moment to recover. 'Yes, I have a book of poems by Robert Burns and would like ...'

'You won't find anything here.' The bookseller turned away.

'I have money.' Patrick wasn't giving in without a fight.

'Try *Warring* in the High Street. Good day.'

Patrick's red hair gave off a wisp of smoke and, with his temper set to explode, he hesitated, then departed giving the door a solid tug.

He found the High Street and the assistant in Isaac Warring's bookshop welcomed him.

'Did you have any poets in mind, sir?' asked the courteous assistant.

Patrick explained. 'I'm just beginning my poetry collection.'

'Well please allow me to recommend the outstanding epic poem *Paradise Lost* by John Milton.'

Patrick remembered his teacher reading a part of this work to the class.

'John Milton was an Englishman,' said the assistant.

Patrick smiled. 'I'm interested in poetry, not politics.'

The assistant smiled back and handed Patrick the volume. Just the feel of the book was enough to set his pulse racing. He opened it and saw the pristine paper, the high quality typesetting, and the expert binding. He turned page after page. They were beautiful with an enticing aroma. He was thrilled and about to announce his decision to purchase his first book when the assistant told him the price.

Patrick's heart went cold. He'd counted his money so often he knew how much he had, to the exact farthing.

The assistant saw the look on Patrick's face.

'May one enquire as to how much money sir has?'

Blinking back tears, Patrick took out his small purse and laid the coins on the table. He was only a few pence short but short he was. The assistant counted the money.

'Oh I do apologise, sir, I've made a mistake. You have exactly the right amount.'

Patrick struggled to understand. The kind assistant looked at Patrick but said nothing. Then the halfpenny dropped, Patrick understood and held out his hand. They shook hands.

'Thank you,' he said. 'Thank you, kind sir. I will treasure this book for the rest of my life.'

Out in the street, Patrick clutched the volume, took a deep breath and headed home.

The bookseller would never know how far the little candle he lit would throw its beams. So shone that good deed in a weary world.

Patrick wanted to stop and read his book. Wrapped in brown paper, tied with string and buried inside his jacket, the book was safe. It would be unveiled when he reached home. He'd eaten the food his mother gave him, which was another incentive to keep moving. *The sooner I'm home, the sooner I'll feed my stomach and soul.*

Walking through a glorious County Down wood with birds, flowers, babbling brooks and dappled sunshine, he succumbed to temptation. He took a drink from a brook then dried his hands. He sat on a mossy tree trunk and unwrapped his precious cargo. *Fastidious* became his middle name.

The world went about its business. Patrick went about his. Placing the folded brown paper and string on the trunk, and opening his tome, Patrick saw words on the title page he couldn't remember from the viewing in the shop. He dwelt on each page. Time meant nothing. Patrick was lost in paradise.

He began to read the epic poem and savoured everything—the theme, the imagery, the vocabulary. He perused the layout of the text, the typeface, the paper, the binding. This one book could teach him so much about understanding and writing poetry. He felt inspired to create his own literary works of art.

He remembered his teacher reading poetry in the small school he once attended. The teacher read aloud. 'Poetry,' he said, 'should be spoken.'

Patrick paused, thought about those words, and turned to the start of the poem. He stepped onto a half-buried rock, raised the book, opened his mouth and performed.

> Of Man's first disobedience, and the fruit
> Of that forbidden tree whose mortal taste
> Brought death into the World, and all our woe,
> With loss of Eden, till one greater Man
> Restore us, and regain the blissful seat,

Patrick's voice drifted into the wood. Did birdsong cease or butterflies stop fluttering? Did brooks babble more softly or plants incline their blooms? The poet was alone with nature, and in love with the written word.

Or was he alone? In fact, a Presbyterian clergyman, the Revd Andrew Harshaw, a relative of the Harshaws who once employed Patrick's father, was walking through the wood when he heard a fellow human. He stopped. Yes, someone was speaking.

> Sing, Heavenly Muse, that, on the secret top
> Of Oreb, or of Sinai, didst inspire
> That shepherd who first taught the chosen seed

Harshaw proceeded with caution. Tip-toeing through a wood seemed unnecessary but, so intrigued with what he could hear, such was his gait. The voice became louder. Harshaw stopped and, from a hidden vantage point, took a back-row seat as the performance continued.

> I thence invoke thy aid to my adventurous song,
> That with no middle flight intends to soar
> Above th' Aonian mount, while it pursues
> Things unattempted yet in prose or rhyme.

Although fascinated with the poem and the performer, Harshaw felt unease at his secret position. He turned to slip away and stood on a fallen branch. Snap, it cracked and the sound echoed through the wood.

The poetry stopped. What was that sound? Harshaw froze. The birds, butterflies and brooks kept performing and Harshaw knew hiding was silly.

'Hello,' he cried, walking into view and approaching Patrick.

'Good day to you, sir,' said a surprised Patrick, stepping down from his stage.

'Forgive me for interrupting. I was passing and felt compelled to stop. It was a most impressive performance.'

Patrick and Harshaw shook hands and introduced themselves. And thus began a relationship, a partnership which can only be described as fortuitous for both men, and for many others. The pair continued their journeys together and found talking and listening to be easy.

Patrick was frustrated working as a weaver, and Harshaw spotted potential in the teenage lover of literature.

'Tell me, Mr Brunty, have you ever considered a teaching career?'

The suggestion thrilled Patrick. 'I haven't, sir, but would love to share my passion for reading and poetry with young minds.'

'Then I have a proposal. I teach in a small school at Ballynafern. If you will attend in the mornings for say, two hours, I can teach you various subjects to help prepare you for a teaching career, leaving you free to continue weaving later in the day.'

Patrick couldn't speak such was Harshaw's overwhelming generosity. Back home, Patrick's proud and emotional parents cried. Their firstborn son was to continue his education and become a teacher.

And so Patrick started each day as a student, before returning home to his weaving. As a dedicated teacher, Harshaw introduced Patrick to several subjects. His progress was excellent and soon brought a reward.

'No lesson, today, Patrick Brunty,' said his teacher. 'I have news.'

'Good news, I hope, sir,' said a curious Patrick.

'There is a Presbyterian church at Glascar Hill, and the school is in need of a teacher. I have recommended you for the position.'

Andrew Harshaw made a habit of rendering Patrick speechless.

He gasped. 'Me, sir?'

'I take it you are still interested in becoming a teacher?'

'Most definitely, and I thank you from the bottom of my heart.'

'Then the reason you have no lesson today is that you are to be interviewed for the post at eleven o'clock.'

'This morning?'

'And I should warn you that not all Presbyterian ministers are alike. You may find this clergyman old-fashioned. So, good luck, Patrick, and being Irish, you have the best luck of all.'

They parted, each with a tinge of excitement.

At Glascar Hill, Patrick sat in the parsonage and the interview began.

'Mr Brunty, the Revd Harshaw recommends you. What is your background?'

The minister, the Revd Alexander Moore, was strict and, although nervous, Patrick spoke with enthusiasm.

'I am a lover of books, sir, and poetry in particular, and believe every child should discover the beauty of language.'

The interview went well with Patrick convincing. He spoke about his studies with Mr Harshaw, his employment as a weaver, and about his family. He spoke with pride but alas, Patrick let slip a terrible fact.

'I'm sorry,' said Mr Moore. 'Did you say your mother is a Catholic?'

'She is, sir. And no kinder or more loving mother ever lived.'

'Then that is unfortunate, Mr Brunty, because I cannot allow the children of my church to be taught by the son of a Catholic.'

Patrick was shattered. He so wanted to be a teacher, and couldn't believe his rejection was due to some age-old prejudice. He went home a despondent young man, and resumed his schooling and weaving.

But not all was lost. Patrick's father, Hugh Brunty, fell on his feet at different times and now, so too did his son.

The teacher appointed to Glascar Hill refused the position, and the parents of the students agitated, telling the minister their thoughts. 'You must appoint a teacher as soon as possible,' they urged.

Unable to find anyone suitable, and forced to swallow his pride and prejudice, the minister offered the post to the red-headed son of a Catholic mother. Arguably, it was the best decision Mr Moore ever made.

'Good morning, children,' beamed the teenage tutor.

'Good morning, Mr Brunty,' they chorused.

'Today we begin a tour of discovery.' The children buzzed. 'Put aside your slate and chalk and line up outside the school.'

This was strange, new and exciting. Patrick turned teaching on its head, and led his students into the countryside.

'Look at those beautiful mountains. Who can tell me their name?'

'Mourne, sir,' replied a child.

'Indeed, and look, what is that bird?'

'That's a ringed plover, sir,' said another child.

'Excellent. Now next week, before we go for our walk, I want you to draw and write the names of three birds found in County Down. Those with the best work will win a prize. Come along; we have much more to see.'

The children tingled with excitement—a walk in the country, a competition and prizes. What kind of a teacher is this man?

Patrick adopted an unusual approach. He saw his students as individuals with their own needs and talents. He set tests and placed each student in a category—bright, steady or slow. He devised lessons directed at the various levels. The bright children weren't bored, and the slow ones weren't frustrated. He enabled every student to succeed.

He created a new timetable, started early and finished late, meaning different students or groups received individual attention. He offered additional classes for which he earned no money.

He brought his growing collection of books to school, and allowed students to take a book home and copy poems or pages of text, returning the book the following day. He was a natural educator and way ahead of his time.

It wasn't easy. Some children stayed home to help with the harvest, or when a new baby arrived. Patrick visited the parents and explained how their child excelled but needed their lessons. The dedicated and brilliant young teacher inspired parents and students alike.

One day, Patrick's mentor, Andrew Harshaw, called at the school. The students worked with barely a sound or distraction.

'Patrick, what has happened here? I've heard great things about your teaching, and this is wonderful.'

'And it's all thanks to you, Revd Harshaw. I would never have become a teacher without your expert tuition and encouragement.'

'And your discipline is excellent. How often do you use the cane?'

'The cane? Why, never,' replied a puzzled Patrick.

'Never? But what about unruly children?'

'Oh, I've found children always respond to kindness and interesting activities. If the teacher is enthusiastic and the work a challenge, the students want to learn and discipline is never a problem.'

Like many others, Harshaw was deeply impressed by the youthful Patrick Brunty. His teaching bloomed, his weaving work ended, and his poetry writing took flight.

The students, their parents and the community were all the richer because of Patrick's teaching at Glascar Hill school, and when it all came crashing down, the loss was so great for so many. The issue was sex.

Patrick was still a teenager when he became a teacher, and some of his students were only a year or two younger than their tutor. One was Jean McAlister, a gorgeous lass with flaming red hair, who developed a crush on Mr Brunty. The feeling was mutual. They made a striking couple and saw each other almost every day allowing love to bloom.

After three years in his first teaching role, Patrick allowed his feelings to lead him towards what was a natural but inappropriate relationship.

Making one of his regular home visits, this time to discuss the work of his enchanting student, Patrick spied the beautiful Miss McAlister. He found her increasingly difficult to resist, and was confident she had romantic feelings for her teacher.

As Patrick strode towards the farmhouse, Jean attended to her horse in a field. She waved. He waved. Patrick stopped, looked around and, seeing no-one, hopped over the fence and walked towards his student.

'Good afternoon, Mr Brunty.'

'Good afternoon, Miss McAlister.'

'Have you come to tell my father my work is not acceptable?'

'The exact opposite, as well you know.'

She smiled and Patrick's heart pumped blood with vigour. He'd often thought about Jean McAlister as he walked to and from school, or at night when he lay in bed. She was the most dazzling girl he'd ever seen.

He often thought about kissing her. But, like his father at that age, Patrick had limited experience in the art of romantic behaviour. He held out his hand. Jean looked at him then held out hers.

The touch was electric. Patrick squeezed her hand and their eyes locked. The teacher moved towards a haystack leading his willing student. The horse wasn't interested.

At least Patrick had the sense to make the encounter private as, on one side of the haystack, they couldn't be seen from the house. Alas, his dream became a nightmare.

Not the romantic encounter—that worked a treat. Jean's sweet lips were even more sensational than he imagined. But unknown to Patrick, one of Jean's brothers had a clear view of the Brunty seduction—such as it was. The brother blabbed to his old man who exploded. 'What! The son of a Catholic kissed my daughter!'

"Hell to pay" was only one of the dire comments. Patrick's case wasn't helped by Jean's father being an elder in the Glascar Presbyterian Church. The new minister was not well acquainted with Patrick's brilliant teaching, and received an exaggerated description of the "evil" deed, which triggered a kneejerk reaction. Some thought it was overkill. Yes, Brunty had to be sacked, but was it necessary to close the school?

Like father, like son. Hugh Brunty was sacked from the lime-kiln for a crime of the heart, and Patrick Brunty suffered a similar fate. What a pity because the young teacher became so successful. Hugh Brunty found new employment and his son too fell on his feet—again.

Andrew Harshaw understood people. He recognised Patrick Brunty's talents and so approached a fellow cleric, the Revd Thomas Tighe. He offered Patrick a new teaching position.

'I know your history, Mr Brunty,' said Tighe. He did, but let the good outweigh the other. Patrick warmed to the man. 'I would like you to tutor my children and, in time, would welcome you as a teacher in my school. Does that appeal?'

Patrick was enthusiastic. 'It does, sir, and thank you for such a wonderful opportunity.'

'Like Mr Harshaw, I will offer you free tuition, only this time in the Classics and Theology. Will that be satisfactory?'

'Most definitely, sir. I am truly grateful, and hope your faith in me will be justified.'

Tighe smiled. 'I have an inkling it will. Now come and meet your new students. My children have heard some amazing stories about the young teacher with the red hair.'

And so Patrick began a second relationship with a clergyman. This union would also prove beneficial for many, not least the redheaded bookworm, poet and former weaver.

Thomas Tighe was a man of letters, a graduate of St. John's College, Cambridge, a priest in the Church of Ireland, and both wealthy and influential. With a strong belief in evangelical Christianity, and as a friend of John Wesley, Tighe held high hopes for the 21-year-old Patrick Brunty.

When Patrick wasn't teaching the Tighe children, he became a student under their father, learning Latin, Greek and Theology. Patrick thrived.

'You are a natural scholar, Pat,' said Tighe after one of their many Greek lessons. 'You have taken to classical languages far quicker than any student I know. Even I took longer to grasp Latin than you have done.'

'Thank you, sir, but surely it reflects on the quality of your teaching.'

'And your progress in Theology studies is first-class. So, tell me, have you given any more thought to what we discussed?'

'I have, sir, a great deal of thought.'

'And?'

Patrick took a deep breath. He'd been studying and teaching with Mr Tighe for three years, and the two men developed a strong bond. Over time and without exerting any pressure, his mentor spoke to Patrick about taking holy orders.

With time passing—Patrick was now 24—his future employment became relevant. He had weaving skills, teaching experience and a passion for writing poetry. But was there a place for God in his life?

There was no Damascene moment for Patrick. With study and reason, he came to believe in the evangelical message of God's redemption through Christ. His natural aptitude for study, his strengthening Christian faith, and the strong support from his mentor, all helped Patrick decide. He would enter the priesthood. This delighted Tighe who, without hesitation, recommended his alma mater.

'But Mr Tighe,' said Patrick, 'Cambridge University is too far distant, and has much too high a standard for the likes of an Irishman like me. My parents are far from wealthy and barely literate.'

Tighe became serious, almost angry. 'You, sir, are the equal of any student I have ever taught. And the sooner you apply the better. Besides, St. John's is one college where talented, but poor young men can hope for an education. Their sizar scholarships are for gentlemen just like you.'

Patrick never considered himself a gentleman, but he applied and was successful. He found it hard to believe. With the letter from Cambridge University in hand, he waited until his parents were alone.

'Father, Mama, I have something to tell you.'

'You've met a girl and want to get married,' said a beaming Alice.

Patrick smiled but shook his head.

'I married your mother before I turned twenty,' said Hugh. 'What's the matter with you boy?'

'I'm going to university.' That got a reaction, silence, which worried Patrick. 'Well say something, please.'

'How wonderful,' said Hugh, who felt his chest swell with pride.

'So you'll be off to living in Dublin,' said Alice.

'No, Mama, *Cambridge* University.'

'England!' gasped Hugh. 'You're going to England?' Patrick nodded.

Naturally Alice worried. 'But what will you do for money?'

'I've been accepted as a sizar. My fees are reduced and my meals and accommodation provided.'

Hugh and Alice looked at their son and then at themselves. They knew little of education. They started married life in a two-roomed cottage with next to nothing. Their ten children lived at home or nearby. Now one of their offspring was leaving Ireland, the land of his birth. And why? Because one of the oldest and most prestigious universities in the world had offered a scholarship to their son.

Tears flowed.

Patrick's parents were proud beyond measure. Being a mother, Alice was concerned. Would her boy be safe living so far from home? Hugh could only wonder at the gulf between his childhood and lack of learning, and that of his son who was such a brilliant student now off to university.

It was an emotional day when Patrick left Ireland.

'I'm proud of you, my boy,' said Hugh. 'You bring great credit to your family. God bless.' They hugged with feeling.

Alice cried as she kissed her son. 'I'm not sure what my Catholic relatives will say, but I have never been so proud.' Patrick hugged and kissed his mother. 'And don't you forget to write.'

Patrick's eyes became moist. He climbed onto a cart beside his brother William, and looked at his parents and siblings. Everyone waved. William flicked the reins, and the horse trotted to the port. Next stop England.

Chapter 6

PATRICK ARRIVED EARLY, landing in England in 1802, three months before the university term began. He "ran away" from Ireland because of the troubles. Many Irishmen agitated against the ruling English. Patrick's mentor, the clergyman Thomas Tighe, opposed the invaders. The 1798 Rebellion was a bloody civil war with thousands killed. Threats abounded. Skirmishes happened. You could get arrested or killed.

Patrick knew people, including members of his own family, who hated the English and were up for a fight. Now, after years of teaching and study, he seized this glorious opportunity to study at Cambridge. He knew about trouble when, as a young teacher, he flirted with one of his students. That incident cost him his job. Now he chose to avoid trouble back home, and set out to make his mark on life.

But landing in England three months early made life difficult. His room at Cambridge was unavailable. With his savings sewn into his homemade clothes, produced by his dear mother, he needed to find work. But where were the jobs? And what about his luggage?

Being an old boy at St. John's, Thomas Tighe gave Patrick some tips. One involved approaching the porter of his college to have his trunk placed in storage.

'Good day, sir,' said the polite porter. So far, so good.

Patrick explained his situation and the porter agreed.

'What name, sir?'

'Brunty.'

The porter ran his finger down the list of undergraduates.

'Hmmm. Would that be Prunty, sir?'

Patrick was in no mood to argue or explain.

'Yes, Prunty,' he replied. 'I shall return in October.'

Trunk deposited, he headed into the countryside. Being summer, crops needed to be harvested. Workers were in demand, good workers in high demand. Patrick would tackle any farm labouring work. Make that digging potatoes and you had the best.

For months, he made a fair or almost fair day's pay, met a good many people, and found his accent becoming softer and his skin darker. In September, he headed back to his new home in Cambridge. At last the big day arrived.

He made his clothes and hair as neat as possible and returned to the porter's room at St John's.

'Good day, sir,' said the polite porter. So far, so good.

Patrick explained his situation and the porter referred to his list.

'What name, sir?'

'Prunty.'

The porter ran his finger down the list of undergraduates.

'Hmmm. Would that be Brunty, sir?'

Patrick was in no mood to argue or explain.

'Yes, Brunty,' he replied. 'May I collect my trunk, please?'

And so, with his possessions in tow, Patrick crossed the quadrangle and climbed the stairs. The room for a sizar was small, but Patrick thought his superb. He unpacked, stowed his trunk, then explored.

The first thing he noticed was his uniqueness. His fellow students were younger, shorter and better dressed—far better dressed. Being a weaver had its advantages, but while his garments were serviceable and cost next to nothing, they screamed "homemade". They were the reason most people suspected Patrick to be Irish. The moment he spoke, his voice confirmed their suspicions.

Trying to maintain a low profile proved difficult. Being tall and having a head topped with bright red hair meant Patrick trumpeted his own presence. His thatch preceded him.

Patrick's peers were old Etonians, Harrovians and Wykehamists. He was an old Drumballyroneyian—not quite the same thing, old chap.

But what was Patrick's surname?

Having a Catholic mother, people teased Patrick, calling him a Mick, despite his choice of his Protestant father's side of the religious divide. Now, living in England, in an institution where the Establishment dominated, Patrick tried to play down his links to Ireland and Catholicism. His name became a sticking point because it advertised his Irishness.

To enrol at St. John's, he approached the bursar. Although mid-morning, the official had already enjoyed a glass or three, strictly for medicinal purposes.

'Name?'

Patrick hesitated. 'Brunty,' he said.

'Branty,' said the bursar as he wrote.

Patrick shook his head in frustration. *Who will rid me of this troublesome surname?* In the register at St. John's College, Cambridge, the bursar wrote *Mr P. Branty.* Patrick's name became officially incorrect.

I must change my name, thought Patrick. He chose Brontë. It was hardly Irish but topical thanks to Lord Nelson, and with distinctive overtones, it suggested a Classical even Grecian lineage. Patrick adopted it not knowing one day it would become famous.

Most of his fellow first-year students were teenagers, he 25. Most came from wealthy families while his lived in genteel poverty.

His fellow first-year students included thirty-four gentlemen, seven noblemen and three other sizars. Patrick saw little of the noblemen at meal times as the toffs enjoyed their own private dining-room. And their lordships received a slight academic advantage. They took their degree without the inconvenience of sitting for exams—the word *title* packed a punch. No such perks for the sizars.

For them, life was tough with no gift of guineas from the pater to tide one over. Heating and lighting were luxuries. On some freezing nights, Patrick wrapped his feet in straw. If candles weren't available, he read by moonlight. Drat those clouds. But read he did and became the proverbial swot. His studious behaviour meant he received awards, scholarships and unusual offers.

One night, someone knocked on his door.

'Come in,' called Patrick, surprised to see this particular visitor.

'Sorry to barge in, old chap. God it's cold in here.'

'Can I help your Lordship?'

'Enough of the Lordship—in here, you're Brontë and I'm Browne. Now, I want to help you improve your station in life. And buying some coal will do for starters.'

The fellow-student fascinated Patrick. A titled, wealthy old Harrovian, struggling academically, came to a humble sizar's cramped room proposing that Patrick be paid to write the visitor's essays.

'For a fee,' said Browne. 'Name your price, man. And don't tell me you don't need the money.'

Patrick imagined problems.

'But if I write your work, how will you explain it to the Dons?'

'I'll bluff my way through.'

'And fail,' said Patrick. His visitor became angry.

'Well damn you, Brontë. Can't you take pity on a chap? I've been jolly civil about this.'

'There is an alternative.' Browne settled. 'Instead of writing your essays, I'll give you lessons and you can write your own work and pass.'

It was Browne's turn to be surprised. 'You think you can teach me?'

'I can teach anyone who wants to learn.' Both men paused. 'Shall we say tomorrow afternoon at two for two hours?'

'For two shillings.'

'Half a crown,' said Patrick. Browne paused then held out his hand. They shook on the deal.

'Good man, Brontë. But do buy some damn coal before tomorrow.'

So the brilliant student earned a modest income tutoring the sons of wealthy Englishmen, who were lazy or dim or both.

At the end of every year, Patrick finished in the top group of students. He won prizes. The leading anti-slavery advocate, parliamentarian and Christian philanthropist, William Wilberforce, donated funds for a scholarship won by Patrick. Prominent Christians regarded him as a brilliant scholar and a leading contender for holy orders.

"Left, left, left, right, left", rang out across the square.

Patrick joined the army. Well, not exactly. Across the Channel, Napoleon remained busy, and many feared for England's safety. The university allowed the students to form a militia. And for someone who detested warlike antics back in his beloved Ireland, Patrick enjoyed marching and firearm drills. He excelled in handling weapons, and looked sharp in his military togs. He met fellow militia students.

'Temple,' said a young man, extending his hand.

'Brontë,' replied Patrick as they shook hands.

The two men became friends, well, friendly acquaintances. In later years, Patrick became a clergyman, and Henry Temple, in the guise of Lord Palmerston, aka *The Mongoose*, bobbed up as the British Prime Minister—twice.

Although his love of poetry never waned, Patrick's future became ever clearer. He had a calling. Not the Army, the Law, Education or Politics, but the Church. He received a Bachelor of Arts degree and was ordained in the Church of England becoming the Revd Patrick Brontë; meet Pat the Priest.

Before taking up his first appointment as curate in the church of St. Mary Magdalene in Wethersfield, Essex, Patrick went home. What a welcome awaited the Irishman who had "done good".

Invited to preach in the little church at Drumballyroney, he found it packed with his parents and siblings, mentors, relatives, former students, neighbours and locals. They flocked to see and hear the Irishman who went off to England a weaver and came home a priest.

After the service, the comments went along these lines.

'He spoke for an hour ... No, it was more like two ... He never once used no notes ... He remembered all them words by heart.'

His parents were overcome with pride and happiness. Alice cried.

'I can't imagine what my Catholic relatives will say about me being in a Protestant church, but Patrick, that was the most wonderful service. Thank you.' She kissed her son.

'Thank you, Mama.'

'And if only you would write more often to your poor old mother, I could tell everyone you are the best son in the whole wide world.'

They laughed and again embraced. Both were thinking this might be the last time they would ever see each other. It was.

Hugh Brunty found the event difficult to comprehend. His brutal childhood and non-existent schooling meant that even today he still struggled to read and write. Yet here was his own flesh and blood, a clergyman, a university graduate and a clever, erudite man. Hugh's pride was so powerful, it hurt.

Patrick returned to England and never again set foot on the Emerald Isle.

In between parish duties, Patrick thought about poetry and sex. The two were not connected. His passion for poetry usually didn't involve passion, and because he was a priest, many of his poems were restrained and "proper like". They were ripe for being damned with faint praise.

THE HAPPY COTTAGERS
By Patrick Brontë

One sunny morn of May,
When dressed in flowery green
The dewy landscape, charmed
With Nature's fairest scene,

In thoughtful mood
I slowly strayed
O'er hill and dale,
Through bush and glade.

In Essex, Patrick lodged with an elderly spinster, Miss Mildred Davy, who conveniently lived a few pews from the church. One morning, he and his landlady were enjoying a cup of tea when a teenage visitor arrived.

'Good morning, Aunt,' she called entering the kitchen.

Patrick stood, instantly smitten. It was like Hugh Brunty arriving at the McClory Christmas luncheon some thirty years ago.

'Mr Brontë, this is my niece, Mary Burder.'

'Good morning, Miss Burder' said Patrick who, unlike his father, could speak from the off.

'And Mary, this is Mr Brontë, the new curate.'

'How do you do, sir,' said Mary, presenting her aunt with flowers, and Patrick with a captivating smile.

They partook of refreshments and enjoyed small talk, during which time Patrick affirmed his belief in feminine qualities being particularly interesting. He was keen to pursue this young woman for all the right reasons. When Mary stood to depart, Patrick's suggestions came alive.

'Miss Burder, I'm about to start my visiting rounds. May I have the honour of escorting you home?'

Talk about the charm of the Irish. Patrick carried his own Blarney stone. Mary accepted his kind offer and the happy couple set off. Patrick walked slowly so as not to inconvenience Miss Burder, but mainly to spend more time in her presence.

Like his father's first meeting with his mother, Patrick wanted to tell Mary he considered her beautiful and lovely and kind and wonderful. He didn't then but would do so later. They parted on friendly terms and Patrick wondered if she cared for him as he for her.

She did. The number of Mary's visits to her Aunt Mildred increased. Patrick regularly escorted the teenage Miss Burder. When apart, the couple wrote often; when together, Patrick became keen to press his suit.

'Mary, I want you to know my true feelings.'

She smiled. 'I'm quite sure they're not a secret, Mr Brontë.'

'A clergyman has a humble calling and I fear I shall never be wealthy.'

'Are you saying, sir, love cannot thrive unless money is involved?'

Patrick smiled and sensed her willingness. He believed a Church of England clergyman should be married, and was convinced Mary Burder would make an excellent wife. Patrick was good at plain speaking.

'I'm saying my heart is filled with love and affection, but I need you to understand the truth about my station in life.'

'How kind you are, Mr Brunty. And I need you to know that my uncle has asked to meet you.'

Patrick flinched. 'Your uncle?'

This sounded serious and Patrick experienced a feeling of dread. *What have I said or done? Why do I think I'm in trouble?*

Mary remained calm.

'He is my guardian, and as I am not yet of age, he asked about your intentions. I told him I am sure they are honourable.'

Patrick was hurt. 'Mary, how could you think otherwise?'

Was history about to repeat itself? Patrick's great-uncle Kevin didn't want Hugh Brunty to marry Kevin's niece, Alice. Now it appeared Miss Burder's uncle and guardian didn't want Patrick to marry his niece, Mary. What was it with these overbearing, sticky-beak uncles?

Mixed marriages can be controversial and difficult. Patrick's Protestant father married his Catholic mother and that union thrived. But Patrick's proposed union was something far worse. Mary was a non-conformist.

Patrick arrived at Mary's home to be introduced to her uncle. He was coarse and spoiling for an argument. He knew his line of attack by heart and fired many questions.

'How long have you been in this county; this country?'

Patrick discovered he'd made a fundamental error, almost identical to the scene where his father, Hugh, made a disastrous loyal toast. Patrick was unaware of the following fact.

Courting a young lady involved a strict set of rules, the first and most important of which was to get the parent or guardian's permission *before* the hand holding began, or certainly before things got serious. Patrick crashed at the first hurdle. Uncle's salvo continued.

'Who is your family? Where is your family?'

Patrick tried to answer but his questioner continued to interrupt. As a farmer, if Uncle allowed Pat to speak, the angry guardian would discover his niece's suitor's father was a farmer too, well, farm labourer.

It was obvious Patrick would fail the "suitable suitor test". Mary imitated a mouse. Her uncle turned accuser.

'You've got no land, no money and no prospects. You're C of E and our Mary's a Congregationalist.'

This was outrageous; a mixed marriage of the worst kind.

Several accusations hurled at Patrick were true, but hardly his fault. *And what have any of them to do with love?*

If given a fair opportunity, Patrick believed he could make a strong case for his good name and noble intentions. But when the fiery uncle let fly with his final comment, Patrick realised all hope was gone.

'But by far your greatest fault, sir,' said the sarcastic Uncle Outrage with finger pointed at the clergyman, 'is that you're Irish!' Here endeth the inquisition.

Devastated, Patrick fell silent as Uncle turned on his niece.

'You, young lady, will come home with me to the farm, and stay there until I say so. And you, sir, you will return Mary's letters first thing tomorrow. Do I make myself clear?'

Uncle bullied his niece into silence, and Patrick made as dignified an exit as possible. What a disaster.

The next day, he posted Mary's letters but added something extra— something of his own creativity. He drew a simple sketch of his likeness and popped it in with the letters. Mary discovered the illustration and read Patrick's message. "Mary, you have torn the heart; spare the face". And that was how it ended—not with a bang but a whimper.

Over the next few weeks, Patrick pondered his position. *Do I truly love, Mary? Should I fight her guardian?*

He believed he loved Mary but obviously her family disapproved. The gentlemanly thing would be to call on Mary, or at least to write and explain his decision to withdraw his promise of love. He dithered. This situation became his second spectacular romantic failure.

Patrick worried. He was a prominent member of the community, a curate in a busy church, and the grapevine would soon be buzzing. Within the village, gossip could be deadly. His reputation would be damaged. He thought long and hard about the matter then took the coward's way out and disappeared—to Shropshire.

Mary was heartbroken, Patrick ashamed, and Mary's uncle took great delight in hearing that the "foreigner" had been sent packing.

Nobody could possibly foretell such an event, but Patrick's decision to "walk out" on Miss Mary Burder, would one day return to haunt him.

All Saints' Church in Wellington, Shropshire, employed an English vicar and a Welsh curate. To that add one Irish curate. Patrick worked closely with his vicar, John Eyton.

'Mr Brontë, apart from the day-to-day business of the parish, my passion lies in helping the sick and the poor, and in running a wonderful school for every child. What say ye to those matters?'

'I wholeheartedly agree and support them, sir.'

'Excellent. Now come and meet your fellow curate, Mr Morgan.'

William Morgan was Welsh, portly, and a damn fine fellow. He and Patrick became firm friends and remained so until death did them part.

William's wit provided much comic relief. Once, when the three clerics were discussing parish matters, William interrupted proceedings.

'I say, gentleman, did you hear the tale about the Englishman, the Irishman and the Welshman?'

There was a moment of hesitation before the others caught the humour in the quip, and all three rocked with laughter.

Patrick enjoyed his time in Shropshire, but still being single, he often thought about his future. The Industrial Revolution thrived and certainly in Yorkshire. The need for clergy "oop north" had never been greater.

He decided. His next move would be north, towards Bradford. As he made enquiries about a possible parish, a letter arrived which threw a cat among his racing-pigeon plans.

Dear Mr Brontë
The position of chaplain on the island of Martinique, West Indies, has
become available and I have recommended you for the post.
Be so kind as to advise me of your interest in this matter.
Yours in Christ
James Wood

Oh dear, what a choice. Now let's see, there's Yorkshire where the winter ends in June to begin again in July, or Martinique where the sun refuses to go on holiday, and the fruit trees cry out for your attention. Would it be snowdrifts or snow-white sands?

Who knows what might have been had the young curate opted for sunny climes? What we do know is that Patrick swapped All Saints' Wellington for All Saints' Dewsbury, and began his life in Yorkshire.

Chapter 7

"PECULIAR PATRICK" became a term used to describe the new curate. Mind you, Yorkshire folk had their fair share of eccentrics, so Patrick must have done something right to win such an accolade. Another nickname for Patrick was *Old Staff* due to the large stick he carried on his many parish wanderings. *Perambulatory Pat* would've worked too.

Without wanting or trying to boost his profile, Patrick found himself centre stage in various events. His reputation grew. Meet Brontë, the have-a-go hero.

One day when walking beside the River Calder, he passed a group of skylarking lads. Old Staff strode on when the boys' laughter changed to screams. Patrick turned. The boys on the bank yelled and waved frantically to another lad in trouble in the river.

Patrick raced back and, tossing his stick aside, leapt into the water. The boy floundered in the swift current. Being almost Christmas, the water and air were bitterly cold.

'Give me your hand,' shouted Patrick. *'Your hand!'*

Now when some people believe they are drowning, they panic making a difficult situation worse. The terror-stricken boy moved further from the bank. Patrick struggled as the water became deeper. The boy went under and Patrick despaired. *Where is he?*

Up bobbed the gasping victim and Patrick threw himself sideways, grabbing a flailing hand and the boy's hair. He hauled the lad towards him and yelled.

'I've got you, you're safe. Stop struggling, stop struggling!'

The boy's fears subsided enough to allow Patrick to drag him to the bank, enabling the onlookers to reach out and help bring the two "swimmers" ashore. The boy who fell in had been pushed, and apologies from his friends came thick and fast.

'Where do you live, boy?' asked the soaked, shivering cleric.

'I know, sir,' said one of the group. 'I can show you. Follow me.'

Patrick picked up the child with the chattering teeth and carried him home. His shocked mother oozed gratitude and thanked the curate time and again.

'Oh Mr Brontë, thank God you were there. Come near to the fire and let me get you a hot drink.'

And so a modest tale of heroism spread amongst the Dewsbury faithful concerning Patrick the lifesaver. Alas that noble reputation was about to lose its lustre.

The vicar was a stickler for keeping the Sabbath holy, and his curate even more so. With the vicar absent, Patrick was in charge. The Sunday evening service finished and Patrick repaired to his lodging. He pondered the next line of his latest poem when the sound of church bells broke the silence of the quiet Dewsbury night. *It's the Sabbath; there can't be bells after Evensong.*

Stunned, a furious Patrick raced to the church. Panting, he reached the door to the bell tower. *How dare they break the Sabbath—and in my church!*

Damn! Patrick banged on the locked door and called. 'Open this door!' The door remained locked and, as if to mock the priest, the bells pealed the louder. Patrick set off to the home of the parish clerk who greeted an agitated curate.

'But I gave them permission, Mr Brontë.'

'You what?'

'There's a bell-ringing competition tomorrow, and the gentlemen wanted to practise.'

'*On the Sabbath!* Sir, I am in charge of the church, and demand the key to the bell tower, *now!*'

A meek man anyway, and faced with the furious Irishman, the key changed hands with speed. Patrick resumed running.

At the church, he fumbled to open the door, flew up the steps three at a time, and burst in on the campanologists. Surprise and fear came alive in response to the curate's fury.

'How dare you,' uttered Patrick multiple times until the bell-ringers fought back.

'But sir, we need the practice for tomorrow's competition.'

'Mr Brontë, we've completed our duties for today's services.'

'How dare you,' said Patrick, yet again.

The heated discussion got hotter and one chap threatened Patrick, storming out vowing never to ring a bell in the church again as long as its current curate remained. The others left and Patrick triumphed.

Or did he? If ever a pyrrhic victory was won in Dewsbury, this was it. Patrick the Lifesaver became, satirically, Patrick the Sabbath-saver.

But all was not lost in the best-of-three competition. The Irish cleric had one more opportunity to show his mettle.

Preaching the gospel was always important to Patrick, with both education and social justice coming a close second. So when a local Dewsbury lad, William Novell, was unjustly arrested and charged with being an army deserter, Patrick entered the fray. The only witness for the prosecution was a soldier named Thackray, who swore he enlisted Lovell.

The local magistrate ignored testimony from witnesses, who claimed young Bill had been miles away on the day in question. 'He was with me, sir,' said several witnesses. 'He couldn't have enlisted, sir.' The magistrate gave them all short shrift.

'We can bring even more witnesses to testify for the accused, sir.'

'Too late,' said the magistrate, 'the prisoner is guilty as charged,' and sent the young man to prison.

People in Dewsbury were outraged, Patrick among them. 'This is a grave injustice,' he said, and set about righting the wrong. With three prominent Dewsbury residents, Patrick set off to see the magistrate.

'Sir, we the citizens of Dewsbury, wish to petition you regarding the case of the alleged deserter, William Lovell,' said Patrick.

'You've had a wasted journey, gentlemen. It is no longer an allegation and the case is closed,' replied the magistrate.

'But we have new witnesses, sir, men who will testify against the soldier who claimed to have enlisted Mr Lovell.'

'I've told you, sir, the case is closed. Good day.'

Patrick was dogged and smart. A humble curate may not impress the magistrate, so find someone with clout. I mean, what's the point of having friends in high places if you can't call on them in time of need?

Patrick wrote to the Secretary at War, Lord Palmerston, aka Henry Temple—the same Henry Temple who marched around Cambridge with Patrick in their student militia days.

Perhaps His Lordship couldn't remember the redheaded Irishman because his reply was not at all helpful. So was it time to surrender? Of course not. *Who's next on my list?* mused Patrick.

His local MP was William Wilberforce, the same man who donated funds for a Cambridge scholarship won by the Irish sizar. Patrick penned another letter. Mr Wilberforce wrote to the magistrate urging him to re-open the case. The magistrate ignored the parliamentarian's missive. Surely now Patrick should quit.

No, because his belief in justice drove him forward. He wrote again to Wilberforce suggesting the MP pop round to the Secretary at War for a personal chat with His Lordship. After all, this affair was a slur on the Army's good name.

Wilberforce did as Patrick suggested and, hey presto, a result. Patrick's persistence paid dividends. Lord Palmerston instructed the magistrate to re-open the case.

The diligent curate rounded up fifteen witnesses including one who testified that the soldier, Thackray, had boasted his claim was a lie. Finally the truth was revealed.

The alleged deserter was set free, and the lying soldier went on a seven year "holiday" to Tasmania. Under sail, the journey took several months with the now ex-soldier enjoying below-deck accommodation, wearing special bracelets, and the company of flatulent bovines.

Yorkshire newspapers gave the story a sizeable splash, and the Irish curate got the recognition he deserved.

The vicar of Dewsbury liked Patrick. They were cut from the same cloth, and the various good deeds Patrick performed impressed the vicar, so when the curate of nearby St. Peter's, Hartshead became ill and resigned, Patrick got the nod. This was a perpetual curacy, another first for Mr Brontë. He now had a position for life.

It was a dark and stormy night in Yorkshire with Patrick only just asleep. The county buzzed with talk of civil unrest. The mills were alive with the sound of new Industrial Revolution-type machines, and workers were up in arms. Many sought alms.

Mill owners now produced more cloth, better cloth, faster and with fewer employees. The rich bosses became richer while the poor remained hungry having children—hungry children. Unemployment skyrocketed and poverty and hardship thrived.

Patrick soon discovered that caring for the soul was sometimes less important than caring for the poor. "Bugger eternity, Father, canst thou spare a ha'p'orth?"

On this particular night, voices outside his bedroom window woke Patrick. He peered into the darkness. What he feared might happen, was happening, in his parish, and on his doorstep.

A week earlier, Patrick had gone to visit a dying parishioner. The elderly farmer was close to death, and Patrick gave what comfort he could. As he prayed beside the old man's bed, he heard voices coming from downstairs.

In a meeting, local folk discussed unemployment, poverty and industrial unrest, all of which were rife in Yorkshire and right here, in and around Hartshead. Patrick crept to the top of the stairs and listened.

'Cartwright's the worst. He sacked another twenty weavers today.'

'There's nowt about. I'm broke and t'wife and kids are starving.'

'Any folk with loom in cottage is doomed.'

Patrick's ears pricked at that last remark. He knew all about the cottage industry of weaving. Then the conversation became darker.

'The only way is t'smash new machines.'

Others agreed.

'The only way is t'kill mill owners.'

Others agreed.

'I say we spread word and get workers t'attack damn mill.'

Others agreed.

'I can get Luddites from Leeds who think like us.'

Most folk, including Patrick, knew about the Luddites who smashed new machinery. And now, their revolution was in Patrick's village. He crept downstairs and slipped away home.

Now, a week later, voices outside his lodgings, woke him at midnight. He dressed and tip-toed outside. In the darkness, he estimated there were dozens, maybe a hundred angry men. Were some of them women disguised as men? They carried farm tools and sticks. A few had ancient firearms. This ragtag army was on the move in the dead of night.

Patrick caught snatches of conversation and recognised voices.

'We'll torch damn mill ... let's see how he likes losing his livelihood ... if I see him, I'll kill him.'

Patrick recognised members of his own congregation. Their anger was palpable making Patrick afraid and confused.

He supported the poor but respected the law of the land. *Should I intervene and reason with them? If I do, will they turn on me? If I don't, will blood be shed?*

The ex-workers headed for Cartwright's mill. Patrick followed.

Close to the mill, they fell silent and stopped. The building reared up against the night sky, and the rioters seemed to have a plan. The only sound was the river tumbling over rocks. Patrick's mind raced. *Surely they won't attack the mill.*

They did. On cue the mob raced to their former place of employment. Many yelled threats and curses. 'Burn the mill!' they screamed.

Crouched in the darkness, Patrick looked on in horror as rocks smashed against the wooden door. If the workers got inside, the mill was finished. Miles away, the owner slept in his bed. Tomorrow he'd discover his major asset a smoking ruin.

Then everything changed. The silent mill awoke. The owner was not at home in his bed, but inside with workers and soldiers ready for any attack. Wooden shutters burst open. Soldiers appeared with rifles, and gunfire echoed through the once peaceful Yorkshire valley. Patrick heard the screams of the injured and terrified workers. What a slaughter, an action approved by the authorities and, right there, hiding behind a tree, Patrick Brontë, the local man of God, the priest with a passion for social justice, witnessed the shocking event.

He froze. Injured protesters screamed and scrambled. The rioters fled into the night, carrying their bleeding comrades. Other than a doctor, the ideal person needed was a clergyman to attend to the dead and wounded. But, afraid for his body, for his career or just afraid, Patrick too slipped away. His thinking became muddled. *Am I a coward? Do I obey the law or help those in need? What is this place called Yorkshire?*

The event became news around the nation and locally was explosive. Afraid to tell anyone he saw everything, Patrick said nowt. How would his bishop react if he knew? Lying in bed, Patrick kept hearing the sounds of screaming workers as bullets rained down from the mill.

It might have been better to die in the riot. Several did, but many survivors were arrested and tried. Perhaps a fine or a short custodial sentence should apply. A fine or a short custodial sentence? Not exactly.

Many of the rioters were executed—hanged by the neck until dead, with the "lucky" ones being transported to Australia. The message from the authorities was crystal clear. It doesn't matter if you've lost your job and can't feed your family, let alone yourself, rioting will not be tolerated.

Bad blood flowed in abundance, and particularly in Yorkshire. Patrick lived and worked in the thick of it.

And people didn't forget. Grudges last a lifetime—longer. A wool merchant, a vocal opponent of the Luddites, rode between mills. He was ambushed and murdered in cold blood. Yorkshire resembled a war zone. Workers were hanged and bosses assassinated. There was trouble at mill, all right. Oh to be a clergyman in sunny Yorkshire.

Telling no-one, Patrick obtained a pistol. His days in the student militia at Cambridge came in handy. He placed the loaded firearm, with his watch, on his bedside table, where it remained a fixture for decades. Each time he moved to another church, the firearm moved too. The Revd Brontë put on the breastplate of righteousness, but right now he became a belt-and-braces mortal who created his own arsenal. Having said his prayers, Patrick checked his piece. Having loaded it at night, he discharged it in the morning. This wasn't unusual; this was Yorkshire.

A week later, late at night, he grabbed his gun. As a light sleeper, Patrick heard noises. Clutching his pistol, he crept out of the farmhouse and crossed the road. He lived only a stone's throw from the church. He crouched behind the graveyard wall. What were those sounds? He peered over the wall.

In the moonlit churchyard, men dug a grave at two in the morning. Could it be witchcraft? Patrick strained to decipher the muffled voices, and discovered the truth. A local man, a Luddite, wounded in the riot at the Cartwright mill, had died and his family wanted him buried in secret.

Patrick crept home and waited for the burial party to leave. He returned to the empty churchyard. It was a strange sight at ten past three in the morning, where the priest stood beside the fresh grave and conducted a shortened burial service. Patrick was both the officiating priest and the only human mourner. A beautiful barn owl sat in an ancient yew tree, the tree from which Robin Hood took a branch to create his last arrow. The owl hooted its own "Amen".

But not all was doom and gloom when Patrick returned to education. The headmaster of a new boys' school near Leeds, first met Patrick during their days in Shropshire. John Fennell moved to Yorkshire, and when he discovered the Irishman preaching nearby, he invited Patrick to examine his students at the Woodhouse Grove School. John Fennell's invitation changed Patrick's life.

'Patrick, my dear fellow,' said Fennell, greeting the Irishman.

'Headmaster, it's lovely to see you after all this time.'

Genuine friendship existed between the two men. Fennell needed his Classics' teacher's work inspected, and Patrick appreciated a break from the poverty and violence in his parish. This new arrangement would soon prove wonderfully fortuitous.

'Come and meet the ladies,' said Fennell, and led Patrick into the sitting-room. Patrick knew Fennell's wife and daughter, both called Jane. Patrick and the ladies greeted one another. 'But you haven't met our guest. Mr Patrick Brontë, may I present Miss Maria Branwell.'

'Good morning, Mr Brontë.' Maria's smile enchanted Patrick.

'Miss Branwell,' said Patrick giving a slight bow, and thinking his long walk was indeed worthwhile.

Maria was Mrs Fennell's niece. Maria's parents were dead, and as the housekeeper at Woodhouse Grove, Mrs Fennell needed help. Having her niece living with them got Maria out of her parentless home in Cornwall, and meant Mrs Fennell had an extra pair of hands to help run the domestic side of the school.

'Well ladies,' said John Fennell, 'if you'll excuse us, I must show Mr Brontë around the school.'

'Luncheon is at noon, my dear,' said Mrs Fennell. 'Please don't keep Mr Brontë too long.'

The men departed. Patrick met the teacher responsible for Classics, and they arranged a time for Patrick to inspect the students. A general tour of the school followed before the two returned to the dining-room for lunch, and Patrick sat beside Miss Branwell.

Patrick and Maria liked one another. Over lunch they spoke at length. He thought her pretty and petite, quietly spoken with a mind of her own, and a delightful dry sense of humour.

She was unlike any of Patrick's previous female friends. Maria was about Patrick's age, a student of scripture and a devout Christian. Patrick felt at ease in her company, yet excited to be close to her. This time he felt confident he'd met not just a possible partner, but a true and understanding friend.

What a refreshing change for the Irish priest. He could work with students and the Classics again, and converse with a woman who caught his eye and captured his heart. Could life be any better? Indeed it could as Patrick discovered over lunch.

'Tell me, sir,' said Fennell, 'what news of our friend, Mr Morgan?'

William Morgan and Patrick hadn't seen one another since Shropshire and both were poor correspondents.

'I heard he too moved to Yorkshire but little else,' replied Patrick.

'We had the pleasure of Mr Morgan's company only last week.'

'Excellent,' said Patrick. 'And how is my old friend?'

'Well if you visit us again soon, you and he may well cross paths.'

Jane Fennell, the younger, blushed. Her mother changed the subject.

Walking home to Hartshead, Patrick had a spring in his step not unlike his father Hugh, who, in County Down, having first met Patrick's mother, skipped most of the way home.

Woodhouse Grove School was a Wesleyan Academy about twelve miles from Hartshead, but covering such a distance became a stroll for Old Staff, he of the species, *longus legus*. Sometimes he would make the round trip in a single day. Sometimes he stayed overnight and enjoyed breakfast with the Fennells and the fascinating Miss Branwell—a particularly delightful experience.

Patrick didn't need encouragement to visit the school. His pleasure at having met Maria increased when he discovered a portly Welshman, the Revd William Morgan, now based in Bradford, was also a visitor to Woodhouse Grove. Morgan arrived as suitor to the headmaster's daughter. For both curates, life took on a special glow.

Back at Hartshead, Patrick lodged with Mr and Mrs Bedford at Lousy Thorn Farm. All three got on famously, and with St. Peter's being across the road from the farmhouse, the Sunday commute was a mere stroll. But Patrick considered the twelve miles to Woodhouse Grove a far more pleasant and even easier journey than the few yards to his church. This was due to a Miss Maria Branwell.

With Patrick now regularly dashing across the county, his landlord became confused.

'Wot's wi' tha' curate?' asked Mr Bedford of his wife, as he smoked a pipe before the fire. 'There's summat wrong wi' lad.'

'Oh, y'big lummox, art thee blind?' T'man's in love.'

Mr Bedford smiled. He rather liked the young parson.

In between visits, the courting couple corresponded. Friendly-formal at first, their writing soon became chatty and intimate. You could trace the development of their friendship by studying the greetings with which Maria started her letters.

They began, "My Dear Mr Brontë" and soon flowed into "My Dear Friend". As the intimacy increased her greeting became, "My Dearest Friend" but that was not the end of her salutations.

On one visit to Woodhouse Grove, with Jane and Jane away visiting friends, Patrick, Maria and John enjoyed refreshments when the headmaster left to deal with a student who had taken a fall. Patrick stood and moved to the window.

'Miss Branwell, did you know it's possible to see the church from this side of the house?' It was a ruse. Maria knew and Patrick knew she knew.

She placed her cup and saucer on the side table and moved to the window. She stood close to Patrick and looked where he looked.

'So you can,' she said. 'I'm glad you pointed out that important piece of fascinating information.'

She looked up at him and smiled. He looked down at her and smiled. They paused amongst the teasing and Maria spoke again.

'Please don't let your tea get cold, Mr Brontë.'

She turned to move back but stopped when his hand touched her arm. Their eyes met and they held each other's gaze. The spell broke as Patrick bent and kissed her cheek. Some would consider the move saucy. It was only a peck, but as they almost say, "A kiss is worth a thousand words".

Before anything happened, and both were hoping something might happen, they heard Mr Fennell returning. As he opened the door, Patrick and Maria were reclining in their chairs.

'No harm done,' said the headmaster, oblivious to the budding romance. 'Now, what have you two been discussing?'

Before long, the romance between Patrick and Maria became public knowledge, and the couple received strong support from all who knew them. This union appeared to be a marriage made in Heaven.

A sign of the depth of feeling between the lovers was the new greeting on Maria's latest letter. It began, "My Dear Saucy Pat". Cheeky chappie.

Courting became easier and more frequent. Patrick considered proposing marriage to the woman from Cornwall, but wanted to make it something special. From the distant past, he recalled the mess he made of a previous marriage proposal.

One sunny afternoon, the couple went to nearby Leeds and enjoyed the parkland around the ruins of Kirkstall Abbey. They shared a light repast beside the River Aire, and Maria sensed Patrick was nervous.

'Did you know, Miss Branwell, the building of the Abbey began over 500 years ago?'

'So I believe, Mr Brontë.'

'And the first monks were Cistercians with an Abbott in charge.'

'I must say, I'm only partly impressed with your knowledge.'

This surprised Patrick. 'Only partly impressed?'

'Yes, I'm convinced you have far more important topics to discuss.'

'I'm afraid I don't follow your thinking, Miss Branwell.'

'Really, Mr Brontë? All this time we've known one another, and you think I can't read your mind.'

Patrick looked at her. *You really are a remarkable woman.*

'I'll tell you what I *do* think,' he said. 'I think I've met my match in you, Maria Branwell, and am sure I can never outwit you.'

'But why must we outwit one another? Why not work as a team?'

Maria handed Patrick the perfect cue. His nerves caused problems, he needed a shove but, to his credit, he threw caution to the wind. With the ghosts of the Abbey looking down, Patrick dropped to one knee and grasped Maria's hands.

'I love you, Miss Maria Branwell. Nothing would give me greater pleasure than to have you share my life.' Tears welled in Maria's eyes. 'Please, dearest Maria, will you marry me?'

She nodded and whispered a teary, 'Yes.'

Their engagement created great excitement. This was a wedding people anticipated with happiness and goodwill. The couple's joy intensified when William Morgan proposed to Jane Fennell, and the couples agreed to marry on the same day. Now that's newsworthy; two clergymen marrying their bride in the same church on the same day.

It wasn't a typical family wedding. Maria's parents were dead and Patrick's far across the sea, but more than the usual number of friends attended because of the two-for-one ceremony.

John Fennell would give away his daughter in the first wedding, and his wife's niece in the second. But who would marry the couples?

'Let's do it ourselves,' said a jovial William.

'Ourselves?' laughed Patrick.

'Yes, I'm sure the ladies will agree.'

'William, I've performed I don't know how many weddings, but this will be a first for me.'

And so in the parish church in Guiseley, West Yorkshire, on a chilly winter's day, Patrick officiated at the marriage of William and Jane with Maria as bridesmaid. Then the four friends swapped roles enabling William to officiate at Patrick and Maria's wedding with Jane becoming Maria's maid of honour.

All four spoke their wedding vows with ease, the rings appeared on cue, and both priests declined a fee for their respective services.

Chapter 8

MR AND MRS BEDFORD FUSSED.

'Move big bed into next room and be quick about it,' she said.

Mr Bedford did as he was told. He was good at that.

'This ain't no place for young couple on weddin' night,' he mumbled.

Mrs Bedford plumped cushions. 'You've no doubt f'got, but there wasn't much admirin' of furniture on our weddin' night, y'big lummox.'

Mr Bedford smiled and kept pushing the bed into the bridal suite.

When finished, the room at Lousy Thorn Farm was a country retreat; cosy, warm and inviting. Patrick and Maria were overcome with the handiwork of the Bedfords.

That night, the newlyweds snuggled up in bed and enjoyed blissful feelings of happiness and expectation.

The candles were out and, in the darkness, Patrick whispered to his new bride.

'I suppose you know we Irish are renowned for our large families.'

'Really?' replied Mrs Brontë.

'Oh yes, in my family we had ten children.'

'You don't say?' replied Mrs Brontë, only this time with a giggle.

'Yes, madam, you've married a man who comes from a fine family of breeders.'

'Ten children, you say?'

'Indeed, ten.'

'Is that all?'

'Is that *all*?'

'Well I come from a fine English family and we had twelve children.'

'Twelve!' Patrick was stumped but, quick as a flash said, 'Well we'd better make a start then hadn't we?' and tickled his wife.

She squealed with delight, and elsewhere in the house, Mr Bedford snored while Mrs Bedford wore a contented smile as she drifted to sleep.

Living with the Bedfords proved to be wonderful as the older couple helped the newlyweds. But soon it was obvious more space was needed and a search began for a curate's dwelling.

Patrick and Maria settled on a large stone dwelling called Clough House about a mile from the church. It had five bedrooms, and maybe this fact encouraged the Brontës to find a way to fill so many of them.

Apart from enjoying married life and attending to his parish duties, Patrick continued to write. His love of poetry remained strong and, as his wife was about to turn 30, he penned some verse to mark the occasion.

'I have no ordinary birthday gift, Mrs Brontë, but wish you to accept this poem as a token of my love. I created it in your honour.'

'Oh Patrick, what a wonderful idea. Please, I insist you read it.'

He did and the poet became the performer. He remembered the way his father used to tell tales in Ireland. Enunciate well, pay attention to detail, and always, *always* speak from the heart.

In their home in Hartshead, Yorkshire, Patrick performed his poem.

Maria, let us walk, and breathe, the morning air,
And hear the cuckoos sing,
And every tuneful bird, that hears the gentle spring,
Throughout the budding grove,
Softly coos the turtle-dove.
The primrose pale,
Perfumes the gale,
The modest daisy and the violet blue,
Inviting spread their charms for you.

'Patrick, that is beautiful. And you wrote it for me?'

She hugged and kissed her husband who wanted to speak.

'There is more, my dear, if you would care to hear it.'

'I could listen for hours but the supper's cooking and I fear may burn.' She returned to the food. 'But how does it end? I hope you leave the reader feeling uplifted.'

'Judge for yourself,' said Patrick and delivered the final lines.

Whilst thou dost love, and still art kind,
No gloomy changes can my peace destroy.

The steam from the pot helped, but Maria's eyes filled with tears as she thought about her life, her spouse and their happiness. She'd found a caring and loving husband. Their future seemed full of promise.

Patrick came home from a parish meeting. En route he'd paid a visit to a sick parishioner. The foul weather saw Patrick dripping and shivering. He didn't grumble—much—but on this occasion he did, and spoke about a busybody parishioner, and another who opposed everything he suggested. Patrick kissed his wife, tried to dry himself by the fire, then gave a rundown on the person who was poorly. After much blathering, he realised his wife hadn't said a word. He stopped and gave her his full attention.

'I'm sorry, my dear. I'm so busy talking about myself, I've neglected my darling wife. Forgive me.' He smiled. 'So, Mrs Brontë, how are you?'

'Pregnant,' she said and keep stirring the pot.

After being so talkative, a stunned Patrick became speechless. Without turning her back, his wife continued.

'You are permitted to speak, sir.'

Patrick couldn't. Instead he embraced his wife from behind and kissed the back of her head. He hugged her for some time.

'The supper is burning, Your Lordship.'

Patrick released his wife and she returned to her cooking. He dragged a chair towards her.

'Now my dear, I want you to sit.'

'Oh Patrick, don't fuss. I'm having a baby. It happens every day.'

'Not to my wife, it doesn't. So is it a boy or girl?'

'Does it matter?'

'All that matters is the good health of my wife and child.' He sat at the table. 'I must write a poem about the new Brontë.'

'You do know pregnancies take several months?'

'Thank goodness,' he said with a grin, 'because that's how long I take to write a poem.'

'Come and eat your meal.'

As Patrick prayed, he added a special note of thanks for his wife's condition. She squeezed his hand.

In time, the first Brontë babe was born—a daughter, Maria, named after her mother.

Life went on, and with another three empty bedrooms at Clough House, it seemed a pity to waste all that space. In due course Maria, that's the mother, gave birth again.

'I'm beginning to feel outnumbered in my own home,' said Patrick when told he'd fathered a second daughter, named Elizabeth after her Cornish aunt.

From time to time, Patrick would attend various religious meetings, often in Bradford. Here he talked shop with his fellow clergy, and on one such occasion the curate from Thornton buttonholed the curate from Hartshead.

'Brontë, my dear fellow, I believe congratulations are in order. Thy flock hath increased, has it not?'

'Thank you, Atkinson, it has. And how are things at Thornton?'

'For the congregation, things are first-rate, but sadly the same cannot be said for the bachelor curate.'

'Oh, are you unwell?'

'Never better, but I have a small problem.' The curate from Thornton drew the curate from Hartshead to one side and lowered his voice. 'I am rather keen on a certain Miss Walker who lives over Huddersfield way.'

Patrick smiled. 'Congratulations.'

'Yes, but you know courting from a distance is jolly hard.'

Patrick enjoyed fond memories of his walks to Woodhouse Grove.

'I disagree. When I met my future bride, I found twelve miles a mere stroll.'

'But my future bride is fifteen miles distant and my legs are only good for ten.'

Patrick laughed heartily. 'Then a horse perhaps, or choose a local lass.'

'Look, I have a proposal, Brontë, which I would beg you to consider.' Atkinson paused then whispered, 'We swap.'

'We swap?'

'Yes, we both hold a perpetual curacy. You move to Thornton and I to Hartshead. You get a church with a parsonage and double the salary.'

'But you'll lose much of your income and there's no parsonage.'

'But I may gain a pretty wife. Please, old chap, I'm sure the vicar will approve.'

Patrick nodded. 'Let me think about it. I'll speak with my wife. Now that's something you must do if the lady from Huddersfield accepts your proposal.'

The men laughed and shook hands.

Before long, with the proposal approved, the curates swapped places. Patrick, Maria and their two daughters set off for Thornton and the start of an interesting adventure.

'Oh Patrick, come and look at this.'

Maria explored her new abode. The parsonage at Thornton was big, old and showing its age. It had many rooms and outside, space in the backyard for livestock. A trip to the privy could include collecting eggs or feeding the horse.

Patrick's wage increased significantly but he needed every penny. He had two bairns, a third on the way, and the house and church needed constant repairs.

'Buckets, Maria,' called Patrick as he found another bedroom with a leaking ceiling. 'God alone knows the state of the roof.'

The church was even worse. Its structure was a danger to life and limb. The musicians in the gallery were afraid to play *furioso* in case they fell through the floor.

'Mr Brontë,' said the lead violinist. 'It's fearful up in gallery. Either close it or get organ.'

Patrick closed it.

Inside, the church was dark, damp and dangerous. The aisles were covered with gravestones, and when moist turned walking into skating. The wealthy paid a premium to be buried within the church resulting in an unusual aroma.

'Tha's strange smell in church, Mr Brontë. Y'outa stop burials in 'ere.'

Patrick did.

The congregation comprised solid Yorkshire folk, many of whom were poor. Numbers swelled when the local canines felt the need for spiritual guidance. All were made welcome.

Patrick's sermons would last a good half an hour, and the thriving Sunday school became his pet project.

'It's another girl, Mr Brontë,' said the midwife once Charlotte was born. 'At this rate you'll be able to open your own girls' school.'

'I did my best, darling,' said Maria as she showed their new daughter to Patrick. 'We'll have a boy next time, I promise.'

'You always do your best, Mrs Brontë. Why do you think I married you?'

'Perhaps we should invite my sister to come and stay. You're so busy, and having someone to help with the girls will be a godsend.'

'She'll come even if I have to carry her here myself,' smiled Patrick as he kissed daughter number three.

And so Maria's sister, Elizabeth Branwell, came from Cornwall and settled in the Thornton parsonage. Patrick called her Bess, and she proved a great help in caring for her three young nieces.

Bess had a fondness for matters social. The Firth family were well-to-do parishioners who enjoyed entertaining. Dr. Firth was a widower, and he and his 18-year-old daughter, Elizabeth, became close friends of the curate and his family.

'You must all come to tea on Saturday,' said Elizabeth.

'That's most kind, Miss Firth,' said Maria.

'Indeed,' added Patrick.

'We shall expect the whole family including baby Charlotte. Is three o'clock suitable?'

The Brontës, especially Bess, enjoyed the Firth family hospitality, and when the teenage Elizabeth produced a bonnet for baby Charlotte, it capped a perfect afternoon.

With Maria again pregnant and Bess returning to Cornwall, life became a struggle for Mrs Brontë, running the house and caring for three daughters under three.

'I need help, Patrick. A servant would be wonderful.'

And so 13-year-old Nancy Garrs joined the Brontë brood. In time her younger sister, Sarah, would become part of the "team", and the sisters would serve Patrick and his family for many years.

Baby number four arrived and finally, *finally* this one had the same sex as its father.

'How did you know it would be a boy?' asked Patrick as he sat beside his wife. She cuddled the new born with his three sisters all craning to see and touch their baby brother.

'We must call him Patrick,' said his mother.

'Oh I don't think so,' said Patrick. 'You'll call for "Patrick" and neither of us will respond thinking you mean the other.'

Maria stuck to her guns. 'I want our son to have his father's name. And to save any confusion, we'll call the boy by his other given name.'

'Which is what, pray tell? And don't say Algernon or Fortescue.'

'I like Branwell.'

So Patrick, son of Patrick, was known as Branwell, and with a family of four children under four, Patrick, his wife and their servants, Nancy and Sarah, got on with their Yorkshire life in the Thornton church known as the Old Bell Chapel. Before long, Maria fell pregnant—again.

Being so close to Bradford, Patrick often met fellow clergy with two being extraordinary.

The Revd Henry Heap, a recent appointment as the vicar of Bradford, was a fine example of someone who acted above his station.

'Mr Brontë,' said Heap holding out his hand in greeting. 'I'm delighted to make your acquaintance.'

'How do you do, sir,' replied Patrick.

'I've heard a great deal about the Thornton curate. Now, I should warn you, sir, I'm on the lookout for first-class clergy who are ambitious and keen to respond to my call.'

Patrick didn't understand the cleric and opted for small talk.

'How have you found Bradford, Mr Heap?'

Lacking listening skills, Heap ignored Patrick. 'I may have the ideal situation for a forward-thinker like you. Are you up for a challenge?'

'I'm always willing to do the Lord's work, sir.'

'Oh taken as read, my good man. No, I'm talking about change, about progress, about grasping the future before it slips into eternity.'

Patrick found the vicar's conversation bewildering, and was glad to get away until he met another cleric, making Patrick's day even worse.

'Redhead,' said the priest introducing himself.

'Brontë,' replied Patrick.

'I say, have you met our new vicar? The man is a breath of fresh air, and I sense wondrous things under his leadership.'

The Revd Samuel Redhead seemed a younger version of their vicar, and Patrick sensed trouble.

He arrived home to the news his daughter tally had risen again with the newborn Emily crying in her mother's arms.

'You're becoming quite good at this, Mrs Brontë,' said Patrick, kissing his wife and gazing at their latest child.

'Five children, in this house, is difficult, Patrick. We need somewhere bigger.'

'It's funny you should mention that.'

He explained his meeting with Mr Heap, and Maria asked questions which Patrick couldn't answer.

'Well it's either a bigger house or no more babies,' said Maria feeding her daughter.

Patrick feigned horror. 'But I'm sure you said you wanted twelve.'

Maria looked for something to throw at her husband.

Several months passed before Patrick again encountered the Revd Henry Heap.

'Mr Brontë, I spoke to the archbishop about you only last week. I have a proposition.'

Patrick listened with interest as the cleric explained a vacancy would arise with the perpetual curacy at Haworth, eight miles from Bradford.

'And you would like me to apply for the position, sir?'

'Oh good heavens, no. My good fellow, I'm the vicar of Bradford, and if I appoint someone to one of my outlying churches, then there's an end to it. What I say goes.'

'I see,' said Patrick with no confidence and many questions.

'I suggest you ride out to Haworth, and tell the church trustees I intend to appoint you to the position. Inspect the parsonage. You have a family, I believe.'

'Five, sir, with another on the way.'

'Excellent. Let me know when you're ready to move. Now, if you'll excuse me.' The vicar spied another potential cog in his machine.

Had Patrick spoken it would have been irrelevant, as Mr Heap heard only his own voice. Patrick told his wife of the developments.

'Move to Haworth?' said Maria. 'Is there a parsonage?'

'I believe so.'

'Is it large?'

'I believe so. But, my dear, I'm not sure about the move.'

'Not sure? Why ever not?'

Maria had been unwell of late, but news of Patrick's offer lifted her spirits.

'I've agreed to visit Haworth and meet their people. I want to be sure we're the right fit for the parish.'

'We?' asked Maria. 'The vicar has chosen you, not your family.'

Patrick looked at his wife. 'You are my rock, Maria Brontë. Without you, I am lost.'

She loved him and was reluctant to tell him about her tender tummy.

Patrick went to Haworth and found the local trustees welcoming but restrained.

'The vicar has asked me to apply for the position of curate in your church,' said Patrick.

'Has he now?' came the reply. Patrick sensed opposition.

'Yes, I believe he has the right to make appointments in the area.'

'That 'e do, Reverend, but we 'ave right t'refuse.'

'Oh.' Patrick hadn't expected that.

'Tell y'what, Mr Branty.'

'Brontë,' said Patrick.

'You come along 'ere on a Sunday and preach us a sermon. We'll be sat in pew an' listen. Now we can't say fairer 'n that.'

The other trustees nodded and agreed. Patrick considered their suggestion then made a counter offer.

'I'm not sure such an occasion would allow you to judge me well. Why don't you come to Thornton to hear me preach to my congregation? That way you can see and hear the man you'll be getting.'

This was a new offer for the trustees, who spoke amongst themselves before announcing their decision.

'We'll think about it, Mr Brunty.'

Oh dear. That didn't sound promising.

Patrick inspected the church and the spacious Haworth parsonage. When he got home, Maria was keen for news.

'So? What did they say?'

He explained the events then shocked her.

'I've decided against the move.'

'But Patrick, you said there's a large parsonage and grounds. Think what that'll mean for the children.'

'I'm sorry, my dear. The setting may be right but not the appointment process. I'll tell the vicar I don't wish to preach for my pulpit.'

He did and the senior cleric was cross. His empire building and the key to his success depended on the lower classes, the curates, following his "requests" without question.

Before long Patrick received a letter and showed it to Maria.

'Mr Heap has gone over my head. The archbishop has commanded me to preach at Haworth.'

'Well get cracking. In case you've not noticed, I'm carrying your sixth child. I'm getting bigger while our house is getting smaller!'

Patrick preached at Haworth. The locals liked him, but the curate sensed trouble in the form of a clash between the vicar and trustees. He didn't fancy being caught in the crossfire, so wrote to the Bradford vicar.

Dear Mr Heap
After careful consideration of your generous offer regarding the
Haworth curacy, I believe, sir, I am not the right person for this
appointment. I therefore respectfully decline your kind invitation.
Yours in Christ,
P. Brontë

Henry Heap was peeved but determined to have his way. He looked at his list. The second name was Samuel Redhead.

Politics thrived in the Church of England, in Yorkshire, in 1820. Haworth needed a curate. This moorland village-cum-town, bitterly cold in winter, was blessed with a parish committee of fine, tough-as-a-dry-stone-wall Yorkshiremen. Just that fact alone should've caused any interested party to tread with care. Patrick did, Samuel didn't.

The vicar of Bradford got his way. He put Patrick's refusal down to the curate being Irish, and lined up the second candidate. If Heap couldn't persuade one redhead, he'd try another. The Revd Samuel Redhead was delighted to be offered the Haworth curacy and accepted on the spot.

Pity because Sam wasn't the brightest candle on the altar and, to be fair, could not have envisaged his fate—and what a fate.

To understand the situation, one needs to understand the beast which is known as "a Yorkshireman". Yes, he calls a spade a spade and yes, he'll do a good turn for a fellow tyke without being asked. "Salt of the Earth" is a fair description of someone from this part of the north of England. But be warned. Do not take a Yorkshireman for granted. Do not assume he will agree with you. Do not decide on his behalf. He is his own man.

That was the fatal error made by the Revd Henry Heap. And poor old—well old in thinking anyway—Samuel Redhead became the lamb in the Yorkshire slaughter sandwich.

The priest arrived in Haworth on his first Sunday. With pate polished and his new vestment an investment, the church was packed; not to the rafters but of empty pews were there none. Let's all meet and greet the new curate.

Sam found it hard to contain his pride and excitement. The vicar of Bradford—friend of the archbishop no doubt—had handpicked this up and coming priest to assume command of a strong and dedicated flock. Sam surveyed his new congregation. *Me; they picked me. I am their shepherd.*

The hubbub dropped then stopped. Silence pervaded the church.

The pulpit at Haworth had different levels, and Sam chose the highest. He wanted to see and be seen. The hush continued as Mr Redhead ascended his throne.

There he was, lord of all he surveyed. He paused and looked out over the sea of eager faces. Thank goodness he'd honed his sermon. Start as you mean to go on, Sam. You only get one chance to make a good first impression.

He cleared his throat, opened his mouth and ... froze.

Before even one syllable of his brilliant first sermon could escape his lips, every man, woman and child in that packed congregation rose and walked out of the church. Their shuffling feet and clacking footsteps made a sound, but the departing worshippers spoke not a word.

To describe Sam as surprised would be a massive understatement. To say he was shattered would be entirely accurate. He now needed to work on the answer to the first question the vicar of Bradford would ask when next they met. "What did they think of your first sermon, Mr Redhead?"

Oh dear.

Now Sam was no quitter. If nothing else he had pride. It wasn't quite, "I'll show these locals who's boss," but rather, "The vicar chose me, I'm a jolly good chap, and I will see this through". A risky philosophy but, if nothing else, Sam should be given full marks for trying.

The next Sabbath rolled around and the Revd Redhead rolled back into Haworth. It's easy to imagine the gossip in the town the previous week, not to mention the speculation on what might happen this week. The church became the Theatre Royal, Haworth, and one needed to be early for a seat to see the best show in town.

Again the church was packed. Seating was less comfortable because so many locals arrived, resulting in squashed worshippers. Children, too big to sit on their parents' knees, sat on their parents' knees. It was standing room only.

In the vestry, Sam downed a quick snifter, his nerves on edge. Then it was time. His plan was to appear nonchalant as if last week's escapade hadn't happened. He would speak from the lowest pulpit. He would be friendly; be one of them. They'd made their point. Now they would accept him and all would be well. Let's let bygones be bygones.

He entered the church, and again the hubbub dropped to a pin-dropping silence. He walked to the steps of the pulpit. Everyone stared at him. Could Sam hold his nerve?

He settled on the lowest pulpit—the Revd Humble. He opened the bible. No movement from the masses; so far, so good. Sam paused. He had control; then he didn't.

A mixture of sounds came from the front of the church. Outside a man called. He pounded on the church door, and an animal joined the ruckus. What was happening? Sam and his flock were spellbound.

Was it a latecomer? Surely everyone from miles around was already here. The church door opened, and Sam's eyes stood out further than the draw knobs on the Haworth organ.

A latecomer made somewhat of a grand entrance. The local, a born and bred Yorkshireman, wasn't alone. The man wore a large collection of hats piled one upon t'other and sat, backwards mind, on an agnostic donkey which was none too pleased to be working on the Sabbath.

The donkey was ridden down the aisle. Perhaps *ridden* is not accurate. With colourful language, the rider urged on the beast who protested in equal measure. The uproar from the congregation would have done a Roman Emperor proud as the lions were let loose on the Christians. Sam was a Christian.

If a walkout was a kick-in-the-guts for the new curate, today's pantomime knocked it into a cocked hat. Sam scampered down the pulpit steps, ran into the vestry then fled. Most parishioners didn't see him go they were laughing so much at the donkey, whose closing gag was to defecate beneath the hymn noticeboard. Number 67 was *Hark! The Haworth Asses Bray.*

Sam would need an amazing answer to the vicar of Bradford's next question. "So tell me, Mr Redhead, how did your second sermon go?"

The situation was out of hand. Word spread that the locals were behaving in a most peculiar way. Well, perhaps *peculiar* elsewhere, but more likely par for the course in Yorkshire. Sam faced humiliation. If he quit now, his reputation would be forever tainted. He needed help. He found it.

By bringing some "heavies", some religious muscle to Haworth, Sam believed he might intimidate the locals and, if that failed, at least his delicate limbs would be protected. It was worth a try.

Next Sunday, the gunslinger and his deputies rode into town. Tickets had sold out long ago. During the week, the organist had never had so many volunteers desperate to join the choir. None of them could sing a note or wanted to, but all were desperate to be ringside for the greatest show on Yorkshire Earth.

In the vestry, Sam discussed tactics with his henchmen. 'I'll make the sermon short. If the masses revolt, I'll need you to form a protective wall between me and the troublemakers.'

'We're with you, Reverend,' said an overweight non-conformist.

The time had come. For the third consecutive week, the curate who accepted the Haworth perpetual curacy, entered the packed church. Twice he'd been humiliated. This was his third and final chance. His "supporters" left the vestry first, and drifted to points around the pulpit. Cometh the hour, cometh the Redhead.

Sam strode purposefully to the pulpit. Today he would ascend to the highest level. The congregation fell silent. They watched as the curate reached his destination. Nobody moved. Nobody entered the sacred building and made an ass of himself. It appeared as if Sam had finally won.

He spoke. No reaction. Yes, the curate had won over the locals. But wait. From the front pew, an inebriated chimneysweep, covered in soot and ash, stood and moved to the pulpit steps.

The curate stopped speaking. The sheep on the moors stopped chewing. Worshippers stopped breathing. Two bodyguards moved towards the sweep, but Sam raised a hand and the muscle fell back. The sweep, without brushes or brooms, and wearing soot from half the chimneys in Haworth, climbed the stairs; a decent climb.

The whites of his eyes sparkled on his blackened dial. Higher he climbed. Sam stared and waited, hoping, praying for a happy ending. Did the fellow intend to harm the curate?

A collective holding of breath began as the sweep reached the level of the clergyman. With no weapon in sight, this must be an apology. And in a sense it was, only in the form of a Yorkshire welcome.

Pausing beside the priest, the sweep threw open his arms, stepped forward, gave the preacher an almighty bear hug then planted a passionate kiss on the curate's cheek.

The audience, er, congregation erupted with outpourings of glee. The curate's costume now required the handiwork of Haworth's finest laundress, while half the priest's face gave the impression he hailed from deepest Africa. The worshippers' laughter rolled around the church and for Sam, the jig was up. It was time to throw in the once-white surplice.

He fled from the pulpit and, with the protective help of his minders, raced out of the church. There were many locals outside—those who couldn't get in—and they surged forward to catch the action. This caused Sam and Team Redhead to veer towards the pub. Jubilant locals gave chase.

The pursued raced into the public house and, in true religious character, shouted for sanctuary. This was a first for the publican, who closed his front door and then had no idea what to do. He'd never served a priest in clerical garb with a two-tone face. Outside, the audience demanded an encore. Sam made a silent request. In prayer form it became, "Please God, help me get the hell out of this den of iniquity".

After several minutes of chanting from the excited fans outside, the circus showed no sign of ending.

Sam turned to the landlord. 'Help me.'

'I'm sorry, your Grace,' replied the publican, knowing full well the curate stood firmly on the bottom of the ecclesiastical ladder, 'but I owes you nothing.'

'But they wish to harm me,' bemoaned Sam.

'No, they wish to *alarm* you. You can walk out right now and all you'll cop is ridicule—a lot, mind, but still only words.'

Sam was shattered. A beating might be better than ridicule. A bruise is a badge of honour. Laughter can sting forever.

'Well, make up your mind, m'Lord. I've got a business to run.'

'On the Sabbath?' snapped the curate.

The publican switched to angry. 'You just don't get it. Stop telling good Yorkshire folk how to behave.'

The "prisoners" huddled in discussion. Then, holding his head high, Mr Redhead declared, 'We are now ready to depart'.

As if they had a choice.

The party moved to the door and paused, the publican opened it allowing Sam and his followers to stride boldly into the lions' den.

The locals were in fine form. They stood outside the pub and lined the street all the way out of the village. Talk about running the gauntlet. Upstairs windows burst open and ridicule, like slops from chamber pots, splattered over the hapless holy man.

As the Revd Redhead departed, he was hooted, jeered, catcalled and barracked, with insults befitting the bluntness of good Yorkshire folk. Sam was halfway back to Bradford before the laughter and insults began to fade. The ringing in his ears lasted for weeks.

With his appointment scheme in disarray, the vicar of Bradford found humiliation not to his liking.

Some serious discussions took place involving the archbishop, the vicar and the much-chastened curate. Mr Redhead now regarded overseas missionary service as highly desirable. Anywhere would be better than Yorkshire.

Eventually, Patrick Brontë received an invitation to become the new perpetual curate at Haworth. He was delighted to accept, and the locals were delighted to have him. For them, honour was satisfied.

Maria delivered yet another daughter making the tally six children in seven years. Patrick gave thanks for baby, Anne, and for his wife's sturdy constitution. She was now half way to her mother's output of an even dozen.

Patrick and co. prepared for the move to Haworth with two carts, two servants, and two dogs and, at the last roll call, six children.

Maria and Patrick were in bed on their final night in Thornton. The children, servants and dogs were asleep.

'Tell me again about the parsonage,' said Maria.

'It's large,' replied Patrick.

'How large? How many rooms? And what about the land?'

'Lots of rooms and lots of room. The children can play in the garden or open the gate and explore the moors.'

'That sounds dangerous.'

'The dogs will love it.'

'You and your dogs.'

'Both the Wesley brothers preached in Haworth. Five thousand attended one of their services—more than the entire population.'

'I hope they don't bury parishioners under the aisles like they do here?'

'No my dear, but there is a crypt at Haworth. When I'm old and frail, you can pop me under the altar.'

She snuggled into him.

'I can't imagine you being old and frail.'

'I'll have snow white hair and fifteen grandchildren.'

'Only fifteen?'

He kissed her. 'Goodnight Mrs Brontë.'

Maria wanted to talk. 'Tell me about Haworth the town.'

Patrick sighed. 'Plenty of mills, plenty of shops, non-conformist churches, public houses and ...' He paused.

'And what?' He hesitated. 'Plenty of what, Patrick?'

He didn't want to talk about it but she pressed him. He replied.

'Alas, my dear, there is plenty of death.'

'Death is not new. What's unusual about death in Haworth? Tell me,'

'In Haworth almost half the children die before they are six.'

Maria gasped. 'Why?'

'Haworth has terrible overcrowding; some say worse than the London slums. Dozens of people share a single privy. Most of the water pumps don't work and often the water is foul.'

Maria sat up. 'Patrick, why are we going to Haworth?'

'There is much sickness and most people die before they're thirty.'

Maria went quiet. 'Will we be safe?'

Patrick went quiet. 'God will watch over us.'

There was a lull. Maria thought about death. Patrick fell asleep.

'Goodnight Mr Brontë,' she said then whispered, 'I love you, Patrick Brontë.'

Chapter 9

MARIA SAID NOWT. It was not in her nature to complain. She was a loving mother and devoted wife who maintained a strong faith in her Christian beliefs. But she was unwell and worried. The family had been in Haworth a few months, and upstairs in the parsonage she remained in bed. Patrick entered and was surprised.

'My dear,' he said, 'are you unwell?'

Maria said nothing. She rolled her head, looked at Patrick and tears welled in her eyes. She nodded. Instantly he was by her side.

'Tell me. Are you with child?'

She shook her head and grimaced as pain jabbed her abdomen.

Patrick felt her brow. 'You have a fever. I'll send for the doctor. Lie still.' He held her hand and said a short prayer. Maria joined her husband in the *Amen* and felt better having shared her news.

She'd been unwell for some time. In the last two weeks she discovered unusual bleeding and knew it was not her regular cycle. Then the severe pain started. Not long or continuous pain but short, sharp stabs. She prayed and hoped the suffering would pass. It didn't. Now she could disguise her suffering no longer.

The doctor came, examined her and advised her to stay in bed. Downstairs in the study, he spoke with Patrick.

'There is no easy way to say this, Mr Brontë. I believe your wife is seriously ill.' Shock gripped Patrick.

'Could you be mistaken, Doctor?'

The medical man shrugged. 'Sadly, I am often mistaken, but in this case I fear an internal condition troubles your dear wife.'

'Internal condition?'

'Her female organs appear infected and I fear there is little hope.'

'Nothing?' Patrick was a mess. His thoughts raced. He felt faint. For a moment he thought he would lose his temper with the doctor.

'Oh, forgive me, Mr Brontë. We have medication to ease the suffering, but I'm afraid there's nothing we can do to stop the disease. I regret, she will die, and sooner rather than later.'

Patrick thought he would vomit. A few months ago his family travelled from Thornton to make Haworth the Brontë home. Their future was full of hope. The house and garden were wonderful, the children happy and now this—this terrible, unspeakable news.

'I'll leave you this laudanum which you should only give your wife every ...'

Patrick wasn't listening. He'd had no warning of this nightmare. From a happy, healthy wife to one who was dying—and so young—was all too much. He collapsed in a chair and sobbed. After a pause, the doctor placed a hand on Patrick's shoulder.

'Breathe slowly, sir. You've had a nasty shock.'

Then an excited Maria and Elizabeth burst into the room. 'Papa,' they cried, 'come and see.'

They froze seeing their father crying. Elizabeth burst into tears.

In an instant Patrick recovered. He stood, wiped his face and ushered his young daughters into the corridor. 'Wait for me in the kitchen. I will be there directly.'

The doctor held out his hand. The men shook hands and locked eyes.

'You're a good man, Mr Brontë. I will call in later this day.'

Patrick walked to the door with the doctor, closed it and rested his head on the door. He prayed in silence. *If ever I needed your help, Heavenly Father, it is now. Have mercy on my family and especially my darling wife.* His lips shaped the word "Amen".

From that day forward, Patrick's life changed dramatically. As much as he trusted the local doctor, he went in search of other medical men. He requested professionals from as far away as Leeds and Bradford to examine Maria. Each delivered the same galling message.

'But there must be an operation you can perform,' pleaded Patrick. His misery knew no bounds.

Word spread about the curate's wife just like her dreaded cancer. In shops, homes and at church, he faced the same questions and comments.

'How is your wife, Mr Brontë?'

'I hope your dear wife is feeling better, sir.'

Maria needed constant care which Patrick couldn't provide. He hired a nurse, Martha Wright. She was sombre in appearance and personality. She may once have been a compassionate and caring person, but those days were long gone.

'I need you to sit with my wife during the day, madam,' said Patrick. 'I will attend to Mrs Brontë during the evenings.'

'I understand,' said the nurse. Talkative she wasn't.

And so began that appalling time of living with a loved one dying before your eyes. To make the situation worse, if that were possible, Maria's suffering was never quiet or peaceful. Her agony was intense and prolonged. Unlike at Dewsbury, Hartshead and Thornton, at Haworth, Patrick had few friends. Each night he sat beside his darling wife, listening to her laboured breathing and muted cries, as pain wracked her wasted body. Prayers became shorter and fewer.

Exhaustion ruled. Patrick's workload was onerous. He was the sole cleric conducting Sunday services, as well as weddings, funerals and baptisms. He had the sick to visit. There were meetings with the trustees and church matters to administer. He slept fitfully as every evening he became his wife's carer.

Once Maria's illness became public, Patrick gathered his children together and asked them to be quiet and listen.

'I want you to be good children because your dear Mama is poorly.'

'Has Mama got a cold, Papa?' asked Charlotte aged five.

'She does and other things too.'

'Is that why you're crying, Papa?' This from Elizabeth aged six.

'There are new rules for everyone. Mama is not to be disturbed. I will tell you when you can visit. And because she needs to rest, it is important not to make a noise when playing in the house. Is that understood?'

The children nodded. They had often sat and listened while their father talked to the family, but this was different. Silence filled the room. Then Branwell, aged four, was the first to speak.

'Is Mama going to die?'

A gasp filled the room. Shock struck his three older sisters while fear gripped the two younger ones.

This was new ground for Patrick. He'd conducted hundreds of funerals for souls of all ages. But this was unique. These children were not just his parishioners; they were his flesh and blood. He had the closest of relationships with the dying person and her children yet, at that precise moment, all his training and experience seemed of little help. With sensitivity, he ignored his son's question and asked the children to bow their heads and pray.

Life became unbearable when his children caught Scarlet fever. For days, Patrick was torn between despair and desolation. Slowly his children recovered removing one of his painful burdens.

But Maria's cancer was unforgiving and Patrick wrote to his sister-in-law, Elizabeth, in Cornwall. Bess or, as the children called her, Aunt Branwell, rejoined the household to become a godsend for Patrick.

As the days drifted by, Patrick became curious about the nurse. One night, when Maria was asleep, Bess and Patrick discussed the woman and her work.

'She is not a caring woman, Patrick.'

'I thought so but what can I do?'

'Today I found her in the kitchen talking to the servant.'

'What? But who was sitting with Maria?'

Bess shrugged. Patrick trembled.

'That is beyond the pale. I'll dismiss her tomorrow and can I ...'

'Please, brother-in-law, you don't need to ask. I will stay as long as I'm needed.'

Patrick burst into tears. He was so stressed, so tired, so drained that any kindness, no matter how small, tipped him over the edge.

The next morning he asked the nurse to step into his study. She was dismissed and at once took offence.

'Is my work unsatisfactory, Mr Brontë?' she snapped.

'No, madam, it's a sensitive family matter.'

Patrick explained to the unhappy woman.

'As you know, my wife's condition is such she may pass away at any moment. I hope you understand that we wish only family members to be present at this dreadful time.'

Martha Wright stood. Patrick joined her. 'And I shall pay you until the end of the week.' He turned to his desk, picked up some coins and handed them to her.

She counted the money then started for the door forcing Patrick to move to open it. Instead of leaving by the kitchen, she turned and walked to the front door. Patrick followed. She waited while he opened the door.

'Good day,' he said. Without speaking, she stormed off in a huff. In years to come, she'd have plenty to say about the Revd Patrick Brontë.

That night, Patrick fell asleep holding the hand of his dying wife. She spoke his name.

'Patrick.'

She spoke in a hoarse whisper. He dozed. She spoke louder but speaking, like most things, was now painful. He woke and moved closer.

'My darling, what can I get you?'

'Patrick, I want you to make me a solemn promise.'

'Of course, my dear, but now you must rest.'

Maria was on a mission and would brook no argument. 'Promise me you will always care for our children. Please, promise me.'

Patrick shook his head in disbelief. *Why would she ask such a thing?* Maria fell back on her pillows and closed her eyes. The pain was powerful and now constant. Patrick tried to calm her.

'Of course I will care for our children. You do not need to ask.'

'And I wish to see them all tonight.'

'But they are in bed and asleep, my dear.'

'I know I look dreadful, but unless I can kiss and hold each one of our children, I will die a sad and lonely woman.'

Patrick paused. His wife was the bravest person he knew. She never complained or cursed God. She was an ideal patient and about to die.

'I'll have Bess bring them to you.' Patrick squeezed her hand and Maria called as he left the room.

'Patrick. Please send Nancy to help with my hair.'

Patrick looked at her pathetic face.

'Yes, my dear.'

He left and closed the door. Tears sprinted down his cheeks. He sensed the end was nigh. He took a deep breath, wiped his face and went downstairs.

The servant went to Maria, sponged her face and brushed her hair. Bess woke the children and gave them strict instructions.

In their nightclothes they waited in the corridor outside Mama's room. Maria and Elizabeth took turns to hold their baby sister Anne who was not yet two.

Patrick opened the bedroom door, saw his children and put a finger to his lips. 'Mama is poorly but would like to say a special goodnight. Will you be brave for her, please?'

'Yes, Papa,' they spoke as one, except Anne who was searching.

'Where's my Dolly?' she asked and Charlotte slipped away to fetch it.

Patrick poked his head around the door and spoke to his wife.

'The children are here, my darling. Shall I fetch them?'

Maria nodded and tried to sit up a wee bit more. The children entered in order of age, and moved towards the bed. The candles gave light to the patient, and her face was strange but serene.

The two oldest girls approached their bedridden mother. Both wanted to cry but remained brave as Papa had asked.

'Goodnight, Maria. Goodnight Elizabeth.'

The girls kissed their mother. 'Goodnight, Mama,' they said and stood back.

Charlotte moved close to the bed. Maria's feeble arms tried to hug the young girl. 'Goodnight Charlotte.'

'Goodnight Mama,' said Charlotte, her eyes moist and her lower lip trembling. 'I will pray and ask God to make you well.'

She stepped back and her brother ran to his mother. She hugged her son who whispered in her ear.

'I love you, Mama, and I always will.' Branwell rushed to his father, buried his face in Patrick's side and sobbed.

Emily held little Anne's hand and Aunt Branwell guided them forward. Bess lifted Emily allowing her to kiss her mother.

'Goodnight Mama,' said Emily, 'and God bless you.'

'Goodnight Emily.'

Anne wanted to show everyone her doll.

'Look, Mama,' she said. 'Dolly and I can walk.' And with that the toddler lifted her doll and walked around in a circle.

Maria smiled through her pain. 'Can Mama give Dolly a kiss?'

Anne agreed and held up her doll to Maria. Bess lifted the child and Maria kissed her baby and her baby's baby.

It was a dying woman's wish fulfilled. Patrick and Bess could not hold back their tears. Ushering the children outside, Bess took them away to their beds.

Patrick sat in the chair beside his exhausted wife, his head in his hands. 'Thank you,' whispered Maria and closed her eyes. Patrick stood and kissed her forehead. He wanted to pray but felt empty. He'd run out of prayer.

Maria died and Patrick despaired. She was his rock, his life, his wife, the mother of his six children and his closest friend. He told her everything, sought her counsel, and loved her as he had never loved anyone or thing.

He couldn't work, shunned food and for two weeks did nothing. Clerics from local parishes took Patrick's services.

William Morgan, who married Patrick and Maria, conducted the funeral service, and Maria was buried in the crypt beneath the church.

But Patrick knew he had to work, for his children, his flock and his sanity. There were mouths to feed, sermons to deliver, dogs to walk and the sick to be seen. And that was just this week.

With six children under eight, he sat alone in his study. He avoided dining with the children because they spoke about their mother, and their words broke his heart. They were motherless and Patrick couldn't be both parents. He needed a wife, but who would marry an impoverished parson with six young children and live in a freezing Yorkshire town? Desperate and sad, and still uneducated in the ways of the world, well in the ways of women of the world, Patrick pondered his fate.

He couldn't marry his sister-in-law, Elizabeth. Church law forbade such a union, and the law of the land ruled it to be incest.

In Thornton, the Brontës became friendly with Dr. Firth and his daughter Elizabeth. They were some of his strongest supporters in the parish, and Elizabeth was godmother to two of the Brontë children.

When Patrick moved to Haworth, he continued to call on the Firths whenever he was in the Bradford area. And when Dr. Firth died, Patrick travelled from Haworth to conduct the funeral service of his dear friend.

Not long after Maria died, Patrick again called on Elizabeth Firth. She was now an accomplished young woman, aged 24, and Patrick noticed how well she ran the household. She knew Patrick's children. They liked her. She liked them. *Why have I not considered Elizabeth?*

He returned to Haworth and wrote to Elizabeth proposing marriage. He was twenty years her senior and unaware that Miss Firth had a suitor. A young clergyman, the Revd James Franks from Huddersfield, courted Elizabeth and his love was requited. Miss Firth was spoken for.

Patrick's pain was real when he received Elizabeth's reply. It wasn't so much her rejection, but her claim he was disrespectful to his late wife. The letter crushed Patrick, and Elizabeth broke off all communication with the Brontës for two years.

But never say die, and life continued. Twelve months later, Bess and Patrick were still caring for the children when Patrick made another half-hearted attempt at finding a wife.

A clergyman in Keighley lived with his spinster sister who had independent wealth. The brother spoke to his sister about the possibility of marriage to his friend in Haworth, but the Keighley cleric had even less knowledge of romance and women than the Haworth curate. The sister was not remotely interested and Patrick got the blunt message. Forget it.

And from such failures you might think Patrick would have learnt his lesson. Alas, no. He had no little black book of former lovers, but his memory recalled the teenage Mary Burder in Essex many years ago. Don't go there, Patrick. *But once she loved me.*

There had been an understanding between Patrick and Mary and, had it not been for her outrageous uncle, she and Patrick might well have wed. Perhaps she still harboured feelings for her first beau. Really?

Poor clueless Patrick. That failed romance was years ago. He'd walked out on her. And what was he offering now? No money, a tribe of young children and snowdrifts all the way to the privy at the bottom of the garden—every single woman's dream.

But Patrick had hope and so wrote to Mary Burder. He deserved points for perseverance. Again he received a reply, and you'd be forgiven for thinking it came from a Yorkshire lass. A modern-day translation of Mary's blunt reply would, in summary, read as follows.

And, sir, if we were to never meet again, it would be too soon.

Mary gave Patrick a piece of her mind, and there wasn't much peace in her piece. Again, a modern-day translation would show that Mary told Patrick where he might "file his proposal".

And so the curate retired from wife-hunting and remained a widower for life.

But there was some good news. Bess remained in Haworth where she became a kind, if somewhat unusual surrogate mother to her nephew and five nieces. Patrick was delighted.

Chapter 10

'HAVE YOU SEEN THIS?' Patrick passed a newspaper to Bess and pointed to an advertisement. She studied the paper.

School for daughters of the Clergy
Reduced fees. Full Board
Patron
The Hon. William Wilberforce M.P.
Headmaster
The Revd William Carus Wilson

'That's the answer,' said Patrick. 'The girls can be educated in a fine, Christian school. Wilberforce, the great anti-slavery advocate, is the patron, and he it was who helped fund my studies at Cambridge.'

'And what about the headmaster?'

'Wilson's a Calvinist and keen on the fiery sermons, but I'm sure his heart's in the right place. And consider the benefits. The school is close by in Lancashire and offers full board.'

'I hope you won't send all the girls. And what will happen with Branwell?'

'I'll send Maria and Elizabeth at first, and I can teach Branwell and the other girls here at home.'

'Education is important to you.'

'It's not important Bess, it's essential.'

'Even for girls?'

'Especially for girls. They have a brain and can reason and express themselves, just like any male.'

'My sister once told me you had unusual ideas about education.'

The mention of Maria stopped Patrick in his tracks. He spoke less of her as the months drifted by, but she was often in his thoughts. The children reminded him of Maria. Sometimes he heard a footstep and, as his study door opened, he looked up expecting his wife.

'I want a solid education for all my children and for the girls, this new school at Cowan Bridge sounds perfect.'

Patrick wasted no time. He contacted the Revd William Carus Wilson then set off on the forty mile journey with Maria and Elizabeth.

The girls seemed happy, Patrick felt grateful and, at Cowan Bridge, he dined with the staff and students and stayed the night. What an excellent situation for the struggling widower. But Haworth beckoned.

'Goodbye Maria, goodbye Elizabeth.' He kissed his daughters. 'Please do your best for your teachers.'

'Yes, Papa,' said Maria.

'Your dear Mama will look down from Heaven, so I want you to work hard and make her proud.'

'I'll do my best, Papa,' said Maria.

'So will I, Papa,' added Elizabeth.

They waved until their father was out of sight.

Months went by and all reports were good reports. Patrick repeated the procedure, this time taking daughter Charlotte, and later Emily to Lancashire, meaning there were now four Brontë sisters at the Cowan Bridge School.

At around this time, 12-year-old Charles Dickens worked in a London blacking factory. In about a decade, Mr Dickens would travel to the north of England to conduct research into schools. As a result of his trip to Yorkshire, he wrote a novel.

Nicholas Nickleby featured a school in which the students suffered enormous hardship. Dickens told the world that life in one particular school was cruel, harsh and unhealthy.

He didn't mention Cowan Bridge in his novel, and that would be left to another novelist, who wrote from first-hand experience.

A typical day for the students at Cowan Bridge went as follows. The girls rose at dawn to add whatever garments they could to combat the bitter cold in their often freezing dormitory. Washing became a challenge as it meant breaking the ice which formed on their water jug. The single lavatory was a hole in the ground. After ablutions came an hour of prayer and only then did the students eat breakfast.

Eating often became optional because money was tight and compromises were made. There were food shortages. "Waste not, want not" applied, meaning the school kept and cooked rancid food—badly. Growing children struggled to grow with hunger the norm.

There was no mention of love, care and compassion in the school's mission statement. The rod wasn't spared with beatings commonplace.

Laughter slipped off the curriculum, and the four Brontë sisters lived in this tyrannical and punishing environment with their father remaining unaware of his daughters' predicament.

Religious education received priority. The girls walked two miles to church on Sundays regardless of the weather. They crossed fields, and their clothing often became wet and muddy. Being Lancashire, it rained with the students soaked by journey's end. They shivered in the freezing, stone house of God, but only for several hours. They remained in the church for two services before repeating the all-weather trek back home.

No prize for guessing the theme of the sermons which thundered down from the pulpit, with Mr Wilson in his element. Simplicity was the key to help young minds grasp the "truth".

'Crying children can be struck dead by God, and evil children will go straight to the fires of Hell,' he declared in fervent Calvinistic tones.

Some of the girls reckoned Hades might not be so bad an option—at least there they'd escape the bone-numbing cold.

Mr Wilson took a perverse form of satisfaction when one of his charges died. At last, she's flown to Heaven with her soul intact.

And the headmaster toiled to promote "healthy" Christian living at every opportunity. His writing for children became well-known. Back at the school, he read to the girls at night as they shivered in their beds, his booming voice bouncing around the dorm.

Do look at that bad child. Oh how cross she looks. And oh what a sad tale
I have to tell you of her. She was in such a rage that all at once God
struck her dead. She fell down on the floor and died. No time to pray. No
time to call on God to save her poor soul. She left the world in the midst of
her sin. And oh where do you think she is now? I do not like to think of it.
But we know that when they die, bad girls go to Hell.

The headmaster snapped the book shut and the resultant gust of wind snuffed out the candle. In the darkness, the man of God whispered, 'Sleep tight, girls.' The only missing touch was an evil laugh.

Back in Haworth, Patrick continued his work, taking services and visiting, and teaching his son and youngest daughter, Anne. Bess helped with Anne's education.

Because there were only two children left at the parsonage, Patrick took advantage of servant, Nancy Garrs, wanting to leave to get married.

'Congratulations, Nancy, and I hear you're to marry a Patrick.'

'That I am, Mr Brontë. And if my Patrick turns out even a tenth as kind a man as you have been to me and Sarah, I'll count myself lucky.'

Patrick helped Sarah find new employment, and the sisters were replaced by Tabitha "Tabby" Ackroyd, a middle-aged spinster from Haworth, who became a much loved housekeeper to the family. She and Bess made a good pair.

Domestic changes aside, Patrick remained ignorant of life at Cowan Bridge. He knew nothing of the appalling food standards, unhealthy diet, filthy kitchen and incompetent cook, the single outside lavatory, the long walks in foul weather, and the beatings and fierce Calvinistic diatribes. But his ignorance disappeared when a letter arrived from the school.

Dear Mr Brontë
I am sorry to say your daughter Maria is unwell.
M. Drewitt
Housekeeper

Patrick exploded. 'What! Bess!'
The letter shocked him. He'd made his dying wife a solemn promise. He would care for all their children. Had he broken that promise?
Bess came running. 'What is it?'
'Maria is ill. I must go to her at once.'
He grabbed his coat and hat.
'But what about ...'
Patrick ran from the house leaving Bess stunned.
'Pray for Maria,' he cried.
She yelled after him. 'Wait for the carrier.'
Wait? Patrick couldn't wait. His darling daughter was ill and needed her Papa. He ran the four miles to Keighley, boarded the coach and slumped beside the driver. There was no time for small talk.
The bumpy roads made Patrick despair, and wild thoughts filled his head. *What is wrong with Maria? Has she seen a doctor? I promised her mother.*
'Oh come on, driver, faster, faster.'
Patrick endured mental and physical agony. Once they drew close to the school, he leapt from the coach before it stopped, ran to the school and burst in, startling staff and students.
'Where is my daughter?' he demanded.

The agitated Patrick was led to a small room with a single bed. His daughter Maria lay still, covered by a single blanket. He fell on his knees beside his girl. Her smile lit up the room.

Patrick gently pulled back the bed-covering and gasped at the sight of Maria's nightdress splashed with blood. He scooped up his daughter and could not believe her weight. She was but skin and bone. *Oh God,* thought Patrick. *Not again.*

Then the door opened and Patrick's daughters couldn't believe their eyes. The school had told Elizabeth, Charlotte and Emily their Papa was here but surely it wasn't true. It was true.

'Papa!' they squealed their delight.

Patrick knelt and was smothered with hugs and kisses from his darling girls as tears fell like rain. The joy of his daughters overpowered Patrick but the health of Maria made him despair. He decided.

'My darling girls, Maria is unwell, and I will take her home where Aunt Branwell and I can nurse her back to health.'

'But can't you stay here, Papa?' pleaded Elizabeth.

'Yes, Papa,' whispered Charlotte.

'Take me home, Papa, please,' begged a crying Emily.

Patrick thought his heart would break. It was torture to look at his daughters' pathetic faces. He felt terrible but stuck to his plan.

'I think it best for Maria if I take her to Haworth. When she is well, I promise I will return and visit you.'

Now the tears became sorrowful. Patrick hugged and kissed the three remaining girls. He wrapped Maria in her coat and a blanket, and carried her to the coach. It was one of the saddest days of his life.

The sight of his desperately ill daughter caused exquisite pain. The cries of 'Goodbye Papa,' and 'I love you, Papa,' from his other daughters were painful beyond measure. He found it impossible to look back.

The journey to Haworth seemed endless. Patrick cradled Maria, and only part of her face could be seen beneath the clothing and blanket. She never complained. Patrick kissed her forehead and whispered, 'I love you, my darling girl.' If he said it once, he said it a hundred times.

Finally the coach arrived in Keighley with Patrick exhausted. As light as she was, he couldn't carry Maria back to Haworth. He prayed and whether by divine intervention or luck, he saw the carrier turning into his yard. Patrick pleaded. He offered extra money.

'No need, Mr Brontë. I can see lass is poorly. Climb aboard.' This simple act of kindness pushed Patrick over the edge. His tears came alive.

Back home, the condition of Maria horrified Bess. The child was bathed, dressed in a spotless nightdress, and put to bed. Patrick and his sister-in-law took turns to sit with the girl. Helping her take broth for sustenance was agonisingly slow.

Memories of another Maria were still vivid, and seeing the little girl waste away tore at everyone's heart. She seldom spoke, coughed often, and made her father bitter and sad.

'Papa,' she said, 'if you pray to God, will He make me better?'

The child loved her father. He taught her to read, told her stories and took her for walks with the dogs. She saw him in church in his religious garb, preaching about God and his infinite mercy. *Infinite* was too big a word for many a child to understand, but if anyone could answer her question, Papa could.

Patrick looked at his dying daughter. Prayer didn't save Maria the mother. Now it was odds on it wouldn't save Maria the daughter. Her mother had cancer whereas Maria the younger had lungs clogged with consumption.

The child slipped away as Patrick held one of her hands and Bess the other. Maria sighed and died. Patrick wept and Bess howled. Through his tears, Patrick waved to Bess, indicating the door.

Branwell and Anne were close by, and distraught adults can frighten little children. Patrick wondered how he would explain to his children at home, and at Cowan Bridge, that Maria had flown to Heaven.

Patrick's friend, William Morgan, came to conduct another funeral service. Maria joined her mother in the crypt, and Patrick reached the lowest point of his life. Despair and the numbing pain of grief and misery dominated his thinking. His sadness caused sharp chest pains.

Thankfully Patrick couldn't foretell the future.

With his wife and daughter dead, Patrick struggled to work but how, he wasn't sure. Perhaps his vocation helped. There were so many things to do. *Doing nothing will drive me mad,* he thought.

A few days after he buried little Maria, when working in his study, Patrick heard knocking. He opened the front door and his heart turned to stone.

He recognised a man and woman from the school at Cowan Bridge. The man held something—or someone—in his arms. The woman spoke.

'Mr Brontë, this time we saved you the trip.'

They handed daughter Elizabeth to Patrick. His mouth opened in disbelief. Only a few weeks ago he saw her at Cowan Bridge. She looked pale, thin perhaps, but was thrilled to see her Papa and kissed him strongly. Now she looked like a replica of her sister, Maria.

Patrick closed the door with his foot. 'Bess,' he called in a voice filled with pain. Aunt Branwell came running and couldn't believe her eyes. They placed Elizabeth in bed and fussed. By now the adults were good at caring for the sick and dying—they'd had plenty of experience.

Elizabeth had the same condition as her older sister—consumption. It attacked her lungs. She coughed, wheezed and gasped for air. She cried, and as the pain throbbed in her chest, Patrick and Bess did everything and nothing. Their prayers went unanswered.

Word spread around Haworth that another Brontë girl was poorly. Many Haworth families suffered the death of a child. Many didn't even make it to double figures. Maria, 11, and Elizabeth, 10, were "lucky".

With a crushing inevitability, Elizabeth faded away and helped swell the Brontë body count beneath the church. Patrick's grief plumbed new depths. How much pain and suffering can one man take?

He'd sent four daughters to the school at Cowan Bridge, with such high hopes for his girls and the school. Now, two Brontë children were dead. Did the conditions at Cowan Bridge contribute to their deaths? Worse, did they cause them?

Patrick took no chances. He set off for Lancashire, and arrived at the school to find it empty.

'There's been an outbreak of typhus, sir,' said a caretaker. 'The children have gone to the headmaster's home on the coast.'

Patrick's nightmare became worse. He arrived at Wilson's home, where Charlotte and Emily rushed to their father. He was afraid to look fearing the worst. Thankfully they were healthy and overjoyed to see him. He told them to wait while he searched for the homeowner.

'My name is Brontë and I wish to speak with the headmaster,' said Patrick to a servant.

'Will you wait here, please sir?'

He waited. The young woman returned.

'I'm to tell you, sir, Mr Wilson is not available.'

Patrick seethed. He was a parent of students at the school and a fellow clergyman. Two of his daughters became ill at Wilson's school and died. *He has to see me.* Patrick called on all his reserves of patience and raised his voice.

'Kindly tell the headmaster I am withdrawing my daughters from his school. If there are any outstanding fees, he is welcome to come to

Haworth and collect them in person. Good day.' He turned to leave but stopped. 'Do you speak Latin, Miss?'

The servant shook her head. 'No, sir.'

'Well please try to remember this additional message—*in loco parentis.*'

In his study, a nervous William Carus Wilson stood still, listening to every word Patrick spoke. Wilson flinched when someone knocked on his door. His servant appeared and Wilson expelled a sigh of relief.

'Mr Brontë has left, sir, and ...'

'Yes, yes, that will do.'

'He had a message in Latin and ...'

'Just go!' shouted Wilson in his best fire and brimstone voice.

Patrick and his daughters set off for Yorkshire, and the girls never returned to the school at Cowan Bridge.

Back in Haworth, Patrick sprang into action. He made new rules. His four children would live at home. The parsonage would become College Haworth. He, Bess and Tabby would become the teaching faculty, and his children would be educated at home. The parsonage became Fortress Haworth, with the children's movements restricted.

'But Papa, why can't we go into the village and play with other children?' asked Branwell.

'Because there is sickness in the village and I want you to be safe.'

'May we go to the moor, Papa?' asked Charlotte.

'Yes, Papa,' said Emily. 'I have to take the dogs for their walk.'

'You may go to the moor provided the weather is fine and you do not go beyond the bridge. And you may only go if I am with you or Tabby or Aunt Branwell. Is that understood?'

'Yes, Papa,' they replied and were secretly pleased. At least the moor was still theirs to explore.

They went out to play leaving Aunt Branwell not well pleased.

'You don't expect *me* to go out on that godforsaken moor?'

Patrick looked at his sister-in-law. This Cornish lass would never be a Yorkshire lass. He smiled for the first time in ages. She smiled too and they both laughed, but neither could remember when that sound was last heard within the Haworth parsonage.

Patrick discovered the old times when he became a teacher again. He treated his four pupils as he did his many students back in Ireland, using a simple routine. In the morning, the children studied, and in the afternoon, they played and went for walks. Patrick got cracking.

'This morning we begin with geography. Please go to the map and discover three countries in Europe and three in Africa. But they must be adjoining countries.'

The three older children moved to the map.

'Please Papa,' said Anne, 'what is a "joining"?'

'Come with me, Anne,' said Charlotte, and Patrick took pleasure in seeing the oldest help the youngest.

After their morning lessons, the sisters went to the kitchen where Tabby taught baking, after which Aunt Branwell taught needlework. A problem arose because Bess reckoned she knew more about cooking, while Tabby reckoned she made a better seamstress. At times, both women were busting to correct the other.

In his study, Patrick gave his son tuition in Latin and Greek.

At lunch, the children discussed their morning studies. Patrick called in to say goodbye en route to visiting parishioners.

'Please Papa,' said Charlotte, 'why can't we study Branwell's subjects?'

'That's a good question,' said Aunt Branwell, challenging the teacher.

'You eat y'lamb stew, young lady,' said Tabby.

Patrick spoke. 'Branwell studies the Classics to prepare for university.'

'Papa says I could go to Cambridge just like he did,' said Branwell.

'I'd like to climb a bridge,' said Anne, spooning more lamb and taters into her delicate mouth.

'Now girls,' said Bess. 'Remember that young ladies who are educated become a governess or teacher. Young gentlemen, like your brother, go to university to become a lawyer or doctor or, like your father, a priest.'

'I wish to become a soldier,' said Branwell.

That statement got the girls talking and Patrick interrupted.

'Very well, I agree.' Everyone stopped and looked at the household head. 'The girls may sit in my study when Branwell is having his lesson.' This provoked much happiness from the girls with their brother a trifle miffed. 'But only to observe. Now please finish your lunch. Goodbye.'

'Goodbye Papa,' they called and resumed eating and talking. Bess made a mental note to include table manners on tomorrow's timetable.

In Haworth, Patrick found death to be commonplace. Consumption, cholera and typhus were widespread, and the health of the locals was further damaged by the town's water supply. At times, it was so polluted, even the cattle refused to drink it.

And while Patrick kept his children away from the sickness and disease in the village, he went out as always. He continued going into homes where the sick and dying coughed and vomited. He never shirked his duty.

And not only in homes, as Patrick visited mills and factories, sickened by the sight of children working at all, let alone in dirty, dangerous places. He saw deprivation in Ireland, and now here in Yorkshire, and believed passionately in education being the key to eradicate poverty.

Patrick entered one of the many Haworth mills.

'Mornin', Mr Brontë,' said the foreman who kept working.

'Good morning, Mr Armitage. I trust you are well.'

'Mustn't grumble.'

'And your wife and family?'

'Aye, they're champion.'

'Can I have a word about the children working in your mill?'

'Aye, but not for schoolin'. Some brings in the family wage.'

'But they're so young. How old are they?'

'I won't take 'em unless they're ten.'

'Ten!' Patrick shook his head.

'And I won't 'ave 'em work more than ten hours.'

This staggered Patrick. 'Ten hours a day, for a child?'

'Aye. Now if you'll 'scuse me, sir, I've got summat important t'do.'

Patrick shook his head, smiled at a bedraggled child and left. That night he wrote letters. Recent government legislation dealt with children working in factories. But often the laws were ignored, which greatly upset Patrick. He wanted the laws enforced, children removed from factories, and sent to school. He showed his letters to Bess.

'More letters,' she said. 'You know nothing will change.'

'But there are children as young as eight working in those deadly mills.'

'They have to because their parents are ill, unemployed or dead.'

'But they'll never escape poverty until they get an education.'

Bess worried about Patrick's frustration. He clearly wanted to help people prepare for Heaven but equally, he wanted to make their life on Earth free from disease, unemployment and poverty.

'I'll post these letters tomorrow.'

'And what about tonight?' Patrick looked at Bess. 'The Church Missionary Society meeting in Keighley.'

'Oh no,' cried Patrick, grabbing his coat and hat and running out of the parsonage. Bess smiled. She wasn't as efficient a secretary as her late sister, but she still kept the curate on his toes.

He arrived at the meeting, took his seat, looked at the clergymen on stage, and felt ill. One of the clerics was the Revd. William Carus Wilson. Patrick's heartbeat raced. He flushed with anger. His evening was ruined. He'd made a pledge to ignore the man who ran the school where two of his daughters suffered so badly they died. Patrick knew it was not the Christian way to behave, but a father's love and loss drove his thinking.

To Patrick, the meeting dragged. He didn't wish to make a scene, and to stand and leave was difficult. He was sitting in the middle of a row close to the front. He felt trapped. Then it happened.

Wilson's eyes met Patrick's, and this threw the headmaster. *Good,* thought Patrick. *Now he's uncomfortable too. Now he may understand some of the pain I suffered and still suffer.* Wilson averted his eyes.

The meeting ended and people chatted over refreshments. Patrick pondered his next move. *Should I confront him? Should I approach him and politely enquire about his school? Being kind might pack more of a punch. I'll go to him and see what happens.*

Patrick headed to Wilson but stopped as a hand tapped his shoulder. The hand belonged to William Morgan, and Patrick's tension vanished in the smile of his dear friend. They warmly greeted one another and shared news. When Morgan left, and Patrick turned to find Wilson had gone.

Travelling home, Patrick thought about the headmaster from Hell, and re-lived the terrible experiences he endured with the death of his girls. In a way, Patrick was glad he didn't confront the man. *Hatred, bitterness and revenge won't make me a better father,* he thought.

It never rains but it pours. Soon after that meeting, Patrick crossed paths with Wilson again. The vicar of Bradford, Henry Heap, died. Patrick saw this as an opportunity to break the tie between the Haworth and Bradford churches. As it stood, his church paid a type of royalty to the church in Bradford, which meant less money for Patrick to help the Haworth poor, sick and uneducated.

The Haworth curate proposed the arrangement be disbanded, but his proposal was defeated, due to the casting vote of one, William Carus Wilson. *Thank you, headmaster; thanks for nothing.*

The mills kept producing cloth and Haworth's children remained exploited and uneducated. Almost half the town's children died before they started school, let alone work. This kept Patrick busy burying and baptising. At some services he baptised up to thirty souls in a single service. With life so short, no-one knew who might die tomorrow.

And through all this time, his offspring were growing—in body and mind. What did the future hold for Patrick's children?

Chapter 11

PATRICK DID MUCH MORE THAN TEACH. He wanted his children to think, to be able to research, to reason and to argue a point of view. He knew reading widely enabled every child to gain confidence, and would help them make their way in the world. One night they were in his study.

'I want you to borrow any of my books,' he said.

The children buzzed in anticipation.

'All of them, Father?' asked Branwell, looking at Patrick's impressive library.

'And that applies also to magazines and newspapers.' The excitement increased. 'I have copies of *Blackwood's Magazine* with many articles you should find interesting.'

'Thank you, Papa,' said Charlotte speaking for her siblings.

'You may care to read a short novel called *The Maid of Killarney* written, I should modestly say, by your father.'

The children gasped with surprise and delight.

'You have written a novel, Papa?' gushed Branwell.

'Why haven't you told us?' asked Emily.

'And many poems,' replied Patrick pointing. 'There are my poetry books on the shelf.' The children looked in wonder. Their father was a published author. 'So please read whatever you wish.'

Anne, being the youngest, felt intimidated. 'Papa, your books will be too difficult for me.'

'Nonsense,' he said. 'Life is full of challenges. Set your mind to achieve success and let nothing stop you.' He stared at his youngest child. 'Anne Brontë, you are a very capable young lady.'

That comment typified Patrick's positive approach—his hidden positive approach. Outside the parsonage, few people knew how well he inspired and educated his children during their years of schooling at Haworth. His choice of subjects, his teaching skills and the different activities he introduced, opened a brave new world of learning for his children, and created an environment where they wanted to learn.

Patrick stimulated their thinking by holding family discussions, a "philosophy class for beginners". He used simple devices, including a mask, to draw out their thoughts.

The curate asked a question, before handing the mask to the child being quizzed. His thinking being that, behind the mask, the child would speak freely. And speak freely they did.

Patrick began. 'Anne, what does a child need most?'

Little Anne held the mask in front of her face and spoke with confidence. 'Age and experience, Papa,' she said.

'Excellent,' replied her father and retrieved the mask. 'Charlotte, what is the best book in the world?'

Charlotte held the mask. She enjoyed the game.

'*The Bible*, Papa, followed by *The Book of Nature.*'

Patrick nodded and Charlotte smiled. She was an avid reader, and loved the days her father brought home a newspaper or book. She was so keen, she even devoured the writing on the brown paper in which the books were wrapped.

'Emily,' said Patrick. 'Sometimes your brother is naughty. What should I do with him?'

This was a brilliant example of the benefits of the mask. Branwell sat there looking pleased. He couldn't see Emily's face but hung on her every word.

'Reason with him,' said Emily. Branwell nodded. 'But if he will not listen, whip him.'

Branwell gasped and was about to object when Patrick gave his son the mask and questioned him.

'How can we know the difference between the intellects of a man and a woman?'

His sisters were hooked. Behind the mask, Branwell spoke. 'By considering the difference between them as to their bodies.'

Charlotte found the answer confusing and annoying, but before she questioned the answer, her father spoke.

'Tomorrow we start lessons on great Old Testament leaders. Who can suggest a name?'

'King David,' said Charlotte.

'Moses,' added Branwell.

'Noah,' said Emily.

Everyone looked at Anne.

'Can I tell you tomorrow, Papa?' she asked and everyone smiled.

'You can, but be warned. Soon we shall have a debate. Each of you must choose a biblical leader and argue why he is the best of all.'

The children's excitement continued to grow.

'I used to give prizes to my students in Ireland.' Another buzz of eager anticipation came from the class. 'Perhaps I could introduce the practice here in Haworth.'

That was the knockout punch in Patrick's sales-pitch. The children were bursting to start their new studies.

'Oh, and I have news about extra teachers. They will come to the parsonage and you will all study painting and music.'

This thrilled the children.

'Thank you, Papa,' said Charlotte. 'You and Aunt Branwell have helped us so much.' The others agreed.

'This is the best school I've ever been to,' announced Anne.

'This is the *only* school you've ever been to,' teased Branwell, and everyone laughed.

Patrick continued. 'Tomorrow I go to Leeds. I shall set you work and inspect it when I return. Is that understood?'

'Yes, Papa,' they spoke as one.

'Now let us pray.' The children closed their eyes as their father spoke a simple prayer. He thanked God for all His gifts, and asked God to bless their house and all its occupants, including the cat and dogs. Emily said "Amen" louder than her siblings.

The children kissed their father and went off to bed, followed by Aunt Branwell, who clacked along the flagstone floor. She found the cold crept into her feet, so wore a type of wooden overshoe which kept her normal shoes and stockings clear of the chills.

The next day, Patrick had parish business in Leeds and, when completed, he walked to the coach for the journey home. He stopped at a bookshop and looked in the window. His eyes played tricks. Was it true? No, it couldn't be. Was that a copy of Patrick's book of poetry, *The Rural Minstrel?* It was. His heart beat faster. Patrick Brontë, a published poet. This was the first time he'd seen his work in a bookshop. He wished his darling wife could see this. He would tell his children. *I wonder if they will be proud of their Papa*, he thought.

He crossed the street and saw something in a toy shop window. Moving closer, he inspected a box of toy soldiers. Patrick did not like to spoil his children and always treated them as equals, but he knew his son would adore this gift.

Patrick entered the shop and asked to examine the soldiers. The kind shopkeeper allowed Patrick to handle the beautifully made toys. Quality craftsmanship was a joy to behold, with its exquisite attention to detail.

'I'm most impressed,' said Patrick, 'but I fear the cost is too great.'

'Not necessarily,' said the shopkeeper. 'Mr Brontë, is it not?' Patrick looked surprised. 'I have family in Haworth, sir, and when visiting, have had the pleasure of hearing you preach from time to time.'

Patrick smiled his appreciation. The shopkeeper continued.

'I'm sure we can reach an agreement, sir. May I enquire as to your offer for the soldiers?'

Patrick's mind raced back to the previous century when he stood in a Belfast bookshop. Now, today, in Leeds, he took out his purse. Surely he didn't have enough. He placed the coins on the counter, then felt in a pocket and discovered two more. He hoped for success.

The shopkeeper smiled. 'A most generous offer, Mr Brontë; allow me to wrap the soldiers. For your son, you say?' Patrick was speechless.

With the railway to Haworth still to be built, Patrick took the coach and carrier, which had to contend with Yorkshire weather and roads.

Tabby had retired for the night, but Bess greeted him as he entered the kitchen.

'How are the children?' he asked. Patrick always spoke those exact words when he returned. He patted the dogs. 'And how are you, Bess?'

They drank tea and forgot parish matters as Patrick delivered his exciting news—the sight of his published book of poems, and the present he bought for Branwell.

'Don't wake him now,' said Bess. 'And what will the girls think when Papa buys something for the son and heir, but nothing for us mere females?'

Patrick looked horrified. 'Bess, that's a wicked thought. They know I love them all.'

'They know and I know, but let's see what happens.'

Next morning, early riser Patrick was not the first out of bed. He heard squeals of delight and lots of chatter. He put on his dressing-gown and opened the door. There on the landing, his four children played with the toy soldiers. Their happiness flowed through the house.

'This is the Duke of Wellington,' said Branwell holding a soldier aloft.

'This is my favourite,' said Charlotte. 'He is a nobleman.'

'I like this soldier,' said Emily, 'because he has not one, but two dogs.'

Anne was her usual polite self. 'I think my doll would like a soldier.'

Patrick saw Bess tip-toeing up the stairs. She caught Patrick's eye and made a face. He smiled and returned to his room. Patrick rejoiced; not so much because the soldiers were popular, but rather that Branwell's gift had become everyone's gift.

Buying material for the children's education was costly. Patrick begged, borrowed and bought books, magazines and newspapers but writing-books, ink, quills and pencils were expensive and needed to last. The curate's income was not generous and, besides, he paid for his children's music and painting lessons, albeit with some help from Bess.

The variety of Patrick's teaching continued apace. He inspired his children to explore drama, with the toy soldiers being the props for their invented plays. Talk about sibling rivalry. "My General can defeat your General. Oh no he can't. Oh yes he can."

One day when the weather was mildly atrocious, the children play-acted indoors. The characters were chosen and the script completed, so with impressive accents, it was time for Act One Beginners.

Duke of Wellington
(Master Branwell Brontë)
And so, Monsieur Emperor, I hear you have called me a bad General.
Napoleon
(Miss Charlotte Brontë)
I have, sir, and only because it is true.
Prince of Orange
(Miss Emily Brontë)
My soldiers will give their lives for you, Herr Wellington.
Irish Soldier
(Miss Anne Brontë)
I am Irish, but in this war I shall fight with the British.

Their knowledge of the Battle at Waterloo came from reports in newspapers and magazines read to them by their father. Here, Patrick became *his* father back in the tiny Emdale cottage in Ireland, telling stories of great battles and victories. The children listened in breathless silence, and then these stories stimulated their dramas.

At first, the toy soldiers were the actors. Then the children took over. Cue curtain, cue lights.

One day, as Aunt Branwell enjoyed her afternoon nap, Tabby baked bread in the kitchen while the cat slept in front of the stove.

The actors performed. Did they ever? The French attacked the British and then the Prussians. The plucky Irish joined the fray. Threats rang out, then demands and finally the physical stuff started.

In a modern theatre-school their activities would be called improvisation. In the Haworth parsonage, it was more a free-for-all. The foot-stamping, the shouting and screaming built in a steady crescendo.

Aunt Branwell snored, the cat purred, but the worried Tabby stopped kneading dough. She opened the kitchen door, and the sounds of the re-enactment of the Battle of Waterloo put the fear of God into her. She ventured a step or two towards the room just as all four actors let fly with their most violent burst of histrionics. It was too much for the housekeeper. She fled.

Gasping for air, she ran, well, waddled away to her family's home in the next street. Her nephew answered the door. Tabby screamed.

'Come and help. The chillun' are killin' themselves. Come quick!'

Tabby's nephew took off for the parsonage and arrived well before his aunt. When she entered the kitchen, puffing, she found four young actors seated at the table, each wearing an enormous grin. Their idea of a joke didn't appeal to the housekeeper, but made no difference to the love she had for "her brood". The cat and Aunt Branwell slept throughout the entire performance.

Patrick heard about the "let's terrify Tabby" incident, and gave his children a restrained reprimand. Secretly amused and delighted, he revelled in their artistic activities.

Discussions in the parsonage often involved politics. Issues debated included children working in factories, capital punishment, the right to vote, and discrimination against Catholics. Patrick read the latest newspaper articles to his children. They listened and asked questions. Patrick had opinions, but insisted his children form and explain their own.

One afternoon, Charlotte came into the kitchen where Bess and Tabby were discussing dressmaking.

'Papa will be so pleased,' said Charlotte.

'I think you mean, "Excuse me, Aunt Branwell",' said Bess.

Charlotte apologised then, showing the ladies an article in a Leeds newspaper, continued her speech.

'New legislation allows for a reduction in the number of crimes which incur the death penalty. Papa has advocated this for a long time.'

'I see,' replied her aunt. Tabby gazed in wonder. Charlotte continued.

'And here, this article is about the injustice of rotten boroughs.'

Aunt Branwell shook her head in amazement at Charlotte's grasp of matters political.

What's a rotten barrow? thought Tabby.

This single event, where Charlotte read from a newspaper, could understand and discuss its articles, knew what her father's stance was on various matters, and could clearly explain all that to two adults, was the Patrick Brontë education story in a nutshell.

As an educator, he was a genius. Because of Patrick's teaching, two remarkable things happened. The children became prolific in their writing, and Patrick knew little or nothing about it.

How could he? He often had no assistant curate so performed all services himself. And in addition to clerical duties, he worked tirelessly to start a day school, to remove children from factories, to improve Haworth's dreadful sanitation and water supply, and did all he could for the poor, sick, dying, bereaved and unemployed; and all that while he taught his own children. And to make all of that even more of a challenge, his eyesight began to fail.

He knew about his children's school work, but not their secret writing. But what was this underground literary activity?

The children were fantastic at fantasy. Alone with the dogs on the moor, they played with the toy soldiers. Branwell placed one on a rock and explained the soldier's battle plans. Charlotte described the family life of her soldier. Emily named the dogs owned by her soldier, and Anne knew the names of the children of her soldier, and the names of the dolls owned by these children. Back in the parsonage, the soldiers morphed into kings, queens, dukes and noblemen, into good and evil characters. What lives they led. Patrick's children created a new world—their own.

They became writers of fiction, dreaming up stories with imaginary characters in imaginary lands. They invented countries and kingdoms, and drew pictures of these people, places and events. They read their stories aloud and so inspired one another.

To anyone watching, it would have been astonishing. It *was* astonishing. Their prolific output saw them create so many characters in all sorts of tales. Sometimes they worked alone, sometimes in pairs. They became scribblemaniacs.

Amazingly, Patrick was ignorant of this hive of activity. And not only did his imaginative offspring write and illustrate their tales, they published them too.

Writing paper was scarce so they improvised. They found scrap material such as old wallpaper, and Tabby saved sugar bags for her brood, from which they created miniscule books. Bookbinding became their latest skill. They wrote their fantastic stories in miniature writing because of the tiny dimensions of their homemade books. And the most amazing aspect of this artistic outpouring was that nobody knew about it.

Patrick and Bess kept a watchful eye on their formal lessons, but the underground literary society remained a childhood family secret.

So why did it happen? What triggered this secret writing? What was the impetus and inspiration to drive four children to become so prolific and imaginative?

It came from a single source—the Revd Patrick Brontë, B.A.

The fact that their father was a published poet and novelist, spoke volumes. And his home schooling underpinned their vast outpouring of literature and art. His four offspring became creative thanks to his lessons, his family discussions, his constant supply of new reading material, the games he played with them, and the toys he gave them. He led by example.

But despite being a natural and brilliant teacher, Patrick could never imagine that all his devotion to their education would bear fruit in a most wonderful and unexpected way. All Patrick wanted to do was encourage his children to be well read, to think for themselves, and to follow their dreams.

On those criteria alone, he was an outstanding parent.

The home schooling continued for years. The children grew to become young adults with outstanding future prospects.

But then it was time. One by one, Patrick's children flew the nest; they left the Haworth parsonage to study and work in the outside world. What they did, and what happened to them, would turn their father's world upside down.

Chapter 12

CHARLOTTE SAT IN PATRICK'S STUDY. 'My darling girl,' said her father, 'I don't believe I can teach you anything else.'

'You have taught me so much, Papa.'

'But if you are to become a teacher or governess, you need to attend an appropriate school for young ladies.' Charlotte looked worried. 'Oh no, I would never send you back to that terrible school at Cowan Bridge.'

'I know that, Papa.'

'So what will you do with your life?'

'I am rather fond of writing, Papa.'

'Praise be; but I fear it may never provide you with any financial reward. So what else?'

'I like teaching, Papa.'

'That's wonderful, because your new school is ideal for a teaching qualification. It's the reputable Roe Head School near my old church at Hartshead, and is run by Miss Margaret Wooler and her four sisters.'

'When shall I start, Papa?'

'All being well, next month. It's not far, and your godparents and Mrs Franks, the former Miss Firth, can keep an eye on you.'

'Thank you, Papa.'

'I'm sure you'll make new friends and I have high hopes for your academic success.'

'May I ask, Papa, how you can afford the cost of my new school?'

'The fees are not your concern and besides, a good education is priceless. Your only responsibility is to work hard at your studies.'

'Thank you again, Papa. And I promise I will do my best.'

'I know that.' They stood. He kissed his daughter and squeezed her hands. 'Your dear Mama would be so proud.'

So Patrick's oldest living child was the first to leave Fortress and College Haworth to make her way in the world. Patrick's expectations were met. Charlotte shone academically and, like her father at Cambridge, became an outstanding student.

Next in the time-to-leave-home queue was the son and heir. Patrick taught Branwell the Classics so well, the two men read to one another in Greek. And while Patrick gave his time and energies to all his children, it was Branwell he hoped who would enjoy a successful career.

Patrick was now middle-aged, ancient in Haworth terms, where most adults were dead before they reached 30. His health was sound although not his eyesight.

If Patrick died, Branwell would take care of his sisters, and to prepare for such an eventuality, Branwell needed a career path.

'You have a flair for art, my boy. Would you like to pursue it?'

'Certainly, Papa, but do I have the necessary talent?'

'There's only one way to find out. I can try to arrange your entry to the Royal Academy in London. You should put samples of your best work in a folio.'

Branwell worried. His father made enormous sacrifices to raise and educate him. Branwell liked painting and made modest progress. But what else could he do? What else did he *want* to do? His father came from a poor, Irish background and graduated from Cambridge University. Could he emulate his father's achievements?

That night, Patrick and Bess sat in the kitchen with the animals for company.

'I spoke to Branwell about going to London.'

'And?' she replied.

'I think he's keen.'

'I think he's under pressure.'

Patrick stared at Bess. 'What sort of pressure?'

'Oh Patrick, please, he's an only son. He's under pressure to make his mark. His sisters don't have that pressure. They may marry and, if not, will do well as genteel spinsters like your favourite sister-in-law.'

Patrick wanted to smile but deep down knew the truth in what Bess said. Was he putting pressure on Branwell? Was he pushing his son?

Schooling continued at home for Emily, Anne and Branwell. He took additional painting lessons in Leeds but slowly, subtly, the pressure to make portrait-painting his profession continued to build.

Branwell thought about his possible career. *What if I'm not good enough? What if I fail? Would it be better to aim for something lower, something less public and less difficult?*

Perhaps Patrick should have sensed his son's lack of enthusiasm. Parents pushing their children can trigger unwanted, even disastrous consequences. But Patrick made a decision and told his son.

'I'll write to some influential people. You might be surprised to learn your humble curate father knows several high-ranking gentlemen.'

'Really, Papa,' said a polite but quiet Branwell.

'I know members of parliament and even the Prime Minister.'

That impressed Branwell but didn't remove his doubts. He found odd jobs illustrating cards and teaching painting to beginners. He wrote poetry. But then came the "good" news and Patrick was over the moon. The Royal Academy offered a place to Branwell. His sisters and father rejoiced while his aunt appeared pleased. Branwell put on a happy face and preparations began for his long journey south.

The house was asleep when Bess knocked on Patrick's study door. He buzzed about Branwell's news.

'It's a grand day, Bess. Tomorrow your nephew is off to London.'

'Grand indeed,' said a less than enthusiastic Bess as she sat.

'You look worried,' said Patrick.

They always spoke freely to one another and this was no exception.

'Are you sure the Academy is right for Branwell?'

'Right? Bess, it's the pinnacle of the art world. It's like Cambridge to an impoverished Irishman. Branwell has the opportunity take his God-given talents to new heights.'

'I agree,' said Bess. 'But is that what he wants?'

Patrick fell silent. He remembered their previous conversation about Branwell being under pressure. Had Patrick misread the situation? Had *he* decided his son's future? Patrick slumped in his chair.

'You mean, he doesn't want to go?'

Bess shrugged. Patrick tried to justify his actions.

'I only want the best for my children, Bess. You know that.'

'I don't have the slightest doubt you love your children dearly and want desperately for them to be happy.'

There was a long pause.

'But?'

'You can't live their lives for them, Patrick. You can encourage and inspire your children, and you are brilliant at that, but they must choose how they will live and where and with whom.' She stood, squeezed his hand and opened the door. 'Goodnight Mr Brontë.'

Patrick looked at her. 'Goodnight Miss Branwell.'

Branwell arrived in London to enrol at the Royal Academy. There would be no bursar calling him Brunty or Branty. There would be nothing like the age or class difference his father found at Cambridge, and there would be no sizar situation with straw to keep his feet warm at night. Alas, there would also be no Royal Academy.

Bess was right. Her nephew lacked the passion to study art, or lacked confidence, or both. He didn't want what his father wanted. Branwell wandered the London streets spending his money on food and drink, consuming more fluids than flour. He discovered nothing about the Academy. He didn't even show.

The shame he felt at having failed to register was nothing to the sadness he felt in failing to fulfill his father's wishes. No son had a more caring and loving parent. Everything Branwell learnt came from the thoughtful and devoted teaching given to him in the Haworth parsonage by his father and, to a lesser extent, his aunt. He owed them everything and here he was, throwing a wonderful, once-in-a-lifetime opportunity back in his father's face.

He wrote a brief note to say he was coming home and would explain everything when he arrived. Patrick showed the letter to Bess.

'You were right, Miss Branwell. I pushed the boy into something *I* wanted and didn't understand his feelings.'

'Goodness, how shocking,' said Bess. 'The Revd Patrick Brontë is human after all.'

He appreciated her gentle sarcasm, and whispered, 'Thank you.'

When Branwell arrived home fearing the worst, he broke down and cried such was the warmth of the welcome from his father, aunt and sisters.

'Now my boy,' said Patrick, 'least said, soonest mended. I have found a newspaper advertisement for the new railway company.'

'Patrick,' said a concerned Bess, trying to prevent another case of the pushy parent. But Branwell got in first.

'That's a happy coincidence, Papa. I spoke to a chap in London about the railways. He thinks they'll expand all over the country and will need men for many occupations.'

Patrick smiled and Bess sighed with relief.

'I'll apply tomorrow,' said Branwell. 'And I plan to continue painting whenever I have the chance.'

To rub salt into Branwell's wound of failure, his older sister excelled. She did so well at Roe Head, Miss Wooler offered her a teaching position at the school. Charlotte the graduate came home.

This brought Emily to her father's study for the next heart-to-heart chat with the Haworth College careers' officer.

'My darling girl,' said her father. 'I don't believe I can teach you anything else.'

'You have taught me so much, Papa.'

'But if you are to become a teacher or governess, you will need to attend an appropriate school for young ladies.' Emily looked worried. 'Oh no. I would never send you back to that terrible school at Cowan Bridge.'

'I know that, Papa.'

'So what would you like to do with your life?'

'I am rather fond of animals, Papa.'

'You have inherited that from your Irish grandfather.'

'And you, Papa. You love dogs more than anyone I know.' Patrick smiled. Emily was curious. 'Did you inherit your fondness for dogs from your father?'

'I must have. When he was young, my father's only friends were dogs.'

'I can understand that. Sometimes I prefer dogs to people.'

Patrick thought about his homeland. He wished his children had met their Irish grandparents.

'But that doesn't help with your future, young lady. You must prepare for work as a teacher or governess.'

'As you wish, Papa.'

'Charlotte has done exceedingly well at Roe Head, and when she returns to the school, it will be as a teacher. And you, Miss Emily Jane Brontë, will go with her to undertake your new studies.'

'Thank you, Papa.' She paused. 'May I ask a question?'

'Of course.'

'If I become homesick, will I have to stay at the school?'

Patrick smiled. 'Let's cross that bridge when we come to it.'

And so Charlotte and Emily set off for Roe Head with one the teacher and t'other the student. And with Branwell away working on the railway, the College Haworth roll now had only one name—Miss Anne Brontë.

After a few months, Emily caught the homesickness disease. Patrick and Bess welcomed her back to Haworth. It was anyone's guess what Emily would do, and this brought Anne to the headmaster's study.

'My darling girl,' said her father. 'I don't believe I can teach you anything else.'

'You and Aunt Branwell have taught me so much, Papa.'

'So what would you like to do with your life?'

'I wish to be a governess, Papa.'

'And a wonderful governess you will be. As you know, Emily has returned from Roe Head, which will allow you to take her place.'

'Will Charlotte remain as a teacher?'

'Yes, and you may even be taught by your sister.'

Despite a break due to illness, Anne remained at Roe Head until she finished her studies. Of all Patrick's children, Anne won the prize for *Most Determined Student*.

Branwell worked as a railway clerk. Anne completed her schooling and found a position as a governess. Charlotte became a successful teacher, and Patrick took pride in his talented children. No-Longer-Homesick Emily was the Haworth dog walker, resident ailurophile and assistant housekeeper, and Patrick was sure she too would find a paid position and do well. Alas, Patrick's pride and dreams were due a hammering.

The wheels fell off the Haworth College bandwagon. Charlotte left her teaching post and came home. Sacked as a governess, Anne came home. Sacked as a railway clerk, Branwell came home. Suddenly Patrick had all four of his children back living in the parsonage. Had they ever left?

Years ago, Patrick helped form a Temperance Society in Haworth. His young son was the secretary. But having failed in London and locally on the railway, Branwell also failed the Temperance Society. He broke the pledge and started drinking.

Patrick faced a dilemma and spoke with his sister-in-law.

'Bess, I'm at my wit's end.'

'It's because Branwell sees himself as a failure.'

'Nonsense.'

'Look at the facts. His father achieved academic excellence at a famous English university, and his sisters are clever, intelligent and successful. He's the odd one out. He thinks he's a failure.'

'No!' cried Patrick. 'That is both wrong and self-defeating.'

Patrick anguished over Bess's comments. She broke the silence.

'Perhaps in a less talented family he would not see himself so.'

Patrick found a little relief when Charlotte approached her aunt.

'Aunt Branwell, I have a proposal.'

'Hmmm?' was all Bess said.

'With my sisters, I would like to start a school for young girls here in the parsonage.'

'Would you?' said the less than garrulous aunt.

'But my French is not good enough, and if I were to study abroad, we could offer excellent lessons and thus attract pupils.'

'Have you mentioned this to your father?'

'No, Aunt Branwell. I wanted to discuss it with you first.'

They both understood why. Patrick was poor whereas his sister-in-law had £50 per annum from her late father's estate.

'Such a trip and schooling would be expensive,' said Aunt Branwell.

'I believe Belgium offers the cheapest alternative.'

'And your father would not allow you to travel alone.'

'Emily has agreed to come with me.'

Aunt Branwell fell silent. Charlotte held her breath.

'I can give you £50.'

Thrilled, Charlotte embraced her aunt who inwardly was excited. Once told the news, Patrick beamed.

'I will accompany you and see you are settled,' he said. 'But first I must rehearse my French.' His accent was passable. 'Bonjour Monsieur, Madame, Mademoiselle.'

Charlotte laughed and her heart beat faster.

Charlotte and Emily began their studies in Belgium. On his way back to Haworth, Patrick took a detour and visited the site of the Battle of Waterloo. He arrived home to good news.

Anne had found a new position as governess with the family Robinson, and Branwell had found work as a portrait painter in Bradford, being "chaperoned" by Patrick's pal, William Morgan.

With his children having once again flown the nest, Patrick could concentrate on serving the poor and suffering parishioners in Haworth.

His happiness increased when told that Anne had recommended her brother as a tutor to the Robinsons, and Branwell became a teacher.

'I told you, Bess,' said Patrick over supper. 'My boy will make something of his life.'

Bess smiled and nodded.

'All he needed was the right profession, and with the education he received here, the sky's the limit for your nephew.'

Bess gave a forced smile and asked to be excused.

'Forgive me, Patrick, I am not myself. I think I'll retire early.'

Patrick stood and opened the door for her.

'Are you not well? Should I call the doctor?'

'No, please, it's nothing.'

Patrick dined alone. Housekeeper Tabby had slipped on the ice and done herself a mischief. She went to recuperate with her sister. The sexton's young daughter, Martha Brown, joined the parsonage, her home and parents only a short walk away.

Next morning, Patrick rose early, opened his bedroom window and pointed his pistol at a headstone in the graveyard. Crack! Bullseye! And while the Luddites and Napoleon were not expected to march up the Haworth Main Street next Tuesday, if ever his family or country needed defending, he was ready.

In the kitchen, young Martha struggled with the porridge.

'Good morning, Martha,' said Patrick. 'How are you settling in?'

'Very well, sir, thank you.'

'No Miss Branwell?'

'I've not seen her, Mr Brontë.'

'That's strange. Will you please pop upstairs and call her?'

Martha did as requested and a short time later gave Patrick a fright.

'Can you please come, sir? Miss Branwell is poorly.'

Patrick flew up the stairs, knocked gently then entered Bess's room. His mind flashed back to the final days of his wife.

'My dear, what is wrong?'

Bess could only shake her head as tears glistened in her eyes.

'I'll send for the doctor. No, I'll go myself. Be brave,' he said as he left.

After the doctor examined Bess, he met with Patrick downstairs. It was a case of déjà vu.

'I'm sorry, sir, but Miss Branwell has a serious problem in her abdomen and I fear the condition is terminal.'

Patrick went numb. He could recite this conversation backwards. He would ask about the possibility of the doctor being wrong, and about alternative diseases and various treatments. That conversation took place and then the doctor spoke.

'These drugs will help the dear lady manage her suffering, but I fear she may not be long for this world.'

Patrick wanted to both cry, and scream with rage, but held himself in check. He thanked the doctor and escorted him to the door, then went to his study and wrote brief letters to Belgium, and to Thorp Green where Anne and Branwell were working for the Robinson family. He sent Martha to post the letters and hurried upstairs.

Bess smiled as he entered her room. 'It runs in the family, I'm afraid,' she said before coughing and wincing in pain.

'I want you to take this laudanum,' said Patrick helping her to sit up.

When she settled, he held her hand and prayed. Then there was silence until Bess spoke.

'Please may I be buried beside my sister in the crypt?'

'Come now; let's not dwell on such things.'

She looked at him. 'Please?'

He understood her wish to be open and honest. 'Of course. *Of course.*'

Patrick didn't mention fighting the disease or praying for a miracle. He knew Bess didn't want that, just as they both knew she was dying. He remembered the months of agony his wife endured, and hoped that Bess's death came sooner rather than later. Patrick broke the silence.

'You do know that I too wish to be buried next to your sister. Should we argue over which side is better?'

Bess tried to laugh at Patrick's humour but ended up crying with pain.

As with his deceased wife and daughters, Patrick sat with Bess through the long, pain-wracked nights. Exhaustion meant he struggled to perform even the smallest of his parish duties. His children headed home. Two made it; two didn't.

Elizabeth Branwell settled in the parsonage at Haworth to care for the six Brontë children when her younger sister, Maria, fell ill with uterine cancer. When Bess died from bowel cancer, quickly fortunately, she had lived, worked and supported Patrick and his children for nigh on 21 years. To them she was less Aunt Branwell, and more Saint Branwell.

Charlotte and Emily left Belgium but missed the funeral. Patrick, Branwell and Anne were the chief mourners, and were desperately sad at their aunt's passing. Branwell was devastated.

'I have lost the guide and director of all the happy days of my childhood,' he bemoaned.

Patrick lost his best friend, his confidant and the one person who understood him. *To whom now can I turn for help?*

Chapter 13

CHARLOTTE RETURNED TO BELGIUM ALONE. Miss Homesickness, Emily, preferred West Yorkshire and her new housekeeping role. Anne and Branwell went back to their employers, the Robinsons. Patrick's eyesight got worse.

Charlotte's French improved but she inherited her father's romantic clumsiness. She fell in love with her Belgian teacher, a married man, and came home suffering from unrequited love.

Aunt Branwell bequeathed £900 to her sister's daughters, but only her dressing-case to Branwell, which further dented his low self-esteem. Charlotte used some of her inheritance to open the school.

'You can help us teach the girls, Papa, or be an inspector of your daughters' handiwork.'

The curate smiled. 'I cannot begin to describe the joy I have at seeing my children running their own school.'

But joy was in short supply when the school failed. It was hard to teach without pupils. Not one student enrolled. Patrick's spirits sank and his eyesight got worse. The local pharmacist recommended rubbing alcohol to slow the rate of his declining vision.

The alcohol was painful and useless with an unwanted consequence. Patrick gave off the aroma of drink and tongues began to wag.

'Did you smell curate? Typical Irish, he's taken to drink.'

'His boy enjoys a tipple and is following the old man.'

Misery settled in the parsonage. With Bess gone, Charlotte became the keep-up-your-spirits person.

'Come, sir,' she said. 'Where is that young Irishman's optimism; he who left his humble home to triumph at Cambridge University?'

And Patrick's optimism did receive a boost when a new assistant curate arrived. With Patrick's ageing bones and encroaching blindness, having a reliable and competent assistant was a huge relief. The men were alike.

Arthur Bell Nicholls was Irish and worked hard, being devoted to his calling. He even had Patrick's ineptitude when it came to understanding the art of wooing a woman. A bachelor, Nicholls boarded with the sexton's family, a short stroll from the parsonage.

Away from Haworth, Branwell copied his dear Papa. Patrick made elementary mistakes in matters of the heart, and his son followed suit. The family Robinson employed Branwell as a tutor and Anne as a governess, and the wife and mother, Mrs Lydia Robinson, was bored.

She took an unnatural interest in the young Branwell Brontë, with such interest being potentially catastrophic. Like Patrick's relationship with one of his teenage students long ago in Ireland, Mrs Robinson and Branwell were playing with fire.

The couple found it easy to meet because Branwell lived in the grounds of Thorp Green Hall. Mrs Robinson flirted with the young and impressionable tutor who lapped up the attention.

Mr Robinson was unaware of this liaison, and Branwell didn't have his father to rescue him from a looming disaster. Mind you, Patrick was hardly an expert in matters romantic.

One afternoon, Branwell complimented the lady of the house.

'My dear Mrs Robinson, how charming you look today.'

'Why, thank you, Mr Brontë. Perhaps you might call me Lydia.'

Branwell enjoyed a frisson of delight. He moved to his employer's wife and, gazing deep into her eyes, lifted her hand and kissed it. Her fluttering eyelids spoke volumes about forbidden pleasures.

Upstairs, in a room overlooking the garden, Anne helped the Robinson daughters with their needlepoint. She moved to a window and saw her brother's behaviour. She felt ill. Her charges moved to join her and Anne ushered them from the window.

That night, she accosted her brother. 'I saw you in the garden.'

'Naturally, I'm often there.'

'Kissing Mrs Robinson,' she hissed.

Branwell was defensive. 'I have done nothing of which I am ashamed.'

'Are you insane? If Mr Robinson discovers your outrageous behaviour, it will mean instant dismissal—for both of us.'

'She loves me.'

Anne scoffed. 'Oh Bran, don't talk nonsense. She's old enough to be your mother.'

'We have become intimate friends.'

'I don't believe you.'

'Believe what you like.'

'Can you imagine what your scandal would do to Papa?'

'He need never know.'

Anne shook her head. 'If you have no self-respect, at least think of our father. He is an old man who does not deserve to have his final years ruined by his son's pathetic philandering.'

That hurt. Branwell got the message. Or did he? Flattery and sex were a heady mix. Anyway, the budding romance stalled when the Robinsons went on holiday, and Branwell and Anne returned to Haworth.

Patrick had all his children at home. He longed for their news.

'And how are things at Thorp Green with the wonderful governess and the brilliant young tutor?'

Anne didn't mince her words. 'I'm sorry, Papa, but I'll not be returning to the Robinsons.'

Patrick winced. 'But I thought you got on well with the family.'

'I don't wish to discuss it.'

That left an awkward silence.

'But you, my boy, you will continue as tutor?'

'Indeed Papa, I leave next week.' Anne glared at her brother.

But trouble awaited Casanova Brontë. He returned to Thorp Green unaware his employer had discovered the affair. Gardeners sometimes see more than blooms. The enraged Mr Robinson castigated his wife and sacked Branwell on the spot. He was to never contact the Robinson family again, and the young suitor returned to Haworth a broken man.

Anne told her sisters about their brother's escapades, but Patrick received a redacted version. He despaired and felt guilty blaming himself for the worries and problems of his children. Although his hopes for Branwell took a hit, the never-say-die father kept being positive.

'Chin up, my boy,' he said.

But Branwell was distraught; not so much from being been sent home in disgrace, or having failed at yet another task, but because his hope for what he mistakenly believed to be true love was ripped from his grasp.

In his room he cried and berated himself. He rarely slept. He'd failed at the Royal Academy, at the railways, as an artist, as a tutor and now as an ardent suitor. Trips to the local public house became more frequent. And Mrs Robinson hardly helped the struggling young man by writing to him after the wretched affair ended. Branwell became a mess.

In his study, Patrick pondered his lot. He'd lost four members of his family, educated four more, and sent them into the world, only for all four to return in a state of unhappiness or failure or both. Two of his children fell in love with someone who was married. *What went wrong?*

To make matters worse, Patrick struggled to read and write due to his failing eyesight. His letters were full of mistakes, and he needed someone to read him the newspapers, and announce who'd called to see him. Now was the time for the curate to feel self-pity, to become angry with God, and to stop fighting the good fight. But not Patrick Brontë; he kept going, and thanks largely to his assistant curate, Arthur Nicholls.

Still the pressure continued to mount, depression set in and Patrick dropped his bundle when his children disagreed. It was rare for his daughters to raise their voices and argue.

Charlotte spoke with her sisters. 'We need to do something. Aunt Branwell is gone, Papa may never see again, and Branwell is drinking himself to an early grave.'

'I won't be a part of any school,' said Emily.

'I'm not suggesting another school,' said Charlotte. 'It's our writing.'

'Not the miniature books,' said Anne. 'We've never shown them to anyone, not even Papa.'

'Definitely not the miniature books,' said Charlotte.

'Then what?' asked an impatient Emily.

'Our poetry,' said Charlotte. Anne and Emily fell silent. 'Why don't we write poetry and have it published?'

Emily scoffed. 'And that's your wonderful idea?'

'We must do something,' said Charlotte. 'Any money we make can go towards an operation to help Papa see again.'

That stopped any argument. The three sisters wholeheartedly supported any project which would help their beloved father. Silence reigned. Charlotte spoke knowing that what she was about to say would cause trouble.

'Em, I think your poetry is excellent.'

Emily flared. 'How do you know about my poetry?'

'Shhh, Papa will hear,' whispered Charlotte.

Emily fumed. 'Have you been looking through my things? You have. You have no right to read my poetry. It's private. How dare you take something which doesn't belong to you?' She slammed her hand on the table.

In his study, Patrick despaired.

'I know and I apologise, Em,' said a humble Charlotte. 'I was tidying and came across them by accident.'

Anne played the peacemaker. 'There's no harm done, Em. Please don't fuss.'

'Don't tell me I can't fuss.' Patrick cringed as the disagreement flared.

'But I'd like you to know, dear sister,' continued Charlotte, 'that I think your poems are beautiful; touching and beautiful.'

Charlotte's sincerity removed some of the tension.

'Oh come on, Em,' said Anne. 'Charlotte's paying you a compliment. And I would like to read your poems too ... please.'

Emily's anger began to fade. She paused, then spoke in a soft but defiant voice. 'I do not want the publicity of being a published writer.'

'Nor do I,' said Charlotte. 'We can write using invented names.'

Both her sisters spoke as one. 'Invented names?'

'And we must choose male names. Other women publish, and are often ridiculed just because of their sex. You remember when the poet laureate wrote to me and said, "Literature cannot be the business of a woman's life".'

'Pompous fool,' said Emily. Charlotte continued.

'But if we adopt male names, or names which aren't obviously female, we won't be identified and thus can avoid that dreadful prejudice.'

There was another pause.

'It might work,' said Emily.

'And we'll never know unless we try,' said Charlotte.

'My poems might not be good enough,' said Anne.

Charlotte ignored Anne's remark and took control. 'First we must work on our poems, select the best examples, and then send them to a publisher. Are we all agreed?'

Emily surrendered. 'Only if we don't use our real names.'

Charlotte's excitement kicked in. 'We need a bland family name, one which doesn't attract attention.'

'What about Papa's curate?' suggested Anne.

'Nicholls?'

'No, his other name, Bell.'

'It's a bland name,' said Charlotte. 'But then he's a bland curate.'

'Who's taken a shine to a certain Miss Charlotte Brontë.'

Charlotte looked aghast as Anne grinned. Even Emily smiled.

'Him!' snorted Charlotte. 'I wouldn't marry him. He's the most boring man in Yorkshire. And who would marry an Irishman?'

'Mama did,' said Emily, and Charlotte froze, realising her faux pas.

Anne changed the subject. 'We need Christian names which might be masculine.'

They settled on Currer, Ellis and Acton Bell, and paid for the printing of their poetry collection. Would it be well received? Would it sell? In a word, no. Like their planned school at Haworth, it flopped.

The girls were disappointed but not half as much as their brother. He was a poet, a published poet. His work had appeared in local newspapers. *Why didn't they ask me? Why wasn't I one of the Brontë poets?*

But if Branwell's misery at having been kept out of the poetry loop was bad, his disappointment would plumb new depths once his sisters wrote novels.

Blindness now became a reality for Patrick with Arthur Nicholls his saviour. Arthur performed his own duties and Patrick's too. Arthur sat with Patrick and read to him, reported on parish matters and encouraged the elderly curate.

'I think you should preach this Sunday morning, Mr Brontë,' said Arthur. 'I'll take the other services.'

'But I can't see well enough to prepare.'

'Many people say you are the finest extempore preacher they have heard.' Patrick smiled and nodded. 'Shall we agree on you preaching at the first service?'

Patrick reached out his hand and Arthur grasped it.

'Thank you, Mr Nicholls.' There was genuine affection between the two clerics. 'You are a gentleman and a friend.'

It was a full house that Sunday morning. Emily and Anne led their father to the church. His parishioners knew their curate was almost blind. For many, he was the only priest they had ever known. He baptised them, married them and buried their relatives. He taught them in Sunday school, called on them when sick, and helped them find work. And importantly, he became an honorary Yorkshireman by learning how to mind his own business.

Arthur Nicholls knocked on the parsonage door. Running late, Charlotte hurried to open it.

'Oh, Mr Nicholls,' she said.

'Good morning, Miss Brontë. I'm here to collect your father.'

'But he's gone already. Did you not see him with Emily and Anne?'

Nicholls worried and appeared flustered. 'I did not. Ah, well, then perhaps I might be permitted to escort you, Miss Brontë?'

Charlotte paused then nodded. 'Very well. Thank you, Mr Nicholls.'

They entered the church with many a head turning in their direction. Emily and Anne exchanged glances. Arthur escorted Charlotte to her sisters then moved to Patrick. Arthur spoke to him then mounted the pulpit and began the service. When it was time for the sermon, Arthur assisted Patrick to the pulpit in an action which touched the worshippers.

Patrick preached a memorable sermon, speaking from the heart, looking out at the sea of faces yet not seeing a soul. Everyone admired the man who preached while being unable to see his congregation.

Back in the parsonage, Patrick and his assistant took tea with the sisters. Upstairs, Branwell slept in a drunken stupor.

'Thank you for an uplifting sermon, Mr Brontë. I believe you should preach every week,' said Arthur.

'But only if you are strong enough, Papa,' said Emily with a sliver of reprimand for Arthur.

Pleasantries continued until Nicholls stood, preparing to leave.

'Thank you for the tea, ladies. I shall leave you in peace.'

'Will you not join us for luncheon, Mr Nicholls?' asked Anne. Emily glared at her.

'Alas, Mrs Brown is expecting me. But thank you for your kind offer. Well, good day ladies and to you, Mr Brontë.'

'I'll see you to the door,' said Charlotte. When they reached the front of the parsonage, Charlotte stopped and faced the curate.

'Mr Nicholls, I have a favour to ask.'

His enthusiasm came alive. 'Of course, Miss Brontë, anything.'

'My sisters and I hope our father will soon have an eye operation. If that occurs, it will mean a lengthy period of recuperation, placing an even greater burden on you, sir.'

'It would not be a burden, Miss Brontë, but an honour to serve your father and his family.'

Charlotte looked at him. *He might be boring but his heart's in the right place.*

'Thank you, Mr Nicholls. As soon as the surgery can be arranged, I'll inform you of the details.'

He smiled and nodded, and she smiled with her eyes. She opened the door just as an almighty thud and scream of pain echoed through the parsonage. The hungover Branwell had taken a tumble. Nicholls looked at Charlotte. It was common knowledge the curate's son was a drunkard.

'If ever I can be of service to you and your family, Miss Brontë, please do not hesitate to ask.'

He left and Charlotte felt a sense of admiration for him. But now it was time to sort out the domestic crisis better known as Branwell Brontë.

When visiting her friend Ellen Nussey, Charlotte spoke with an experienced surgeon and asked about her father's eyes.

'It depends, Miss Brontë,' said the surgeon. 'The cataracts need to harden before any operation may proceed.'

'But how will we know that condition has occurred?' asked Charlotte.

'An examination will inform the surgeon, but it's likely to be the right time when your father's sight is almost gone.'

At least there appeared to be hope. Charlotte and Emily went to Manchester to meet a surgeon regarded as the finest oculist in the city. The sisters made plans for their father's operation. Back home, they gave Patrick the good news.

'We met Mr William James Wilson, Papa,' said Charlotte.

'He believes you have every chance of regaining your sight, Papa,' added Emily.

'My darlings, I cannot tell you how glad I feel,' replied the old curate. 'Your mother would be so proud of your love and kindness.'

In the weeks before the procedure, the Brontë males led identical lives—Patrick in his study and Branwell in his bedroom. Both were miserable; one because of blindness, the other, depression.

Branwell's drinking took root and he became a fixture in the Black Bull public house. In the church, his father preached on the virtues of temperance and godliness. Next door in the pub, with drink in hand, the curate's son stood by the fire and proclaimed his prejudices. The locals regarded him as the town drunk. Misery consumed his father.

On many nights, the parsonage door received a soft knock, with the visitor making a polite request for the Revd Brontë to fetch his inebriated son.

Patrick didn't have far to travel. The church, pub and parsonage rubbed shoulders with one another, and on those certain nights, Patrick, with his failing eyesight, would lead his son home. It was a case of the blind leading the blind—one sober but sightless, the other dead drunk. Branwell's future looked grim; was grim.

Apart from the obvious, there was another benefit of Patrick's proposed cataract operation. The surgery enabled him to escape the morose, self-harming and tragic behaviour of his beloved son.

Charlotte accompanied Patrick to Manchester and took her father to meet the surgeon.

'Miss Brontë, how lovely to meet you again. And this fine gentleman must be your father. My name is Wilson, sir.'

'How do you do,' said Patrick peering towards the voice but seeing only a shadowy outline.

'Please sit over here, Mr Brontë.' Patrick was helped to a chair.

'Thank you for agreeing to operate on my eyes, Mr Wilson.'

'Well first I need to examine you, sir.'

Charlotte perched in a corner as her father sat still to be examined. After several minutes, Wilson spoke.

'Your eyes are ideal for a cataract operation, Mr Brontë. I suggest it takes place next Monday morning at ten o'clock. Will that be suitable?'

'I am completely in your hands, sir,' said Patrick, 'literally so.'

'And may I ask where you are staying in Manchester?'

'We have found a hotel,' said Charlotte.

The surgeon moved to his desk and made a note. 'I'm sure you can do better in this boarding house. It's close by, reasonable, and the landlady is a former patient of mine. Here is the address.'

'Thank you, sir, that is most kind and helpful,' said Charlotte.

'Indeed, most kind,' added Patrick.

'Until next Monday then,' said Wilson, and Charlotte guided her father back to their hotel.

Mr Wilson accurately described the boarding house, although the landlady was poorly, and recuperating at her sister's home in the country, meaning Charlotte had additional tasks to perform.

In Haworth, about half the population didn't make it to thirty. Patrick, now in his seventieth year, became Methuselah. This added to the risk factor. An elderly patient might not survive the operation.

On the day of the procedure, three gentlemen stood ready to operate on the curate. Charlotte sat in her corner seat.

'I regret, Miss Brontë, family members may not be present during the operation,' said the surgeon.

This troubled Patrick. 'Oh, Mr Wilson, sir, I'd be most grateful if you could make an exception for my daughter.'

The surgeon looked at the curate and his daughter. 'Very well, but you must sit still, Miss Brontë, and not say a word.'

'Thank you, sir,' said Charlotte, and made her small frame even smaller. The curate and his daughter were a team.

'Now, Mr Brontë,' explained the surgeon, 'I intend to use a modern technique where the cataracts are removed. In many cases, surgeons use a needle to push the cataract, causing it to drop from your field of vision, yet remain inside your eye. That procedure works well, but has the risk of the cataract popping back up and making you blind again.'

'I understand,' said Patrick.

'The procedure I use involves making incisions, enabling the cataracts to be extracted, thereby removing them once and for all. Do you have any questions?'

'No sir.'

'First, I will add drops from the plant belladonna. This will cause pain for a few seconds. The entire procedure should be complete within half an hour. Are you ready, Mr Brontë?'

'I am.'

Charlotte held her breath as Mr Wilson and his colleagues began. They used no anaesthetic. Chloroform and ether were available, but sometimes they induced vomiting, and the resulting convulsions could cause the wounds to rupture.

The belladonna drops caused Patrick to flinch. He suffered mentally not knowing what to expect—the fear of the unknown. Helpless, he sat still while a highly sensitive part of his body was prodded and probed.

The surgeon made incisions and worked on the perfect patient. Then it was over and Patrick, like his daughter, had remained silent. Almost blind before the procedure, Patrick became totally blind as the surgeon wrapped heavy bandages around the curate's head.

'May I congratulate you, sir,' said the surgeon. 'Your operation was a great success.'

Patrick offered his profuse thanks with Charlotte mightily relieved and grateful. Patient and carer returned to their boarding house.

'Now, Papa, remember what the surgeon said.'

'Take to my bed for four days and nights in my darkened room, and speak as little as possible.'

'Unnecessary movement must be avoided at all costs.'

'I don't believe Mr Wilson said anything about trips to the privy.'

'It's only four days, Papa. I've heard you preach about "girding your loins". Here's your chance to practise what you preach.'

Patrick wanted to laugh but didn't, fearing he might tear at the wounds. In Patrick's day, because the incision to remove a cataract was not stitched, the surgeons relied on the skin to heal itself; hence the heavy bandages and immobility of the patient.

The surgeon performed one "modern" medical practice as Patrick had leeches applied to "help" with the potentially harmful bloodletting.

Recuperation in Manchester lasted several weeks. Patrick called on his reserves of patience. His daughter did everything and more to care for her father. But as he rested in his darkened room and ate and drank very little, she wrote. She remembered her youthful experiences at the Cowan Bridge

School, and invented another school of horrors. Like Charlotte and her sisters, the fictional Jane Eyre suffered horrendous deprivation.

The surgeon continued to monitor Patrick's eyes.

'You are making excellent progress, Mr Brontë. How is your vision today?'

Patrick lacked conviction and faith. 'I believe I have forgotten how to use my eyes, Mr Wilson. The bandages and darkened room have given me a clear understanding of what life must be like for a blind person.'

'You are a remarkable man, sir, but I will speak plainly. I am confident you will soon be able to see your family, and know exactly how many of your dedicated parishioners have come to hear you preach on any Sunday.'

Patrick thanked the surgeon again, and the curate's happiness increased when he received Mr Wilson's bill. The oculist charged Patrick less than half the normal fee.

After several weeks in Manchester, Patrick returned home to a hero's welcome with Branwell particularly pleased to greet his father.

In Patrick's absence, Arthur Nicholls had performed heroics making Patrick's homecoming even more enjoyable. Nicholls took great pleasure in greeting the senior cleric, and even greater pleasure in greeting the returning daughter.

'I want you to take a holiday, Mr Nicholls,' said Patrick. 'You sir, have most definitely earned a break.'

Arthur smiled and, once Patrick had fully recovered, did travel and enjoy his holiday. Throughout the break, Arthur couldn't stop thinking about a certain Miss Charlotte Brontë.

Chapter 14

PATRICK BECAME A NEW MAN. He took three services a Sunday plus weddings and funerals. With his new eyesight, his letter-writing lost those scratches and most of his spelling mistakes.

But one awful thing spoilt his new freedom; his ability to clearly see his son's destructive behaviour. What he saw turned Patrick's heart to stone. His darling boy had aged. Emily and Anne reported to their father.

'He's worse than ever, Papa,' said Anne.

'That's true, Papa, but we must help him overcome his demons.'

'We must indeed,' said Patrick. 'Now please, tell me everything.'

'The apothecary told us he asks for drugs, promising to pay the next week. But he has no money,' said Anne. Patrick's eyes filled with tears.

'I fear it's more than the drink, Papa,' added Emily. 'He's given up. He thinks his life's a total failure.'

Patrick shook his head. Branwell's death would be beyond belief. *But is not my son's current condition even worse than death?*

'Thank you, my darlings. Now, on a brighter note, tell me your news.'

'I have been writing, Papa,' said Anne.

'More poetry?' asked her father.

'And some prose too.'

'But that is wonderful,' said Patrick. 'And Emily, what of your news?'

'I've been walking the dogs, Papa.' Patrick laughed. 'But with a little writing as well.'

Patrick bubbled with excitement. 'That is better than wonderful. Tell me the details. What are you writing? When may I read your work?'

'Perhaps when your eyesight is fully recovered, Papa,' said Anne, and she stood and kissed him.

'Our writing is but nothing, Papa, knowing you have your sight restored,' said Emily. She kissed her father then added an instruction. 'I told the dogs you are an expert walker, Papa, and they expect to see you on the moors tomorrow. Please do not disappoint them.'

Patrick squeezed Emily's hand, smiled and felt proud. But in the back of his mind he couldn't forget the dreadful condition of his boy.

Patrick relished sleeping in his own bed again. His vision improved with every day. He wanted his four children to be happy and settled. The girls were fine but the huge worry was Branwell.

One night as Patrick slept, he awoke to a commotion—shouting, rich with fear. Screams filled the parsonage. Patrick struggled out of bed and followed the voices. They settled.

He bumped into Charlotte coming out of Branwell's room holding a basin.

'Branwell set fire to his bedclothes, Papa.' Patrick gasped.

'It's all right, Papa,' said Anne joining them. 'The fire was only small and Branwell wasn't hurt.'

Emily appeared. 'Please go back to bed, Papa. We'll take care of Branwell.'

A decisive Patrick gave a clear order.

'Take the boy to my room.' His daughters looked at him and hesitated. 'Please, do as I say.' They did as instructed.

It was an unusual sight. The septuagenarian, still recuperating from his cataract operation, babysitting his 31-year-old son, whose main health issue was alcoholism, with drug addiction and depression thrown in for good measure.

Patrick lay awake as Branwell snored. The clergyman had grounds to abandon or curse his God. His wife, two of his children and his sister-in-law had died in his arms. Patrick did his fair share of sitting beside a bed, as one after another of his family slipped away. Now his son was in mortal peril. At least Patrick could lie on his bed.

Branwell started coughing. It was frightening. Alarmed, Patrick got out of bed and moved to his son's side.

'Branwell, wake up.' He shook his son. 'Branwell!'

He turned Branwell on his side and slapped his back. He slapped harder. Branwell coughed the more and expelled horrible phlegm.

Patrick wanted to cry out to Bess but remembered the dear woman was dead. He refused to call his daughters and, using every muscle in his ageing body, pushed Branwell onto his back, and then pulled his son's feet towards the edge of the bed. The drunk awoke.

'I want to die,' he moaned. 'Please, Papa, let me die.'

Patrick faced many a crisis throughout his life, but never had a family member made such a terrible request.

Over the weeks, within the parsonage, the son and heir stumbled, collapsed, shouted and gave an excellent impersonation of a drunk. In the mornings, he appeared uttering crude absurdities.

'It's amazing,' slurred Branwell. 'The old man's still alive and so am I. Heaven be praised. Now, somebody please pass the gin.'

He wasn't acting, and obtained opium from the apothecary. This combination of alcohol and drugs turned Branwell into a monster. He terrified his sisters and devastated his father. His life became a tragic, senseless waste.

Then came the delirium tremens, the DTs, where chronic alcoholics hallucinate, become fearful and disorientated. Branwell believed Satan wanted to kill him. Life at the parsonage became a living hell. Patrick's suffering entered a new dimension. Night after night he couldn't sleep as, by his side, Branwell coughed, vomited, cried, and pleaded for death.

Incredibly things got worse. Patrick received a demand from a Halifax publican for Branwell's unpaid debts. If the money wasn't paid, Patrick would be taken to court. The curate begged his sexton for help.

'Please, John, take these ten shillings to the landlord in Halifax. Tell him I will settle the remaining debt as soon as possible.'

'I'll leave straight away, Mr Brontë.'

'Thank you. And John, please use your powers of persuasion. If the gentleman takes me to court, I shall be ruined and off to the Workhouse.'

With Patrick able to see again, his daughters alternated between helping their brother and writing novels. They continued to use their pseudonyms. A dubious London publisher accepted Emily's *Wuthering Heights* and Anne's *Agnes Grey* but, for whatever reason, rejected Charlotte's *The Professor*. More fool him.

During her time in Manchester, while caring for her father, Charlotte had worked hard on another novel, and when *Jane Eyre* was submitted to a reputable London publisher, the book was accepted immediately and became an instant success.

When Branwell got wind of his sisters' publishing success, he slipped deeper into woe. All his sisters were using their talents to shine; he'd squandered whatever talent he had. His self-pity became self-loathing. For Charlotte, telling her father about her literary success needed careful explaining. She had communicated with her publisher in secret. Now she had this tremendous success. Concerned, she knocked on his study door.

'It's your favourite daughter, Papa.'

'Really, and who might that be?' He enjoyed their little joke. 'Come in, my child and tell me your news.'

'It is good news, Papa.'

'Excellent.'

'I have written a novel.'

'I am not surprised. Emily and Anne have told me they too have been busy with their writing. Now you must read me your novel.'

Charlotte paused, and then placed a copy of *Jane Eyre* on the desk in front of her father. In shock, he looked at the published tome.

'But this is a published book.'

'It is, Papa.'

'But where are the manuscript pages?'

'In my room, Papa. They became this book with its title *Jane Eyre*.'

'*Jane Eyre*,' he repeated with pride. He picked up the book and saw the author's name. 'But what is this name, Currer Bell?'

'It is a pseudonym, Papa. All your daughters have written under a pseudonym. I am Currer Bell, Emily is Ellis Bell and Anne, Acton Bell. I hope you are not disappointed.'

'Disappointed? My child, I am thrilled beyond measure. Your mother and Aunt Branwell would be overcome with happiness and pride.'

'That is your copy, Papa. I have inscribed it for you.'

Patrick opened the novel and saw his daughter's handwriting.

> *To my darling father who taught me everything*
> *Your loving daughter, Charlotte*

Speaking became impossible. Patrick found it hard to swallow and tears filled his eyes. Charlotte placed her hand on his arm. He recovered and queried the book.

'So you have paid for the novel as you did with your book of poetry?'

'No Papa. I have not paid for it.'

Confusion gripped the curate. He looked at Charlotte. 'But how then did it come to be?'

'A London publisher, Smith, Elder, offered me a contract.'

Patrick's jaw dropped. 'A London publisher offered you a contract?'

'Yes, Papa, and I accepted their offer.'

'Then this is the finished book?'

'Yes sir, exactly that.'

'Then my daughter is a published novelist?'

'Not your daughter, Papa, your daughters, plural—all three of them. You are the father of three published novelists.'

'All three?' Patrick's tears broke free. His tongue locked. His feelings of pride and happiness were overwhelming. The lump in his throat got lumpier. His cheeks glistened. He clutched the copy of *Jane Eyre* as Charlotte stood and embraced her father. Words were redundant.

Branwell was on a mission. Death wasn't his preferred choice so much as his only choice. Patrick watched as his adult child, who behaved as a child, edged ever closer to the grave.

To add to his addictions and depression, Branwell fell ill. With his family at church and as sick as he was, Branwell stumbled outside to beg for opium or alcohol. His addiction and ruin were public knowledge, but most of the sympathy was for the boy's father and sisters.

His coughing and shortness of breath indicated the end of his life. It may have been bronchitis or consumption or alcoholic poisoning, or all three. Even with someone helping him, Patrick fell over in the street.

One Saturday, too sick to get out of bed, Branwell wailed. The Haworth doctor came, examined the pathetic patient, and told Patrick his son was close to death. This medical opinion was old news to Patrick. Surprise and shock were not a part of his reaction.

'I can provide your son with drugs for pain relief, Mr Brontë, but I fear they would be of little use.' Patrick could recite that refrain backwards.

He farewelled the doctor, and when he turned from closing the front door, his three daughters, stood in a group, watching him. What could or should they say or do? Without speaking, Patrick entered his study and closed the door. The sisters heard their father sobbing.

Charlotte went to the sexton's house and asked for Mr Nicholls. She refused to enter and waited until Arthur appeared.

'Miss Brontë, how can I help?'

'I fear my brother may soon die, Mr Nicholls and my father is ...'

Arthur took hold of Charlotte's hand.

'Please don't speak, Miss Brontë. Tell your dear father I will take all services tomorrow, and all his parish duties, and will continue to do so until he is able.'

Charlotte wanted to smile but couldn't. There were many things to say but silence seemed appropriate. She nodded her heartfelt thanks and returned to the parsonage.

That night, unable to sleep, Patrick listened as Branwell made strange wheezing noises with his laboured breathing. A hacking cough shook his body. The doctor's comments made perfect sense as Branwell's body slipped into shut-down mode.

The Sabbath dawned and Patrick had barely slept. He knelt beside his son and prayed—again.

'Heavenly Father, we beseech you to hear our prayer. Have mercy on the body and soul of thy servant, Branwell. Grant him thy forgiveness and everlasting peace.'

There was a shuffling sound outside Patrick's bedroom as his daughters gathered to see what they could do. Knowing their brother was close to death, they listened without speaking. All three siblings wanted an end to the suffering Branwell had endured for months—or was it years? Charlotte moved closer to the door and heard her father praying.

'Thank you, Oh Lord, for thy boundless love and the gift of thy Son, Jesus Christ.'

Patrick hesitated. He began to cry softly. He wanted to pray but grief dominated. Branwell made a sound. Patrick looked up and was about to ask if Branwell wanted something when the penny dropped. Branwell too was crying, not coughing or moaning but crying.

Patrick sat on the bed and embraced his child.

'Be brave, my boy, be brave. And always remember that God loves you. God loves Patrick Branwell Brontë.'

Branwell moaned and emptied his body of tears. Patrick held his son and gently placed his forehead against Branwell's. With their tears intermingling, Patrick prayed.

'Hear our humble prayer, Heavenly Father, forgive us our trespasses, and take us into thy loving arms for all eternity.' Both men wept. 'We pray in the sure and certain knowledge that God's mercy and forgiveness extends to every sinner who repents; in the name of the Father, the Son and the Holy Ghost. Amen.'

Charlotte strained to hear and caught her brother speaking.

'Amen,' was all he said.

His father appeared to be happy, almost rejoicing. Then came silence.

'What's happening?' whispered Emily. The silence continued.

'I'm not sure,' whispered Charlotte.

Suddenly a sickening wail erupted. Grief had found its voice.

'My son, my son,' howled Patrick, and the sisters knew the truth.

Can you compare the suffering and death of different people within the same family? Did Patrick grieve more for his wife than his daughters or his sister-in-law or his son? What nonsense. Each death diminished him.

Each death plunged a fresh dagger into his heart. Each death was unique, and each caused stinging pain and grief.

His parents had five sons before five daughters. What might have been if Patrick fathered three sons and three daughters? More nonsense.

But with Branwell an only son, and because sons were expected to have careers, and because Patrick had been Branwell's teacher, mentor and father, the death of his boy burnt deep into Patrick's soul. He shut down.

After the funeral, led again by William Morgan, Patrick remained alone and aloof. He refused all visitors, and seldom ate or drank. His daughters grieved for the death of their brother, and grieved even more for the wretched and devastated man they loved with a passion; their father.

But, in time, Patrick Brontë did what Patrick Brontë had done so many times. He rose again. He stood, took his hat and walking-stick and went out to greet the world. He prayed, he preached and he persevered. This simple deed alone bore powerful testimony to his character and faith.

Those who knew his life story, or at least his tale since arriving with his family in Haworth, wished him a better life. They hoped his final years would be less traumatic, less painful and more peaceful. In his dotage, might there even be a grandchild to play with and educate? Was Patrick Brontë's tale of woe finally at an end?

In a macabre and cruel way, Patrick experienced life imitating life. It never rained but it poured. In the past, when death struck his family, it struck again. History now repeated itself. It's true that for Patrick, when sorrows came, they came not single spies, but in battalions.

Emily was always a loner. Forget teaching, travelling and tea parties; living at home and walking alone on the moors with her dog for company, meant bliss for Emily Jane. Had she been an only child, one imagines she would have been content.

They interred Branwell. He joined his mother, aunt and sisters beneath the Haworth church floor in late September, when Yorkshire's autumnal storms brought an added chill to the sombre parsonage. Everyone caught a cold but Emily's persisted. How diabolical the irony, that Emily should become fatally ill at her brother's funeral.

The sisters sat in the dining-room.

'Let me send for the doctor, Em,' said Charlotte.

'I can go,' said Anne. 'I am much better this morning.'

'I don't want the doctor,' snapped Emily and wrapped her shawl even tighter. 'Kindly leave me alone.' Her sisters exchanged worried looks.

Charlotte went to her father.

'Papa, we are worried about Emily. Her cough is persistent, yet she refuses to send for the doctor.'

Witness a familiar scene—Patrick hearing news of the unhappiness of one or more of his children. Did he raise his voice, ordering them to resolve their problems? Did he tell them to stop pestering him? Never, and yet again he looked for a solution.

'Does she take any medicine or even homemade remedies?'

'Nothing; she claims they are useless. If we offer to help, she becomes angry. Sometimes when we speak, she refuses to answer.'

Patrick pondered the problem. 'I fear this malady.'

'She has to be seriously ill, Papa. She remains indoors, and Emily never fails to take Keeper for his walk upon the moor.'

'Perhaps we send for the doctor without asking Emily's permission.'

'Thank you, Papa. Perhaps too you might offer a separate prayer.'

Charlotte asked Anne to fetch the doctor, leaving Patrick to pray yet again for the failing health of a member of his family.

When the doctor arrived, Charlotte told him of Emily's truculent behaviour. He nodded and followed Charlotte into the room.

'Em, the doctor is here and ...'

Emily stood in a fury. 'How dare you. I told you I have no need of the doctor.' She stormed from the room, leaving her sisters aghast and the doctor speechless.

Two things continued—Emily's stubbornness and her consumption. The weather worsened as did her health. Her infected lungs made breathing difficult. Her body ached and she moved with slow and pathetic steps. Her skin and eyes appeared strange. Her sisters despaired, and her concerned faithful hound refused to leave her side. His motto—*If my mistress sits by the fire, then I shall sit by my mistress.*

Charlotte and Anne went to their father.

'Is there any hope, Papa?' asked Charlotte.

In this situation, Patrick might well have been a doctor. He saw consumption at first hand. His daughters, Maria and Elizabeth, wasted away before him. They died as children, whereas Emily was 30.

'We must be brave,' said Patrick who recognised the symptoms and could predict the end result.

Christmas approached. The sisters sat together in the quiet parsonage. Emily worked on her needlepoint. Outside the winter weather lost its temper. Then, without warning, Emily spoke in a whisper.

'Perhaps I will see the doctor today.'

Charlotte moved to Emily's side. 'Oh Em, is the pain so bad?'

'I'll go,' said Anne leaving the room.

Charlotte helped her sister to lie on the couch. Keeper moved to be closer to Emily.

Anne told her father of developments, and sent young Martha to fetch the doctor. Soon Patrick, Charlotte and Anne gathered around Emily. Patrick prayed and each of his daughters said "Amen". Keeper looked at the others then back at his mistress.

The clock ticked, the fire crackled and the family waited. Patrick grimaced and pain burnt his chest as he offered a silent prayer.

Make me strong, O Lord, to be strong for them.

What a setting. What did you do today, Mr Brontë? Oh I sat with my daughters while waiting for another one of them to die.

There was no sign of the doctor. Emily's breathing became shorter and her face contorted with pain. Patrick sat close beside her, holding her hands. Charlotte brushed Emily's hair and Anne coughed.

Keeper made a crying sound, and then his ears pricked as he heard someone moving outside. 'This way, Doctor,' said Tabitha.

The doctor entered, looked at Patrick and, from the curate's face, realised his services were not needed. The doctor had no cure for grief.

As with their brother' death, Charlotte and Anne were, in one sense, pleased their sibling died. Their grief was raw, but the one saving grace was that Emily's pain and distress were no more.

Arthur Nicholls conducted the funeral service with the four main mourners being Patrick, Charlotte, Anne and Keeper.

Back in Thornton, Patrick often had canine worshippers, and as Keeper was Emily's pride and joy, it was essential the dog attended the service. Emily adopted him as a pup who became her devoted companion for years. He seemed to understand his beloved mistress was in the coffin and that she would appear sooner or later. But when the coffin disappeared beneath the floor of the church, Keeper became anxious, and only multiple pats and distractions enabled him to be led back to the parsonage.

In the kitchen, Keeper dined on his favourite food and enjoyed more patting. But his anxiety continued. He scratched at the kitchen door and, when it opened, scampered upstairs to sit by Emily's room. Then the howling began. He was taken outside for bodily functions, but for the next two weeks, he returned again and again to the door of his mistress, where he sat and howled. Emily's Irish grandfather would have understood.

What a Christmas. Patrick lost two of his children in less than three months and believed, when he died and went to Heaven, one of the first people he would enjoy swapping tales with would be Job.

In Victorian times, one of the evils of consumption was its slow but insidious progress. Anne was already consumptive when Emily died of the pernicious disease. After Christmas, Anne's health deteriorated.

'What shall we do, Papa?' asked a worried Charlotte.

'There is a doctor in Leeds who treats consumption. I will write to him.'

And so a Doctor Teale examined Anne. Alas, he told Patrick the same old story, one he'd heard many times. 'Your daughter has consumption, sir, but the condition is not yet at the final stage.'

'Then there is hope she may recover?' asked a desperate Patrick.

'I fear not and wish I had better news. I regret to say the best you can hope for is a period of several months.'

After the doctor left, Patrick and Charlotte and Charlotte's friend Ellen Nussey, sat with Anne who looked remarkably bright and brave.

'So Papa,' said Anne, 'what did Mr Teale say?'

Patrick loved all his children but his youngest remained the baby.

'Little Anne,' he began, but stopped as he choked.

Charlotte took control. 'Nell will stay at Haworth and help me to help you. So, "little Anne", we are at your service.'

Patrick nodded and smiled grimly. He was too emotional to speak.

Mr Teale gave a correct diagnosis. Despite becoming thinner and weaker, Anne carried on for several months. She wrote poems and Patrick became distressed when reading her work.

For Thou hast taken my delight
And hope of life away,
And bid me watch the painful night
And wait the weary day.

What father, living with a dying child, could read that poem, her creation, and not know his grief had yet to begin?

When they were alone, brave Anne spoke plainly to her sister. 'I do not want Papa to bury another of his children.'

Charlotte looked at Anne and nodded. 'He will not thank you in this life, but I know he and many will in the next.'

As the end drew nigh, Anne asked if she might travel to the seaside. In happier times, when working for the Robinsons, Anne spent time at Scarborough, so they made plans for a return trip.

Charlotte and Ellen would accompany the invalid. As they prepared to leave, Patrick and the two servants said their goodbyes.

Motherly Tabitha spoke first. 'Now then Miss Anne, you keep warm and eat all your vegetables. An' may God bless thee, lass.'

Young Martha cried. 'I hope you has a lovely holiday, Miss.'

Patrick was treading on eggshells. He didn't think this was the last time he would see his youngest child, he *knew* it was the last time. He was well rehearsed in the art of final speeches.

'Little Anne,' he said hugging her. 'I love you Miss Anne Brontë, and I look forward to reading all those letters you write to your old Papa.'

He kissed her and wept as Charlotte and Ellen helped her to the coach. Patrick retreated to his study. He'd become an expert at weeping alone.

Anne enjoyed her short stay in Scarborough, which included a donkey-cart ride on the wide expanse of sand. On the fourth day her condition became much worse. She came downstairs complaining of being unwell. A doctor was sent for and when he arrived, Anne had trouble breathing. Lying on a sofa she spoke.

'Please sir, will you tell me plainly? Am I dying?'

Taken aback at so frank a question, the doctor looked at the other two women, and then spoke to his patient.

'I fear, Miss, that death is close.'

Charlotte stifled a wail, but Anne raised a hand and spoke with a constricted voice. 'Be brave, dear Charlotte, be brave.'

Anne's hand flopped and she sighed. She closed her eyes and her breath came in short gasps, then stopped.

When the initial crying ceased, the doctor said that Anne had suffered from consumption for many months.

Patrick received Charlotte's letter and knew its contents before reading them. In the kitchen, the servants looked at one another and, from the sounds in the study, knew the curate had lost yet another of his children. What had he done to deserve this fate? Was it now time to curse his God?

At least Anne's gesture spared her father the pain of seeing the crypt opened a seventh time. They buried Anne in a daffodil-strewn churchyard in Scarborough by the sea. The inscription on her headstone contained several mistakes, including her age of 29 as 28.

Was that of any interest to the Haworth curate? Hardly, and of Patrick's six children, only one was alive.

To highlight the pathetic scene at the parsonage, when Charlotte returned, the excited dogs rushed about believing that with one mistress home, the others would soon follow. Their excitement was in vain.

Chapter 15

THE QUIET PARSONAGE housed two dogs, two servants and two Brontës. With Patrick in his study and Charlotte in the dining-room, conversations were few and far between.

When the residents did speak, Patrick chose his words carefully.

'My darling girl, now we are only two, I want you to know I could not have wished for a more loving daughter. You have been my rock these past years, and every day I thank God for your love and support.'

'Thank you, Papa.'

She promised her ongoing care and companionship, and spent her days writing letters and her latest novel. *Jane Eyre* had become a brilliant success, way beyond her wildest dreams. But once it became known Currer Bell was a parson's daughter from Yorkshire, the literary world clamoured to meet Miss Charlotte Brontë. From her publisher, she received an invitation to visit London.

'Papa, I am unsure. It's such a long way, I have never mixed in literary circles and besides, how can I care for you if I am far from home?'

'I disagree, my child. You are now a celebrated novelist, and your readers want to meet you. In fact, I would say it is your duty to go. And I have Tabby and Martha to cook and care for me. Go, I say, fetch your bag and bonnet and go.'

The shy, small and self-conscious Charlotte procrastinated. Reluctant to smile because of unattractive teeth, she had no interest in fame. But Patrick insisted and so to London she went.

Patrick urged Charlotte to go because he was old and set in his ways, and he enjoyed his own company. He offered little for his daughter. She was relatively young and, having lost three siblings, needed company. The empty parsonage reminded Charlotte of all she'd lost. By encouraging her to venture into the world, Patrick believed this gave her life meaning and purpose, and stopped her dwelling on the death of her siblings.

In London, she enjoyed the sights but dreaded meeting literary luminaries. On one occasion, the celebrated William Makepeace

Thackeray introduced his mother to Miss Jane Eyre. It could have been worse; it could have been Mr Currer Bell.

Back in Haworth, Patrick performed his usual tasks. With his devoted assistant Arthur Nicholls, Patrick got stuck into parish life despite being in his 73rd year.

The Haworth water supply had long been a major cause of sickness and death in the town.

Countless thousands lay buried in the graveyard, the corpses riddled with such diseases as typhus and cholera. Water seeped into the graves, washed over the deceased's infected remains, and formed part of the ground water, which was pumped, when the pumps worked, to become the town's drinking water. The fatal irony in Haworth meant the dead killed the living with many not knowing or caring.

Sanitation was basic and usually appalling. Major changes were essential, and a leading light in the quest to fix the Haworth water and sanitation problems, was the long-serving curate. Patrick's children wrote poetry and novels. He'd dabbled in those fields, but now his main scribbling activity became letter writing.

He was doggedly persistent with Haworth's water being a case in point. When Patrick wrote to an authority and received no reply, he wrote again. When he still got no reply or an unsatisfactory one, he wrote again. Officials and bureaucrats groaned as another letter from the ever-writing Patrick Brontë landed on their desk.

Charlotte returned from London. 'Papa, the sights I saw and the people I met, I don't know where to begin.'

'I am so pleased you went.'

'You look well Papa. How have you managed without your ... I was going to say "favourite daughter" until I realised.'

'Only or favourite, they are one and the same. So you met Mr Thackeray and Miss Martineau. Tell me about them.'

Charlotte told Patrick her news. He delighted in her animated demeanour, but worried that in the parsonage, Charlotte would be lonely. Patrick knew his daughters discussed their writing, and Charlotte's latest novel, *Shirley*, could never be enjoyed by her siblings. Now he wanted to help Charlotte find new interests.

Someone who did enjoy *Shirley* was Arthur Nicholls; his main response being uproarious laughter which intrigued Mrs Brown, his landlady and the mother of Patrick's servant, Martha. Contrary to public opinion, the assistant curate did have a sense of humour.

Charlotte's writing appealed to the literati of London and to a select few in Haworth. But once newspapers reported Miss Charlotte Brontë to be the authoress of *Jane Eyre* and *Shirley,* the curious came calling.

James Kay, a Lancashire lad born in Rochdale, led a remarkable life. His father was a wealthy Mancunian cotton merchant, but son James shunned the family business and headed north to study medicine at Edinburgh University.

As a brilliant student, he became a brilliant doctor. His passions in life were education and medicine, and he particularly wanted the poor to be healthy and educated. He worked tirelessly to help the lower classes avoid disease and go to school. These two passions and goals exactly matched those held by the perpetual curate at Haworth.

Kay married well and, by royal assent, took his wife's name. She was the wealthy heiress Janet Shuttleworth, and her new husband became Doctor James Kay-Shuttleworth. Created a Baronet later in life, he was addressed as Sir James.

As far as class, wealth and occupations go, James Kay-Shuttleworth and Patrick Brontë were poles apart. What brought them together was Miss Jane Eyre. Charlotte's novel enthralled vast numbers of readers including the Kay-Shuttleworths.

On a sunny St. David's day morning, Martha Brown answered the door, showed the visitors to the dining-room, and then went to inform Patrick.

'More visitors, Martha; who is it this time?'

Martha struggled with her memory and pronunciation. 'He might have said, Sir James and Lady Kay-Shuttleworth, Mr Brontë.'

'Baronet Kay-Shuttleworth?' asked the startled curate.

'But I'm not sure, Mr Brontë.'

'Good heavens. Where is my daughter?'

'I'm sure she took the dogs for a walk, sir.'

'Well please hurry and find her and tell her to come home directly.'

Martha departed in haste, and Patrick adjusted his attire before greeting his guests. Actually they were his daughter's guests, and the sole reason for the visitors coming to out-of-the-way Haworth was to meet the brilliant new novelist.

Charlotte arrived and welcomed her guests. They warmed to her and invited Charlotte to visit their home, the spectacular Gawthorpe Hall, forty miles away.

'That is most kind of you, Sir James,' said Charlotte, who didn't want to go. She looked to her father for help in resisting the invitation. From Charlotte's point of view, Patrick failed and badly as he replied.

'That is most kind indeed, Sir James. My daughter has received many invitations and met several well-known writers.'

Lady Janet believed Charlotte needed a mentor and subtly expressed that thought.

'Sir James and I are close friends with the novelist, Mrs Elizabeth Gaskell, and I'm sure she'd be delighted to meet you, Miss Brontë.'

Everyone, except Charlotte, supported the invitation.

The Kay-Shuttleworths departed and Charlotte studied her father. She loved him dearly but wished he wouldn't push her into the world of famous strangers. He, on the other hand, was delighted.

'They live in a magnificent Elizabethan stately home, my dear, and that alone will be worth the visit.'

Charlotte smiled meekly. 'If that is your wish, Papa.'

And so the much-talked-about daughter left her beloved father and parsonage and travelled. She went again to London and then to the Lake Windermere holiday house occupied by the Kay-Shuttleworths. Patrick remained at home to serve his parishioners.

Alone in the sitting-room in the Lake District house, a nervous Charlotte heard the sound of new guests arriving. The door opened and Lady Janet arrived oozing bonhomie.

'Do come in, Mrs Gaskell and meet Miss Brontë.'

The women entered the room and stopped. Their husbands followed and all four looked at the unoccupied furniture.

'Oh,' said Lady Janet, 'I expected Miss Brontë to be here.'

'Ah,' said Sir James. 'There she is, admiring the view of the lake.'

She was and she wasn't. A shy and nervous Charlotte was hiding behind a curtain, and the gallant host gave his timid guest the opportunity to make a dignified entrance.

'There you are,' said Lady Janet leading Charlotte to the Gaskells.

Introductions complete, the party sat but after the usual pleasantries, Sir James stood.

'My dear, and Mr Gaskell, I'm sure our two novelists have literary matters to discuss.' Lady Janet and Mr Gaskell took the hint, stood, and left with Sir James. Charlotte and Elizabeth were alone.

'Miss Brontë, I must congratulate you on the splendid success of *Jane Eyre*. I found it quite ... invigorating.'

'Thank you, Mrs Gaskell.'

'I'm fascinated to learn how three sisters in an isolated parsonage created such ... powerful novels.'

Charlotte smiled and Mrs Gaskell noted the young woman's missing teeth.

'Everything can be attributed to my father, Mrs Gaskell.'

'To your father, did you say?'

'He's a most remarkable man. His early life in Ireland was one of poverty and hardship, and yet he became a teacher, a graduate of St. John's College, Cambridge, and has been a Church of England clergyman for nearly fifty years. Everything I know, I learnt from my father.'

'But did you not attend any schools?'

'I did, but it was my father who allowed me to read widely, who taught me to reason and to think for myself. He encouraged his children to write, paint and draw and to play music and, despite his modest income, paid for all our lessons including those extra subjects. As I said, he is a truly remarkable man.'

Mrs Gaskell asked more questions about Charlotte's upbringing and then they discussed her plans. The women liked one another and got on well.

After dinner, Charlotte retired, the husbands strolled in the garden, and the wives discussed the young novelist.

'So what is your opinion of Miss Jane Eyre's creator?' asked Lady Janet. 'Was she who you expected?'

'She told me much about her childhood, and I believe Miss Charlotte Brontë is the real-life version of the youthful Miss Jane Eyre.'

'Really? But she's so unworldly for the writer of such coarse and passionate tales. I suspect her eccentric father is responsible.'

'Actually Miss Brontë spoke highly of her father. He appears to have given his children a remarkable and well-rounded education.'

'But is that the truth? You see, I have heard otherwise.'

'Oh?' Enthralled, Mrs Gaskell listened as Lady Janet continued.

'I know a nurse, living in Burnley, who was employed by Miss Brontë's father and several of the nurse's experiences are quite shocking.'

Mrs Gaskell's curiosity grew as her friend told all.

'The nurse said the father was so overbearing, the children cowered in silence.'

'I'm not surprised. They say the Irish can be fiery at times.'

'The nurse worked in the parsonage for some time, yet not one of the six children ever made a sound. I ask you, how can six youngsters play and not make a noise?'

'You say the father is a brute?'

'The nurse told me he refused the children meat.'

'Good heavens. Perhaps their harsh upbringing explains why all three sisters created fearsome characters and violent scenes with such unladylike behaviour.'

'He fathered five daughters and not one of them married.'

'I heard two died as children.'

'And that may explain his over-protective behaviour, keeping his children under lock and key.'

'Well if true, let us hope Miss Brontë can escape her domineering father.'

Patrick worried about Charlotte's health. Having lost five of his six children, it was easy to think about losing them all, and the thought terrified him. Charlotte fell ill while staying with her friend Ellen Nussey, and Patrick was so concerned he sent one of his parishioners to Ellen's home, several miles away, to check on his daughter.

Patrick worried about Charlotte's finances. Her new income thrilled him but he fretted, thinking she might squander it. He worried about his own health. If he died, who would encourage and advise his daughter?

Patrick worried about Charlotte's marital status. As a relatively wealthy woman, eligible gentlemen would consider her a good catch. Who would protect her from unscrupulous suitors?

When Mr James Taylor, an employee of her publisher, proposed marriage to Charlotte, Patrick knew about the situation but said little.

Charlotte didn't ask his advice and anyway, poor Mr Taylor had no hope. Charlotte considered him ugly with "a nose designed to frighten little children".

But Charlotte received another proposal of marriage, and this one triggered an amazing response from the Haworth curate. The reaction was akin to that shown by the Glascar Hill Presbyterian minister in County Down more than fifty years ago.

Arthur Bell Nicholls was a decent chap. He was kind to old people, to all people; he preached a jolly good, if somewhat pedestrian sermon, and was a marvellous assistant to the Revd Patrick Brontë. Arthur was industrious and pious, although possibly too pious.

Several of Haworth's washerwomen chose to hang their laundry in the churchyard. Apparently it better caught the drying sun, and none of the residents housed beneath the gravestones ever complained.

This domestic arrangement angered Mr Nicholls, who fought hard to end the practice, and his stance upset several locals. Arthur behaved like Patrick with his anger over the enthusiastic campanologists in Dewsbury.

One evening, Arthur and Patrick were discussing parish business, with Charlotte alone in the dining-room. The men finished their business and Arthur left for his digs. But instead of departing the parsonage, he stopped at the dining-room door and knocked ever so lightly. Charlotte felt a strange feeling in the pit of her stomach.

Arthur entered with his usual apology. His appearance surprised and worried Charlotte. The tall, almost statue-like curate was a nervous wreck. She suspected the cause of his angst and became tense in anticipation. Her heart rate increased while his was out of control.

'Miss Brontë,' said Arthur in a soft, almost trembling voice. His hands were shaking.

'Good evening, Mr Nicholls.'

'I would be most grateful for the opportunity to speak with you.'

'I believe you are doing so already, sir.'

Arthur didn't treat this remark as flippant. He tried desperately to remember his lines. He'd rehearsed this performance for ages but struggled as his nerves became anarchists.

'Over the many years I have had the privilege of assisting your father at Haworth, I have always regarded you as a fine Christian woman.'

Now this statement by Arthur Nicholls has never been listed as a popular romantic opening pitch, but for Mr Reliable it was the best he could muster.

Charlotte now definitely knew the purpose of this conversation.

'That is most kind of you, Mr Nicholls.'

She didn't make it easy for him, and remembered the time her sisters teased her about Mr Nicholls being keen on Miss Charlotte. Obviously her sisters got it right.

'Miss Brontë, I have admired you from afar for a very long time.'

Obviously Arthur was trying to propose, but Charlotte had not realised that, for men, well for some men, the business of making a marriage proposal was little short of an ordeal. Drowning in turmoil, Arthur blundered through his script.

'I would like, or rather I would beg to ask, if there is any hope for me?'

Arthur was now so stressed that Charlotte wanted to ask about his wellbeing. Deciding that might be cruel, she said nothing. In truth the poor man was suffering, not so much from a medical malady, but from fear of rejection. She tried to assist him.

'Are you making a proposal of marriage, Mr Nicholls?'

Arthur nodded and spoke with immense gratitude.

'I am, Miss Brontë, albeit in a confusing yet sincere manner. Please, do forgive me.'

'There is nothing to forgive, sir.'

'I wish you to know that my feelings towards you, my sincere and gentle admiration of you, have been present for a considerable time.'

'I see.' Charlotte had only one question. 'May I ask if you have raised this matter with my father?'

The mention of Patrick's name produced a look of terror on Arthur's face, as he went from being nervous to suffering intense pain.

'I ... I have not, Miss Brontë. I doubt if I would ever be courageous enough to raise such a subject with your father.'

By now Charlotte's main concern was the health of her suitor. The man seemed in danger of collapse. She tried to help the petrified parson by standing. That simple action stalled Arthur's tailspin towards disaster.

'Mr Nicholls, thank you for your kind words. Please allow me some time to consider your proposal.'

'Of course, of course,' blabbed a mightily relieved Arthur, who took the absence of a refusal as being almost the same as an acceptance.

'I shall give you my decision tomorrow.'

Arthur's gratitude overflowed. 'Thank you, Miss Brontë, thank you.'

Then he stalled, unable to remember his lines. Charlotte stopped speaking and that jolted Arthur into life. He moved to the door, turned and spoke.

'Good night, Miss Brontë.' He wanted to say more, much more, but realised departure was the better part of valour and so left.

Charlotte stood motionless. After the door closed, she spoke to the empty room. 'Good night, Mr Nicholls.'

The walk from the dining-room to the study took Charlotte at least six seconds. She dreaded the journey wondering how her father would react. She was right to be concerned because, once she described Arthur's marriage proposal, Patrick stood and roared.

'He did what?'

The volume of her father's voice and his facial expression frightened Charlotte. In recent years, she'd seen him weep openly, and heard him speak out on issues he considered unjust and cruel. But his reaction to Arthur's proposal was unlike anything she had ever seen or heard.

'Please do not distress yourself, Papa.'

'How dare he, how dare he,' hissed Patrick as his face turned crimson.

'I have told Mr Nicholls I will give him my answer tomorrow.'

That remark only increased Patrick's fury.

'Tomorrow? Why not tonight; now?'

Charlotte played down the proposal, trying to prevent her father from having a stroke or heart attack.

'I think you should sit, Papa. You look unwell.'

Patrick was snorting rather than breathing and finally sat.

'That man has deceived me. He has worked beside me for years and never once told me of his intentions.'

'I believe he was afraid to do so, Papa.'

'How could he even think himself worthy of taking such action?'

'He behaved in a most polite and proper manner, Papa.'

Patrick ignored her remarks and took another tack.

'Charlotte, my dear girl, you can do far better than a simple, country parson. You are now a famous novelist. Many of the nation's finest literary minds salute your storytelling and artistry with words. Why throw all that away on a dullard from the back blocks of rural Ireland?'

Charlotte thought her father had lost his mind. What about *his* roots?

'Please Papa, do not fret so. I will decline Mr Nicholls' proposal in the morning.'

Patrick calmed a little—slowly. There was an awkward pause. He reached out his hand and Charlotte moved to him.

'Dear child, you are the last of my family. I have no-one else. I do not want to lose you.'

She kissed his forehead and squeezed his hand.

'I will not leave you, Papa, ever.'

Charlotte lay in bed pondering the evening's events. Which was worse; the unexpected and stressful marriage proposal from her suitor, or the unexpected and vitriolic response from her father?

Why did Patrick respond as he did? Was he angry with Arthur for remaining silent about his intentions, or did Patrick fear that, in his dotage, his only child would abandon him? Was he simply shocked by the unexpected nature of the event, or had he become a snob, and now wanted his famous daughter to marry someone of her newly elevated station? Was he worried that marriage, and possibly childbirth, might be dangerous to Charlotte's health?

Whatever the reason or reasons, Patrick's response set off a chain of events which left a sour taste in many a mouth.

Charlotte politely declined Arthur's offer and his dismay cut deep. Patrick was decidedly impolite. He wrote to Arthur, who lived a stone's throw away. Arthur copped a double blow. Charlotte refused him and Patrick chastised him. This caused Arthur to fall into a deep depression. He refused to eat, locked himself in his room and resigned from his post.

Patrick created the situation and now had to live with it. So did everyone else. The two men stopped speaking. Patrick fractured, seemingly forever, what had been a friendly and supportive relationship. Obviously Charlotte and the servants knew about the matter, as did the sexton and his family. Soon parishioners discovered the acrimonious split.

In church, it was common for the two men to assist one another. Now Arthur refused to make eye contact with Patrick and, when a service was over, Arthur drifted into the congregation to exit with the masses. When it was Arthur's turn to preach, he cried ill, and arranged for other clerics to replace him. He dared not ask Patrick.

Arthur was like the Revd Samuel Redhead who, having endured a nasty experience at Haworth, contemplated missionary service abroad. Arthur fancied Australia as his preferred destination. Only New Zealand was further from Yorkshire.

Patrick remained steadfast in his anger. He ignored the basic Christian virtues of forgiveness and loving your enemies, neighbours and everyone in-between. And this vigorous anti-Arthur stance contrasted with the alleged crime. Nicholls hadn't absconded with church funds—as had one of Patrick's previous curates—seduced his daughter, or sought to replace the senior curate; no, Arthur had made a sincere proposal of marriage to a woman he loved and respected.

What was wrong with Patrick?

Charlotte tried to ease Arthur's suffering. She wrote to him and, while leaving no doubt as to her refusal, wished him well.

That note, with its droplets of humanity, helped Arthur, and he asked Patrick, in writing of course, if his resignation might be withdrawn. A sullen Patrick agreed but with conditions, the chief of which being that Arthur must never again broach the issue of marriage. The frost began to thaw—very, very slowly.

With Charlotte's latest novel, *Villette,* about to be published, she was again invited to London. It allowed her to flee the highly unpleasant scenes at home.

Patrick wrote to Charlotte making it clear the disagreement between the curates was still alive. The letters revealed Patrick's cruel behaviour.

"The gentleman is considering the colonies ... I pity any woman to whom he might propose ... He even refuses to walk the dogs."

Patrick's comments were callous and wrong. Arthur was a dog lover, a man who kept his word, or both, as he and the hounds continued their regular explorations of the moor.

Arthur applied for a job as a missionary Down Under. He needed referees and had to include one from his current colleague. Patrick faced a problem.

If he said his assistant curate was a bounder, Patrick's displeasure with the man would become public knowledge, and might lead to further enquiries. That would be tricky. But could he bring himself to praise Arthur? At the end of his standard reference, Patrick stated that Arthur would make an excellent missionary.

Whether he believed that, or just wanted to help get the man out of Yorkshire, is hard to gauge. Perhaps it was both.

At least one referee knew of the clerical falling-out and so wrote a glowing reference for Arthur.

The Patrick and Arthur no-speaking show continued to run. There was no "Final Weeks" sign posted on the church noticeboard. Arthur abandoned his overseas missionary plans and applied for a curacy, any curacy, other than Haworth.

Embarrassment clung to both curates when the local bishop arrived. Dr Charles Longley, who later became the Archbishop of Canterbury, preached to a massive Haworth crowd of almost 1,000 souls, without a single donkey or chimney-sweep in sight. Patrick and Arthur avoided one another in the vast congregation.

The bishop stayed overnight at the parsonage and you can imagine the dinner guests seated around the table. Meet the bishop, the novelist and the two feuding priests. Sitting opposite his assistant, allowed Patrick to turn scowling into a new form of communication.

'So tell me, Miss Brontë,' asked the bishop, 'where do you get the ideas for your novels?'

'I suppose in the same way all novelists do, Doctor Longley.'

Arthur contributed. 'I hope you have the opportunity to read Miss Brontë's novels, Your Grace. They are truly splendid.'

Patrick glowered at his assistant. 'More wine, Doctor Longley?'

The bishop picked up the hostile atmosphere between his clerical colleagues and sensed Arthur's misery.

With supper over, Charlotte retired. As she headed for the stairs, a desperate Arthur followed.

Standing by the kitchen door, Martha Brown, the servant turned gatekeeper, gave Arthur that certain stare—if looks could kill. Charlotte escaped. Arthur retreated.

Martha's father became furious with his lodger, and told others he would willingly shoot him. Arthur was a pathetic and shattered man, and it was all thanks to a certain Patrick Brontë B.A.

Elizabeth Gaskell was keen to continue her friendship with Charlotte.

'Papa, Mrs Gaskell has invited me to visit her home in Manchester,' said Charlotte.

'Then go you must,' replied her father. 'Now you are a woman of letters, it's important you mix with other distinguished writers.'

Charlotte chose not to argue. She considered herself anything but distinguished, and preferred to remain in Haworth to care for her ageing father. She was shy; like Emily, like Charlotte. Despite her reluctance she did accept the Gaskell invitation then cancelled due to a nasty bout of flu.

But if Charlotte couldn't go to Manchester, Mrs Gaskell could come to Haworth, and the servants prepared the parsonage for the famous novelist. She arrived, having formed an opinion about Patrick, thanks to her friend, Lady Janet Kay-Shuttleworth. Now Mrs Gaskell could meet the man in person and test her beliefs.

She arrived during the great clerical standoff. Charlotte struggled with her father's cruelty, and his assistant's despair. Would this warfare influence Mrs Gaskell's opinion?

'I see you have an interest in firearms, sir,' said Mrs Gaskell, looking at a rifle on the wall and a pistol beside him on the table.

'I am interested, madam, and have been since my university days.'

She studied the elderly priest and felt afraid. His eyes seemed angry. Patrick's feud with Arthur still continued, and Mrs Gaskell observed Patrick looking defiantly over his spectacles at his daughter.

This visit allowed Mrs Gaskell to witness the curate in action. Her initial opinion was confirmed. *He ought never to have married. He did not like children.*

The real purpose of Mrs Gaskell's visit was to discover more about Charlotte and her writing. Naturally the two novelists spent time alone.

'I feel I should apologise, Mrs Gaskell. My father and I have been at odds over the behaviour of Mr Nicholls, the assistant curate.'

Mrs Gaskell was all ears. 'I see,' she replied, not seeing at all but impatient for details.

'I have recently received a proposal of marriage from Mr Nicholls, and my father does not favour the match.'

'But you do?'

'I declined the proposal, but disagree with my father's attitude to Mr Nicholls.'

Charlotte changed the subject and they discussed her latest novel, her sisters' writing and Charlotte's plans. Mrs Gaskell saw the plaque in the church, listing the family's tragic deaths. Promising to maintain contact with Charlotte, Mrs Gaskell returned to Manchester with tales to tell.

It was time for Arthur to leave Haworth. He preached his final sermon to a full church sans Patrick. Charlotte was there. Many folk had a soft spot for the bearded Irishman even if he did give the laundry ladies merry hell.

In the pulpit, Arthur preached but stopped mid-sermon. His emotions took control. He broke down. The silence was loud and after a long pause, the clerk moved to the pulpit and spoke quietly to the curate.

'Are you ill, Mr Nicholls?' Arthur said nowt. 'Then you should pull y'self together man and finish service.'

Arthur looked at the clerk, nodded, and struggled to complete his duty. Speaking in little more than a hoarse whisper, the worshippers were stunned. Several women wept and Charlotte became distressed.

Did her father know the impact his behaviour had on his assistant and the parishioners? Arthur managed to complete the service—just.

The Haworth parishioners decided to give Arthur a farewell party.

'Papa, I don't believe you should go,' said Charlotte. 'People know about your disagreement with Mr Nicholls.'

'Disagreement is it? The man treated me with total disrespect. And now he's been arguing with the school inspector.'

'I shall tell the clerk you are unwell.'

Patrick grunted and Charlotte breathed a sigh of relief. She'd given up hoping that peace would ever be restored, and feared the stress from her father's unchristian behaviour might give him a stroke or heart attack. Yet, despite all that, she felt an overwhelming obligation to support him.

Many folk gathered to farewell Arthur, where he received an inscribed gold watch.

The next day, in the parsonage, Arthur entered Patrick's study. Both men dreaded the occasion. Eye contact was not on the agenda. Arthur gave Patrick the school documents, and the two men mumbled a cursory farewell.

There was no expression of gratitude from Patrick for all the support Arthur had given him over the past seven years. Not even a wish for future happiness or success. Arthur offered his thanks for the opportunity to work at Haworth then left. He walked out of the parsonage having never felt so sad and lonely.

He paused at the gate and cried. His tears became sobs. He was a blubbering wreck when he heard footsteps. Blinking through his tears, he turned and saw Charlotte approaching. He wasn't ashamed or acting.

'Mr Nicholls, I wish to say goodbye in person,' said Charlotte.

Arthur had difficulty speaking. As he wept he muttered. 'If only I had the smallest of hope, Miss Brontë, only the smallest.'

Charlotte thought his behaviour pathetic yet touching. Only children wept like this, and yet Charlotte knew she was a major player in Arthur's desolation. She was well acquainted with unrequited love.

They parted, and Arthur left Haworth early the next morning. His replacement, Mr George de Renzy, arrived and began work. With Arthur gone, Charlotte hoped her father's anger would soften. It didn't.

'He's an unmanly driveller,' snapped Patrick.

This made Charlotte doubly sad. *Arthur may weep like a child but my father is wrong to belittle him,* she thought.

Arthur Nicholls was a man who might easily die of a broken heart.

Not long after Arthur departed, Charlotte and Martha were in the kitchen and heard a thud. They looked at one another then rushed to the study. Patrick lay on the floor gasping and partly paralysed. It was not his first stroke but certainly his worst.

'Papa, do not move. I will send for the doctor.'

Martha looked at Charlotte then vanished.

Patrick was distressed. 'I cannot see. I am blind.'

Charlotte knelt beside him and cradled his head. *This is why I can never leave Haworth. I could not bear to have my father die alone.*

The doctor came and ordered Patrick to bed. Downstairs, a worried Charlotte asked questions.

'Please, Doctor, what has happened to my father's eyesight?'

'It may be a temporary blindness, and the best treatment is rest.'

'He has argued a great deal of late in a dispute with another cleric. Could this have caused his illness?'

'It wouldn't have helped. Has the matter been resolved?'

'It has.'

'Good. Now I recommend you concentrate on his recovery.'

Charlotte wished Arthur Nicholls was still in Haworth. The new assistant curate was not a patch on the banished Irishman.

In time, Patrick recovered although not completely. He regained some of his sight but it would never be perfect. He resumed light duties.

George Smith, Charlotte's publisher, announced his engagement. Charlotte admired the man who discovered her writing, and made her a published novelist. She felt sad he'd chosen a wife many years younger than herself. Alone, the curate's daughter pondered her situation. *Will I ever marry? Is the teary Mr Nicholls not such a bad choice after all?*

Patrick was elderly and suffered from indifferent health. If he died, she would be alone. With a husband, Charlotte would have companionship and possibly love.

Ellen Nussey, Charlotte's friend from her schooldays at Roe Head, came to stay at the parsonage. The two friends often exchanged visits where they excelled at rabbiting.

'So has your father stopped hating that dreadful curate?' asked Ellen.

'I'm thankful he has other things to worry about and besides, I wouldn't describe Mr Nicholls as dreadful.'

Ellen sat upright in shock. 'Charlotte, don't you dare tell me you have a soft spot for Mr Nicholls.'

'I wouldn't call it a soft spot, but he does have some noble qualities.'

'Charlotte Brontë, if you marry that curate, if you marry at all, our friendship will never be the same.'

Charlotte looked at her friend. Ellen was serious. She foresaw a future where Ellen and Charlotte would, as spinsters, grow old together.

'Nell, that's a terrible thing to say.'

The conversation faltered with Charlotte surprised and hurt by her friend's comments. They parted without their usual love and affection.

'I'm glad you have Miss Nussey as a friend,' said Patrick. 'Good friends are hard to find and harder to keep.'

'Yes, Papa, you are quite right.'

Martha entered the study. 'I've brought y'mail, Mr Brontë; oh, and one for you, Miss Charlotte.'

Charlotte took her envelope to read in private. She recognised the handwriting and her pulse became more rapid. Alone, she read the letter.

Dear Miss Brontë

I hope this letter finds you well. I have heard Mr Brontë has been poorly and hope and pray he soon returns to good health.

I have read the excellent reviews of your latest novel and wish to congratulate you again on your splendid and well-deserved success.

After some time in the south of England, I have obtained a posting as assistant curate at Kirk Smeaton near Pontefract.

With every good wish

Sincerely yours

Arthur Nicholls

Charlotte re-read the letter and considered her lot. She'd rejected several marriage proposals and been in love, or thought as much, with men, one of whom was married and the other engaged. Her elderly father was unwell. Her obligation to care for him had never been stronger. But what harm was there in replying to Arthur Nicholls? And if she did, must she tell her father? In secret, she wrote to the bearded Irishman.

What would her father do if he knew?

Chapter 16

CHARLOTTE'S CONSCIENCE troubled her. She had deceived her father. She replied to Arthur's letter and they started a polite correspondence. It was respectful and kind but secret.

This created a troubling conundrum. If Charlotte told her father about the postal relationship, would this trigger another stroke? Would her news cause the death of her beloved Papa, and destroy her cherished friendship with Nell?

Charlotte agonised over the issue in-between thinking about Arthur Bell Nicholls. She knew his feelings for her, but what were her feelings for him?

She decided. Honesty was the best policy. Tip-toeing through life was stressful and potentially soul-destroying. She knocked on the study door.

'My dear, come in,' said Patrick. 'Tell me your news. What wondrous writing are you creating today?'

Charlotte was nervous. She could not love her father any more than she did at that precise moment. So why do something to cause him pain—or worse? She began.

'Papa, there is something I need to say which may cause you sadness.'

Patrick was never more attentive. Despite his age, poor eyesight, stiff joints and other ailments, his mind was youthful.

'Please do not tell me you are poorly. I could not bear to lose the last of my children.'

'I am well, Papa. But I want you to know I have received a letter from Mr Nicholls.'

Patrick's eyes flashed and Charlotte despaired, realising his anger towards Arthur was as strong as ever.

'I see.' He paused, unsure of what to say. 'I trust you have destroyed the letter and ignored the wretched man.'

'No, Papa,' said a quiet but bold Charlotte. 'I have kept the letter and replied to Mr Nicholls.'

Patrick's breath became more rapid. Charlotte's stress level rose, thinking her words might trigger another stroke in her father. He relaxed a little then began what he considered to be a reasoned attack on Arthur.

'If proof were needed, Mr Nicholls has revealed his true character. He has broken his word. In this very room he agreed to never again broach the subject of marriage to my daughter. The man has no honour.'

'Papa, that is not correct.'

This was new. Charlotte had never spoken to her father like that—ever. She remained respectful but determined, using reason and logic, the very same skills of deduction she acquired from her father.

'Do you dispute that Mr Nicholls did not make such an undertaking?'

'No, Papa, but that undertaking was a condition of his remaining at Haworth. It does not apply now he has left.'

Patrick had taught his daughter too well. She made a valid, relevant and succinct point. He lost the argument.

'Am I to understand the so-called gentleman has again proposed marriage?'

'He has not, Papa.'

'Then why are we having this conversation?'

'Because, Papa, I do not wish to do things behind your back. I will be much happier telling you that Mr Nicholls and I have exchanged polite correspondence, in which marriage has never been discussed.'

Patrick, the straw man, struggled. Huffing and puffing now would be ludicrous. To give him credit, he stopped criticising his former assistant.

'Thank you for telling me about the situation.' He picked up a newspaper and held it close to his face.

'There is one other matter, Papa.'

He kept reading. 'Yes?'

'Do you have any objection to Mr Nicholls coming to tea one afternoon?'

Charlotte held her breath. Would her father explode?

'Do as you wish,' he said without looking at her.

Charlotte sat, waiting, but not another word came from the curate's lips. Charlotte stood and moved to the door.

'Thank you, Papa,' she said and left.

Arthur positively glowed with happiness. It wasn't so much that Charlotte had written to him, again, but that she had agreed, as apparently had her father, to him, Arthur, paying a visit to Haworth. Bliss.

'Diary, where is my diary?' he cried, rummaging in his desk. He needed a date when he could next travel across West Yorkshire, and gain admission to the Haworth parsonage. Oh, let joy be unconfined.

As it happened, he received an invitation to stay with a fellow cleric in Oxenhope, about two miles from Haworth. The time was ripe. It was January with cold but fine weather, and Arthur followed the routine of Patrick Brontë, who once walked everywhere, and boasted to have covered forty miles in a single day. From nearby Oxenhope, Arthur set out, and the snow and frost crunched beneath his boots.

Patrick and Martha had plenty of notice regarding the visit and both said nothing. Their silence spoke volumes.

With jangling nerves, Arthur climbed the steep Haworth hill, walked past his former digs and headed for the parsonage. Call him Mr Punctual. If one can knock on a door in a formal manner, then Arthur did just that. He waited. With smiling eyes, Charlotte opened the door.

'Good afternoon, Mr Nicholls.'

'Good afternoon, Miss Brontë,' said the nodding, nervous curate.

'You are most welcome, sir, and I'm sure you know where to place your coat.' She watched as he removed his winter garments. 'Please come through to the dining-room and we shall have tea.'

Approaching the dining-room, Arthur steeled himself for a confrontation with Patrick. What a relief. He wasn't there.

'Papa will be along directly. Please be seated.'

'Thank you,' he said and, once she sat, he sat.

There was a pause. Who would speak first and what would they say? Then both spoke at once. Oh dear.

'I apologise, Miss Brontë,' said Arthur. 'I interrupted you.'

'I was about to ask if you are well.'

'Thank you, I am. And you and your father?'

'We are both well but, as you know, the winter in Haworth generously donates a variety of pesky ailments.'

'It does, it surely does.'

Another pause. Both were thinking of the last time they were alone in this room, with suitor Arthur a nervous wreck, and possible-bride Charlotte in shock.

'I gather from your letters you are enjoying your time at Kirk Smeaton.'

'I am, although I must say I miss the people and work here at Haworth.' He paused. 'I especially miss your company, Miss Brontë.'

The fire crackled but its heat paled beside the romantic temperature in the room.

A door knock sounded and Arthur felt ill. Instinctively he stood and dared not look at the person about to enter. He suffered a massive let-down as Martha came into the room.

'Shall I fetch the tea now, Miss Charlotte?'

'Yes please, Martha. You remember Mr Nicholls.'

Charlotte wanted to kick herself. Of course Martha remembered him. He lived in her parents' house for seven years. She saw him every Sunday in the pulpit. She took against him and wanted then and even now to give him a slap. Of course she remembered him!

Martha nodded and started to leave.

'Oh and Martha, please ask Mr Brontë to join us.'

'Yes Miss,' she said and, as she departed, threw a look of smallish daggers at Arthur.

Cometh the hour, cometh the man, and Arthur asked the question that had haunted him for months.

'Please, Miss Brontë, may I ask if your father is less inclined to be so against me?'

'I'm sure you know my father well, Mr Nicholls. The fact that you are in this parsonage suggests at least the possibility of rapprochement.'

Arthur felt a wave of relief wash over him, which vanished in the blink of an eye when the door opened and the curate entered.

This time Charlotte avoided her classic faux pas of "You remember Mr Nicholls". How could either gent ever forget the other?

In an instant, Arthur stood. 'Good afternoon, Mr Brontë.'

Patrick walked to his chair by the fire. 'Good afternoon,' he said with a coldness which matched the weather. He sat.

It was so far, so good as Charlotte spoke.

'Tea will be here in a moment, Papa. Mr Nicholls tells me he is enjoying his time as assistant curate at Kirk Smeaton.'

Silence. Arthur grabbed his chance.

'As you would know, sir, Mr Grant is a fine curate.'

More silence. Then Patrick leant forward in his chair and looked straight at Arthur.

'I want you to know, sir, there is no chance whatsoever of you ever marrying my daughter.'

My goodness. Was there ever a better example of a conversation stopper? The cold snap outside slipped inside. No-one spoke. What could Charlotte or Arthur say? With his blunt speaking, Patrick became an honorary Yorkshireman.

Just as the atmosphere slipped into the excruciation zone, Martha arrived with the tea. Talk about perfect timing. Martha departed and Charlotte fussed with the bits and pieces, and the subject of future nuptials was forgotten. No, not forgotten, buried. It was most definitely not forgotten.

After a sip of his tea, and ignoring the repast, Patrick excused himself and left in a huff. The huff had been filed in the drawer marked, *Even Clergymen Can Be Obnoxious.*

But despite Patrick's exit, three people remained in the room. The third was called Silence. He or she hogged the conversation. Finally Arthur decided to push ahead—in for a penny, my good fellow. But Charlotte got in first.

'I apologise for my father's abrupt behaviour, Mr Nicholls. But at least you know exactly where he stands.'

'I have always known his opinion, Miss Brontë. But it is your opinion in which I have the greater interest.' She looked at him. 'May I ask again, if there is the slightest hope?' He and Silence held their breath.

'I would be happy to receive your letters, Mr Nicholls, and, if you are in the area, to have you call and see me.'

That did it; did it ever? That was the answer he craved. Now speechless, Arthur stood and smiled like a child on their birthday. He both wanted to stay, and yet quit while he was ahead. He'd been given his promise of hope. It was a speck of light at the end of a long tunnel but it did exist. Hope existed. A man can live on hope.

'Goodbye, Miss Brontë, and thank you for a wonderful afternoon.' He'd only been in the parsonage for eight and a half minutes.

She accompanied him to the front door and helped him with his coat.

'Goodbye, Mr Nicholls, and I look forward to reading your latest letter.'

What a remarkable change; what a transformation. The last time he departed the parsonage, he did so as a bawling, blubbering parson to be pitied. Today his tears were tears of joy.

Elizabeth Gaskell and Janet Kay-Shuttleworth were taking tea.

'So what did you make of the father, my dear?' asked Janet.

'He was as you described, only worse.'

'Worse you say? How so?'

'There were firearms on public display.'

'Firearms? In a living-room?'

'Exactly, and apparently he discharges a pistol from his bedroom every morning.'

'Good lord. The man's a lunatic; an Irish lunatic.'

'I saw him glare at his daughter.'

'He glared at her?'

'Several times. And I felt afraid when he fixed his eyes on me.'

'So all the things the nurse from Burnley related are true?'

'Those things and more. He rules his daughter with a rod of iron. But what caused me the greatest concern was how she allowed him to do so. It appeared to me as if he still considers his daughter to be a child.'

'How astonishing,' said Lady Janet.

'I discovered the assistant curate recently proposed marriage to Miss Brontë, and her father refused point blank to countenance the union. He dominates like some overbearing monster. I fear she will never write well, or at all, being ruled by that cassocked savage.'

'There must be something we can do. Could she escape the tyrant if she were to marry?'

'You mean marry and leave Haworth?'

'Precisely, so how can we outwit the father and allow his talented daughter to escape?'

'I'm afraid a major obstacle is the lowly pay of the courting curate. If he could find a better position with more money and a fine parsonage, perhaps the old curate might give Miss Brontë his blessing.'

'A better position, you say?' Lady Janet's mind buzzed with ideas. 'Let me think about it.'

Arthur was working on next Sunday's sermon when his housekeeper told him a visitor had arrived.

'Did you say a Member of Parliament?'

'Yes, Mr Nicholls.'

'And he wants to see me?'

'He asked for the Revd Arthur Nicholls.'

Arthur entered the parlour and met The Honourable Richard Monckton Milnes, the Conservative Member for Pontefract in the West Riding. After introductions, the curate invited his visitor to sit.

'How may I help you, sir?' asked Arthur.

'Thank you for receiving me, and no doubt you are wondering why your local Member of Parliament is seated in your parlour.'

'You must be a mind-reader, sir,' said Arthur with a smile.

'I am the bearer of good news, Mr Nicholls. A dear friend of mine, Lady Janet Kay-Shuttleworth, has asked me to call and offer you not one, but two offers for advancement.'

Surprise and confusion greeted Arthur.

Milnes was the ideal person to help Lady Janet help Charlotte Brontë overcome her father's obstinacy. The parliamentarian was wealthy, a poet, a supporter of writers, a friend of Tennyson and destined to become a Baron.

When Lady Janet informed him of Patrick's opposition to Charlotte's possible marriage, and her idea to rescue the novelist, the MP popped next door to the House of Lords to chat with a bishop or three. It's not what you know but who. Arthur then received the good news courtesy of his MP.

'I am authorised, sir, by leading members of the church, to inform you that two well-paid curacies, each with an excellent parsonage, are available in Scotland and Lancashire, and either is yours for the taking.'

Arthur's eyebrows lifted. 'My first response, sir, is to offer my sincere thanks for such a generous offer. My second response is to enquire why such an offer has been made at all, and to me.'

Milnes smiled. 'I am a poet, sir, and understand the value of poetry and literature. Lady Janet is acquainted with Miss Charlotte Brontë, a brilliant novelist with whom I am told you have a close friendship.'

Arthur heard several dropping pennies.

'You appear to have the advantage, sir,' said the bewildered curate.

'I appreciate the matter is delicate, Mr Nicholls, but I wish you to know my visit results from the friendship and admiration Lady Janet and Mrs Elizabeth Gaskell have for Miss Brontë.'

'Ah, I think I no longer see through a glass darkly,' said Arthur.

'Both the offered positions provide a far better living than your present situation, and will thus allow Miss Brontë's father to look more favourably upon your prospects.' He paused. 'I hope my meaning is plain, sir.'

'It is certainly plain, sir, but Lady Janet and Mrs Gaskell appear to have overlooked one important fact.'

Milnes frowned. He expected gushing thanks, with the only problem being whether Arthur preferred Lancashire Hotpot or Haggis.

'I'm afraid I don't understand, Mr Nicholls.'

'It is straightforward, sir. I could never accept a position which would remove Miss Brontë from her duty of care to her elderly father.'

Oops. The best laid plans of wealthy women, their friends and high-ranking clerics can sometimes gang aft agley.

Patrick was in trouble. He'd lost his temper over Arthur's proposal of marriage to Charlotte. He'd caused Arthur to despair, Charlotte to worry, and his parishioners to choose sides.

The bitterness of his ruling lingered. Charlotte and Arthur kept exchanging letters, and Charlotte grew in stature when facing the father she adored. She again raised the issue of marriage and its consequences.

'I beg to differ, Papa. When you die, I will have some money but no home. I will become a homeless spinster.'

'But you can do so much better than a curate,' pleaded Patrick.

'I am no longer young, Papa, and have never been beautiful. Where, pray, will I find a curate, or any man, who will wait for seven years, offer me a life of love and companionship, and insist on me remaining at Haworth to care for my ageing father?'

Furious at being outpointed, Patrick's rage made a bad situation worse, and he dug himself into a deeper hole. He introduced the same silence routine he thrust upon Arthur. Now Patrick refused to speak to his daughter. Alone, he shouted his pathetic response.

'I will never have another man in my house.'

The servants heard it all. Young Martha, like her father, had taken against Arthur. But the older Tabby, the worldly-wise Miss Ackroyd, had lived at the parsonage long enough to tell Patrick what she thought, and being a Yorkshire lass, her native tongue was plain speaking.

'So then old man, blind an' stubborn as ye be, art thou plannin' on killin' the one person who loves you like no other?'

This stunned Patrick; not that a servant should address him so, but rather that she spoke the truth. He told himself he only wanted to help Charlotte, but deep down he knew his selfish behaviour caused deep distress.

And when Arthur told Charlotte about the offer of upmarket curacies, and Charlotte told Patrick, the denouement drew nigh.

'Papa, may I speak with you, please?'

'You may but I hope we will not argue again.'

'Mr Nicholls has written and told me of an interesting situation.'

Patrick sighed. What a mess he'd created over his former assistant. Charlotte told her father about the offers made to Arthur.

'So which curacy has the man chosen?'

'Neither, Papa,' said Charlotte. 'He has refused both because, as he clearly stated, he could never do anything which might harm you.'

'Harm me?' replied an astonished Patrick.

For the first time in front of her father, Charlotte used his former assistant's first name. That in itself was a telling blow. 'Arthur refuses to do anything which might entice me to leave and thus stop caring for you.'

Ouch. Patrick's shame brought on his silence. How can you oppose or disrespect someone who treats you with the utmost respect?

The chastened curate struggled. The pressure on Patrick to admit he'd behaved badly, and continued to do so, grew stronger. His conscience became the voice of a Hell-fire preacher. Charlotte took control.

'Papa, I wish to invite Mr Nicholls to call when he is next in the area, but only if you have no objection.'

Patrick said nowt. His nod of assent and silence represented a major admission of guilt and his lack of any objection.

And so Arthur's star continued to rise. The latest letter from Charlotte set his heart afire. His joy produced tears; his happiness unrestrained.

There have been many moving and romantic marriage proposals throughout history. And if a competition existed to choose the best such proposal, Arthur's would have been eliminated in the preliminary rounds. His qualities did not include smooth talking. And although that clumsy effort many moons ago had been declined, he didn't need to "pop the question" again. The couple had, as they say, an understanding.

Charlotte knew his intentions. Arthur only needed to know her intentions, and if the Haworth curate had changed his mind. Patrick had changed his mind, and Charlotte, like Barkis, was willin'. She sounded somewhat Jane Eyre-ish when writing to Nell with, "I am engaged".

Several months passed before Arthur returned to Haworth. Letters between the lovers continued on a regular basis, but it was Spring before Arthur appeared with a spring in his step.

He would stay at the parsonage for a few days, with the wedding and life thereafter to be discussed sensibly and without rancour.

Patrick came to accept his guilt in behaving as he had. He knew he had to make amends, but dreaded the thought of a man-to-man chat with his former assistant and future son-in-law. Having a bad cold didn't help. The curates met in the Haworth study.

'I am sorry to see you are not well, sir,' said Arthur.

'Thank you,' replied Patrick, which was a giant step forward in the interests of a harmonious relationship.

This became one of those meetings where previous unpleasantness was never mentioned. Both accepted an unspoken agreement that neither would mention the past. They set about planning for the future.

'I fully support your request to have your privacy sacrosanct,' said the groom-to-be.

'Thank you,' said Patrick for the second time. 'And I am grateful to learn you refused those well-paid curacies.'

'My love for your daughter, Mr Brontë, includes my wish for you to be looked after for the rest of your life. I would be pleased to assist Charlotte in any way I can.'

'Thank you,' said Patrick for the third time. He was being shamed by love. A less-stubborn man might have shaken hands with his future son-in-law, and thanked him for his kindness, but not Patrick, who moved straight to the mundane.

'Of course you will return to Haworth and resume your duties as assistant curate.'

'I will be honoured, Mr Brontë.'

'Some renovations are required to create a study for your convenience.'

'That is most kind, sir.'

And so planning began for the marriage and beyond. Charlotte signed a new will which stated that, if she died childless, her estate would go to her father, not her husband. Arthur supported this wording and, with Martha Brown, was one of the witnesses.

Patrick's rudeness and opposition evaporated. He wasn't the happiest curate in Christendom, and struggled to wear his new outfit of sackcloth and ashes; but wear it he did.

Remarkably, he felt better playing his new role. Admitting his faults proved difficult but ultimately rewarding. He discovered that having a reliable man about the house offered many benefits for him in his dotage.

The wedding in late June would be as quiet and as low-key as possible. The parishioners knew about the long-running clerical dispute, and so telling the world of the marriage might prove embarrassing for the elderly cleric. The solution? Tell nobody.

Well not quite, as the two invited guests, Miss Margaret Wooler and Miss Ellen Nussey, rounded off the wedding party.

Arthur finished his time at Kirk Smeaton, and Charlotte's dress was finished. A clergyman friend of Arthur's would officiate, and all that remained was for Patrick to steel himself in his role as father of the bride.

It had been a long and rocky romantic journey, but at last the happy finale drew nigh. This now perfect scenario could best be described in the words of the Bard—*All's well that ends well.*

But will Patrick remember his lines?

Chapter 17

ON THE NIGHT BEFORE the wedding, Charlotte, Miss Wooler and Ellen Nussey were chatting about the big event when Patrick knocked on the dining-room door and entered.

'Good evening ladies,' he said, squinting towards the trio.

'Good evening, Mr Brontë,' chorused the women.

Charlotte studied her father, and moved to him as her heart rate accelerated.

'Papa, are you unwell?' She helped him to sit.

'I fear I may let you down,' he said, looking into her eyes.

'Shall I send for the doctor?'

'No, it's not serious but I have this ...' He coughed and clutched his chest.

All three women gathered around him, expressing concern.

'Let me send Martha, Papa. Your cough is still distressing.'

'Please, Charlotte, if I need the doctor, I shall tell you.' He paused and took a deep breath. 'I must tell you something sad. I fear I cannot attend your wedding.'

What a shocking statement. The women stood there, speechless. What can one say in that situation?

Charlotte recovered first. 'Perhaps if you take to your bed with one of Tabby's hot remedies, you will be better in the morning.'

Patrick replied by coughing again, more deeply and more often. The three women looked at one another. Charlotte took one of her father's arms and helped him stand. Nell took the other arm and they ushered him from the room.

They returned with glum faces. Nell was particularly upset and moaned.

'Oh Miss Wooler, whatever shall we do? We have the bride and groom, the bridesmaid and the clergyman but no father of the bride.'

'Is he that bad?' asked Miss Wooler.

Charlotte sat and dabbed her eyes. Her courtship and engagement had been through so many trials and tribulations, she couldn't believe her marriage would be cancelled within hours of the ceremony.

'I'm sure Arthur would know what to do,' she said. 'But it's too late to ask.'

The women sat in silence. Then Miss Wooler stood and walked to a bookshelf. The others watched as she perused the titles. She removed a book, opened it and read its Table of Contents. She flicked through some pages, found what she wanted, and began reading. She stopped, looked at Charlotte and Nell and smiled.

'Here it is,' she said.

Charlotte and Nell had no idea what she was talking about.

'Listen,' said Miss Wooler. 'From The Book of Common Prayer—Rites and Ceremonies of the Church of England—*The minister shall receive the bride from her father's or friend's hands.* Don't you see?'

Charlotte was stunned. 'You mean it doesn't have to be the bride's father who can give away the bride?'

'It can be a friend,' added a now excited Miss Wooler.

'But do we know a man who could perform the role?' asked Nell.

'Some perhaps,' said Charlotte, 'although it is such short notice.'

'But it doesn't have to be a man,' grinned Miss Wooler as she tapped the book. 'It says nothing about the sex of the friend.'

Charlotte and Nell understood and joined the grinning game.

'Oh Miss Wooler,' said Charlotte. 'Would you give me away?'

Miss Wooler added head-nodding to her repertoire of expressions. What a sight. Miss Wooler offered her arm to Charlotte, who took it, and the couple walked around the room as Nell sang to la, what sounded like a bad processional. The laughter drowned out the organist.

With his chest infection, Patrick slept badly, his throat seemed on fire, and to top it off, misery haunted him knowing he might miss his daughter's wedding. He could hear his late wife speaking.

"Patrick, it's our Charlotte's wedding. She will be so proud walking down the aisle beside her dear Papa."

Tears rolled down Patrick's cheeks, and he coughed again before drifting towards a fitful sleep. He awoke early on a glorious summer's day. The Haworth birds were in good voice when he heard a soft tapping on his door. Charlotte's head appeared, she entered and smiled.

'Good morning, Papa.' She moved to his side. 'It's a beautiful day for a wedding.'

Patrick coughed again then spoke with a croaky voice.

'Will you forgive your old and feeble father?'

'Forgive you for what? Caring for me as a child, as a young woman, and now as a mature woman on her wedding day? You have my undying gratitude and love, Papa. Now please try your best to get well. Arthur and I expect to see you at our wedding breakfast.'

He clasped her hand but couldn't speak. She kissed him, made for the door then made light of her next words.

'I assume you know that later, if you look out a certain window, you might catch a glimpse of your daughter in her wedding dress? Or even on the landing if you're quick.'

She blew him a kiss and left closing the door. Both felt pain in their breast. Both were sad on a day which should have been overflowing with joy. But the bride had no time to waste.

Nell and Miss Wooler helped Charlotte with her white muslin wedding dress, bonnet and veil. She was nervous but happy. When leaving for the church, she made a point of being quietly noisy on the landing. She heard the floor creak in her father's room and paused long enough for him to open his door a fraction.

Leaving the parsonage, she hoped he could see her heading towards the church.

The celebrant was Arthur's best friend, the Revd Sutcliffe Sowden, and both men arrived on time. The punctual bride arrived having walked the short distance from her home and, in front of the smallest collection of wedding guests ever seen in the Haworth church, Charlotte and Arthur exchanged vows.

When the married couple came out of the church, the bells rang, and that turned some curious locals into stickybeaks. Patrick too heard the bells and felt, well, proud. His only child would now be cared for after he died, and this brought him peace. He was 77 and often poorly.

The wedding breakfast was a small gathering in the parsonage, and as things drew to a close, the curate made a discreet entrance which, when seen, froze every conversation. Charlotte moved to her father.

'Papa, how lovely it is to see you.'

She kissed him. He squeezed her hands. Arthur moved to her side. She stood back and, after a brief pause, Patrick offered his hand, and the two men shook with firm grips and nods of appreciation. This produced a short but enthusiastic smattering of applause from the guests.

But the celebration ended because the honeymooners had a train to catch. Nell helped Charlotte change, and the coach arrived to take them to the train at Keighley.

The guests waved and called their good wishes with Patrick remaining indoors. Martha cleared away plates, and Tabby came over to the curate. For the first time in her many years at the parsonage, Tabby sat beside Patrick. He was a mite surprised and looked at his new neighbour. She looked at him, then, with her eyes sparkling, she nudged the curate.

'Eee by gum, parson, tha' were champion.'

Patrick drew back a little as if to reprimand the woman. He seemed to frown at the elderly servant, but then nodded and mimicked her broad Yorkshire accent.

'Aye lass. She'll be reet.'

Tabby threw back her head and guffawed.

The newlyweds spent a month in Wales and Ireland, during which time Patrick's health deteriorated. He picked up once Charlotte and Arthur came home with their presence the tonic he needed. His daughter looked happy and healthy. His son-in-law proved to be helpful and reliable. For Patrick, life was good.

The locals, having missed the wedding, threw a party, and 500 Yorkshire folk filled the schoolroom. What a grand celebration with the happy couple delighting in the parishioners' good wishes. For Patrick, life was good.

But across the Pennines, the game was afoot. Elizabeth Gaskell and Janet Kay-Shuttleworth discussed a plan, the aim of which was to help Charlotte escape.

They believed her overbearing father stifled her career. The Kay-Shuttleworths had financed the construction of a new church near their family seat, close to Burnley, and the church needed a curate.

'Go and see him in person, James,' said Lady Janet. 'Convince the man his future lies elsewhere. Get him to leave Haworth.'

And so Sir James Kay-Shuttleworth went to Haworth and met with the new bridegroom. It was a case of déjà vu for Arthur.

'Mr Nicholls,' said the Baronet, 'this is a brilliant opportunity to make your mark. It's a brand new church, a brand new congregation, and you can feature as curate, the leading man. The parsonage is delightful, your stipend excellent, and the whole situation will allow for your good lady wife to relax and write more of her wonderful novels. Say the word, dear fellow, and the position is yours.'

Because Arthur was a gentleman, he didn't slip into the vernacular and shock his visitor with a few choice words. But he still made plain his feelings.

'I thank you, Sir James, but as I told Lady Janet's parliamentary friend, my wife and I owe a duty of care to Mr Brontë, and we shall remain in Haworth to serve and look after him as long as he lives. Now, may I offer you some tea?'

The bumpy trip back to Gawthorpe Hall matched the Baronet's mood. When he related Arthur's response, Lady Janet shook her head in frustration. Her plan to become patron of the brilliant novelist seemed destined for failure. When Lady Janet informed Mrs Gaskell of Arthur's response, the novelist softened her disappointment by taking a greater interest in Miss Florence Nightingale.

When Patrick heard of the latest failed attempt to lure Arthur away, he felt an even greater debt to his daughter and son-in-law. He began to enjoy his final years, knowing his family had become his carers. For Patrick, life became extremely good.

Christmas for the happy Haworth couple came and went. The Yorkshire winter came and stayed. And in the parsonage, a familiar scene was staged with a bedridden woman unwell. Patrick's wife and her sister had played that role, and four of Patrick's daughters followed suit. Now it became Charlotte's turn, and her husband became ill with worry.

He sat beside his wife, held her hand and offered a short prayer, before sending Martha to summon the doctor.

Arthur knocked on Patrick's study door and just the look on Arthur's face told Patrick something was wrong.

'She complained of being poorly and Martha has gone to fetch the doctor,' said Arthur.

Patrick became anxious. 'How long has she been unwell?'

'Perhaps a day or two; it's difficult to know because she's reluctant to complain.'

Patrick had a sinking feeling in his stomach. The two men prayed then Arthur returned to sit with Charlotte. The doctor came and declared her fever was not serious and should pass. It didn't. Arthur requested a well-known Bradford doctor. He too believed Charlotte was not in danger, but her condition might continue for some time. It did.

For Patrick, this recurring nightmare involving visits from doctors, no patient improvement, and the slow spiral into death, became almost unbearable.

In Charlotte's case, her pregnancy caused her suffering. She was nauseous and struggled to consume even the plainest of broths. Arthur despaired.

Patrick wrote to Charlotte's closest friends. Grief stricken, Arthur sat beside Charlotte and prayed.

'Heavenly Father, in this our hour of need, we humbly ask for thy healing hand on ...'

He broke down and silently cried. Charlotte stirred and turned to her weeping husband.

'Arthur? What is it?' He looked at her through his tears. 'Am I dying?'

She was, and wanted to change her will. Arthur told Patrick.

'I think that is most sensible,' said Patrick.

Charlotte created a new will making one simple change. Originally she bequeathed her estate to her father, but now it was bequeathed to her husband. She trusted Arthur to care for Patrick. She trusted well. The two witnesses who signed the new will were Martha Brown and Patrick Brontë.

Tabby didn't witness the new will because of poor health. She was so ill, that in the midst of the grief within the parsonage over Charlotte, Tabby died. She had served the Brontës for more than thirty years.

She saw Patrick's children live and die, and after Bess died, Tabby became Patrick's rock and advisor, and a real friend to the children. When she slipped on some ice and broke her leg, Patrick's children made it their business to visit and help Tabby. They wanted her to return and remain at the parsonage. They caught their father's bug of caring for those in need.

Arthur steeled himself and conducted Miss Ackroyd's funeral. She was laid to rest in the churchyard like tens of thousands of Haworth residents before her. She was 84.

The winter in February lingered into March and so did Charlotte. Her 39th birthday approached, and Martha tried to feed her mistress while talking about the baby and how it would be so welcome in the parsonage.

'Mr Brontë will be a wonderful grandfather, Miss Charlotte. Now just one more spoonful,' said Martha.

Arthur copied his father-in-law, becoming a full-time carer for his dying wife. Other clergy took his services. Arthur's desolation was raw. Patrick fell again into that awful abyss. God's mysterious ways were certainly consistent.

A few weeks after Tabby's burial, the tragedy of death in the parsonage was seen yet again. Charlotte died. Patrick and Arthur's hearts were as cold as the Yorkshire snow. Charlotte literally wasted away and two deaths occurred. Patrick outlived his six children, and now his only unborn grandchild. He found it hard to say the words, "Thy will be done".

The curate, who married Charlotte and Arthur, Arthur's friend Sutcliffe Sowden, conducted the funeral service. Nine months earlier, in the same church, he joined Charlotte and Arthur in holy matrimony. Now Charlotte joined her mother, aunt and siblings in the crypt.

How did Patrick bear his grief? The sight and smell of the crypt being opened, yet again, must surely have been too much for anyone, even a man of the cloth. That forthcoming chat with Job was taking on an even greater significance.

Charlotte's wedding attracted a tiny crowd. Charlotte's funeral attracted a massive crowd. The mourners, mainly locals, filled the church with many standing outside in the churchyard. You see, the outside world didn't know Currer Bell was dead. To Haworth folk, Charlotte was less the now-famous novelist, and more the last of the long-serving curate's children.

Unbeknown to Patrick, Charlotte became a sponsor of a young blind girl. When the child heard her benefactor had died, she insisted on walking several miles to the funeral. The little girl's tears and floral tribute broke the stoniest of hearts. By example, Patrick taught his children to care for those in need.

Chapter 18

WHAT A CHANGE TOOK PLACE IN HAWORTH. The once bustling parsonage now housed two widowers and a servant. No children, no wives, no dogs and no joy.

Patrick put things aright on the animal front and, from locals, bought two Newfoundland dogs he named Cato and Plato. At the very least they got the younger curate out of the house on dog-walking duties.

The clerics took comfort in one another's company. Once estranged, they reconciled, and Charlotte's death brought them even closer.

Patrick understood mortality. He made a new will and bequeathed money to Martha Brown, and to his brothers and sisters in Ireland. The remainder he bequeathed to his son-in-law, he described as "beloved". Now, finally, Patrick could wind down and end his days in peace.

Alas, not so.

Had Charlotte been only a curate's daughter and an assistant curate's wife, few people would've been interested in her death. But Charlotte was a famous novelist, and even more so in death. People wrote about her and her family, and thus created the Patrick Brontë myth.

It became a game of *Chinese Whispers* in print. In commenting on the life and work of Currer Bell, a writer criticised the novelist's father.

Another writer repeated, even embellished that critical comment. Were the comments true? Who cares? They made good copy. And so the myth developed. The comments were cruel and wrong, but who would correct them? Who would defend Patrick Brontë?

On her trips to London, Charlotte met successful writers including Harriet Martineau. She wrote an obituary of Charlotte and included comments about Patrick. According to Miss Martineau, who had never met the Haworth curate, Patrick was unworldly and so absorbed in his own life, he had no idea Charlotte and her sisters were writers. The family lived in a parsonage in which newspapers didn't exist.

Really?

What a powerful opening move in the quest to portray the father of genius as a cross between an oddity and an ogre. Patrick Brontë unworldly? Hardly.

He was active in local affairs, spoke often at public meetings, read voraciously, and wrote countless letters to newspaper editors, bureaucrats and church officials trying to make things happen. Often he did make things happen. Miss Martineau's prefix was redundant. She should have described Patrick as worldly, not *un*worldly.

Miss Martineau's obituary found its way to Haworth. The widowers discussed its content with Arthur becoming angry.

'These comments, sir, are untrue and unfair.'

Patrick remained calm. 'They matter not. I am old and soon to die.'

'Matter not? The woman says you are unworldly. You, a man who has risen from an impoverished Irish home to become an outstanding classical scholar, who has seen sickness and death on a vast scale, championed health and education reform, and who taught his children to think and reason, with three of his daughters creating works of outstanding literary merit—that man is unworldly?'

'Be still, sir. It is of no importance.'

'She says this is a house where newspapers are never seen? Is that a bizarre joke? You showered your children with newspapers, books and magazines. How can this lie remain unchallenged?'

Patrick didn't reply, and Arthur's boiling fury was reduced to a simmer.

True, Patrick did not stick his nose into his daughters' novel-writing activities but, having taught and encouraged them so often for so long, of course he knew they loved reading and writing. Of course he knew they read their writing to one another. And besides, his daughters were well described as secretive creators.

But the "literary" *Chinese Whispers* continued. Sometimes the comments were published anonymously. One article described Patrick as, "a wild-tempered eccentric, unfit to raise young children".

These strong and wrong criticisms prompted some to take action. Furious with what she read, Ellen Nussey wrote to Arthur urging him to ask Mrs Gaskell to pen a defence. That was akin to putting the fox in charge of the hen house. Elizabeth Gaskell had long been a fierce critic of Patrick. In fact it was Mrs Gaskell's letters criticising Patrick, which became the trigger for some of the *Chinese Whispers* in the first place. Ignorant Nell was requesting the attacker to attack herself!

Arthur was distressed and ordered a magazine in which Patrick was criticised. Arthur read the article aloud to Patrick. Would his father-in-law fly into a rage as a "wild-tempered eccentric", and thus prove the claims of the anonymous scribbler? Not quite. Patrick laughed uproariously. So much for the power of the pen.

'I haven't laughed like that for ages,' said Patrick wiping tears from his eyes.

'I am pleased you take such an attitude, sir,' replied Arthur. 'I believe the best response to an unfounded comment is to make no comment.'

Patrick nodded. 'Well said, Mr Nicholls.'

But Patrick didn't mean what he said. He thought about the matter, and decided to reply to his critics. Rather than do so himself, he believed a figure of authority would make a better advocate. Patrick's plan was not so much to defend his reputation, but rather to promote the achievements of his talented daughter. To Patrick, the ideal person to perform such a task, would be both an excellent and experienced writer, and a friend of his daughter.

He wrote and asked Elizabeth Gaskell to pen a definitive biography of the late Currer Bell. From Patrick's perspective, this was arguably a terrible decision.

In her Manchester home, an excited Elizabeth Gaskell entered her husband's study, waving Patrick's letter.

'You will not believe what I have received.'

'I am a clergyman, my dear, not a soothsayer.'

'Old Mr Brontë has asked me to write a biography of his daughter.'

'But I thought you planned to do that anyway?'

'I did, but now I have the father's backing and access to all her papers.'

'Does he say that?'

Mrs Gaskell wasn't listening. 'I can't wait to tell Lady Janet. She will be overjoyed at my news.' She was.

And so a long writing journey began. Like any keen biographer, Elizabeth Gaskell wanted as much source material as possible. Patrick and Arthur had letters from Charlotte. So too did Miss Wooler and Charlotte's publisher, George Smith. Ellen Nussey had more than 500.

When Arthur heard about the biography, he was wary.

'Are you sure about this, sir? I mean, is the book only about Charlotte and her writing?'

'It's a biography to be written by a fellow novelist,' said Patrick.

'Yes but the public are curious. They enjoy the intimate aspects of people's lives. Do you want your daughter's private affairs published for the entire world to read?' Patrick's mouth fell open. 'I would be most reluctant to provide letters which contain sensitive information.'

'I agree, Arthur, but Mrs Gaskell is the wife of a Unitarian minister. Her father likewise, a man of the cloth. She is a woman of impeccable character.'

Arthur didn't say what he thought.

The widowers spoke with the biographer when Mrs Gaskell came to Haworth. The discussion didn't go well. It wasn't because they argued about the proposed book, or its possible contents, but because of grief. When the men spoke about Charlotte, their awful sadness came flooding back, and both openly wept.

Before she left, Mrs Gaskell took a few of Charlotte's letters. But she wanted more, so wrote to Ellen Nussey. Ellen shared Arthur's concern about intimate details being revealed in the book. When Mrs Gaskell called to see Ellen, Charlotte's friend had erased certain details from the 300 letters she reluctantly handed to the biographer.

Mrs Gaskell chose not to tell the Haworth clerics she had amassed a huge number of Charlotte's letters. What they didn't know couldn't hurt them.

Then the biographer's charm went to work on Miss Wooler and George Smith, who both handed over Charlotte's letters.

Soon, Mrs Gaskell struck gold. She discovered Charlotte's feelings for her teacher in Belgium, and left for the Continent. Madame Héger ignored her, but Monsieur Héger discussed his memories of Charlotte.

Elizabeth Gaskell wanted the biography to sell. She knew dull didn't work. One reason Charlotte Brontë's books enjoyed such success was her portrayal of powerful human emotions. The characters were passionate and created by a woman. How could this be?

After all, the poet laureate had summed up society's feelings. Women in Victorian society must know their place. Literature and female writers were mutually exclusive.

When Charlotte smashed those opinions, people took notice. Now they wanted to know the novelist. What was she like? Why did she write such emotionally charged tales? What's the story behind the story?

For Elizabeth Gaskell, that meant a warts 'n all exposé; too many letters with intimate details would never be enough.

Soon the research produced the prose as the book took shape. But of communication came there none. Patrick worried. He heard rumours about his life as a curate, and was afraid they might appear in the book. He wrote to Mrs Gaskell.

Dear Madam
It has come to my attention that stories concerning my career have been mentioned in certain quarters. Such stories relate to my early days at Haworth, and the work of my predecessor, Mr Samuel Redhead.
I wish to inform you, I was never dismissed from my position, never in dispute with the Trustees regarding my salary, and the Trustees and people of Haworth were most happy to welcome me to this parish.
If you should need further details about my family, and my daughter Charlotte in particular, I am most willing to help.
Yours sincerely
Patrick Brontë

Patrick was right to be concerned. The plot thickened.

Six months had passed since Mrs Gaskell called to visit the curates in Haworth. The priests discussed the matter.

'I am concerned, Mr Brontë, that we have not heard from the lady for so long,' said his son-in-law.

'I have every confidence in Mrs Gaskell,' replied Patrick.

'But she has only a handful of letters. How can she make a biography from that?'

The clerics remained ignorant of the biographer's stash of source material.

'I shall write to the lady,' said Patrick, and he did.

Dear Madam
Mr Nicholls and I worry you have so few resources. It must be difficult having to rely on your few meetings with my daughter. Perhaps your task might be easier if you wrote more about her books than her life.
Patrick Brontë

Mrs Gaskell kept the widowers ignorant, sensing their possible opposition to her book. Arthur would oppose it, and he and Patrick had no idea the biography was almost complete.

George Smith and Ellen Nussey received a first draft of the manuscript. Independently, both stated that Patrick's description was wrong. "Readers will have to be taught to think kindly of Mr B," wrote Ellen.

Mrs Gaskell used her husband as a sounding-board.

'I'm not sure why I bothered asking George Smith and Miss Nussey for their reaction to the book,' said the biographer.

'Because they knew Miss Brontë very well,' replied her husband.

'They say I've been unfair on the father.'

'And have you?'

'I must tell the world about Charlotte's upbringing. Her father's domestic peculiarities made her what she was. They explain the wild passion and coarseness in her writing.'

'Would you describe the writing as passionate and coarse if Miss Brontë were a Mr Brontë?'

Mrs Gaskell was adept at not answering certain questions and did so by changing the subject.

'Mr Brontë is the key. His tyrannical behaviour is to blame.'

'The man is a tyrant?'

'I have facts from a nurse he employed. Lady Janet interviewed her.'

'And have you spoken with others who worked for the Brontës?'

'One's dead and the other's in America.'

That wasn't the whole truth, and Elizabeth's foul mood worsened. She needed more material. She knew it existed and where. Getting it was the problem. Someone had to go to Haworth.

'I shall go and see Sir James and Lady Janet,' she said and left.

Her husband replied to an empty room. 'That'll make a change.'

'You need a plan, Mrs Gaskell,' said Sir James. 'It involves arriving unannounced and in force.'

'I don't quite follow, sir,' said Mrs Gaskell.

'Don't tell Mr Brontë you are coming, or with me.'

'You, Sir James?'

'I shall accompany you. Those Haworth curates can refuse a woman, but will not so easily repel a member of their own sex, and one with an outstanding history of achievement in the public good.'

'And with a title,' added his wife.

Elizabeth Gaskell smiled. She liked the plan. The novelist and the Baronet set off for Haworth.

When Sir James knocked on the parsonage door, he took everyone by surprise. Martha interrupted Arthur in his study, and disturbed Patrick, who rested in bed, thanks to his painful rheumatism. The two visitors waited in the dining-room where Arthur joined them.

'Forgive me, Sir James; we were not expecting your visit.'

'Good morning, sir,' said the Baronet. 'Please accept our apologies for this unannounced intrusion.'

'Good day to you Mrs Gaskell,' said Arthur. 'I regret Mr Brontë is unwell and confined to his bed. How may I be of service?'

'Mrs Gaskell has asked me to help her obtain essential material for the biography of your dear late wife.'

'But we have already given Mrs Gaskell several letters.'

'Alas, Mrs Gaskell feels she cannot do justice to her subject without further written material.'

Arthur was unhappy. He didn't approve of this unannounced meeting. He disliked a titled gentleman being the spokesman for the biographer. And he abhorred the idea of his late wife's intimate thoughts and deeds being published under any circumstances. He said what he thought.

'Mr Brontë and I are hoping the book will concentrate on the novels written by my late wife.'

Arthur politely told the visitors they would get nothing more. Their trip was in vain. Sir James grew angry and Mrs Gaskell worried. Just as tensions reached boiling point, the door opened and Patrick entered.

'Please forgive me,' he said. 'I did not know we had visitors.'

With more strained pleasantries completed, Sir James turned his guns on Patrick.

'I am sure, sir, you would want the book to extol the virtues of your daughter, and be a source of great pride for you and Mr Nicholls.'

Patrick nodded. 'Indeed we do.' Arthur said nothing.

'To enable that to happen, Mrs Gaskell would be most grateful to receive additional items produced by your daughter.'

'Additional items?' queried Patrick.

Mrs Gaskell explained. 'Manuscripts, notes, letters, sketches; anything Miss Brontë may have written related to her novels.'

Arthur's reluctance rubbed off on Patrick who hesitated. Nobody spoke, so Sir James played his ace.

'Forgive me, Mr Bronte, but did you or did you not, sir, earnestly require Mrs Gaskell to write the life story of your daughter?'

Arthur's anger edged higher with Patrick numb with shock.

'I did require that, sir,' he said.

'Then why obstruct this outstanding novelist from doing as you asked?'

Arthur was tempted to borrow a phrase or two from his father-in-law's booklet, *Even Clergymen Can Be Obnoxious.*

Patrick appeared dazed with this latest attack being too much. He was unwell and had no warning of the visit. He did want the book to be written, and it was not in his nature to offend. He gathered his thoughts.

'I can assure you sir, and madam, Mr Nicholls and I wish to assist you in whatever way we can.'

Sir James smiled and Mrs Gaskell felt a warm inner glow. Arthur fumed. The visitors got what they came for—manuscripts, complete and incomplete, with annotations and, best of all, a treasure trove of the miniature books that Charlotte and her siblings wrote as children.

Brontë 0, Gaskell 2.

Several writers took an interest in the Brontës. Elizabeth Gaskell researched and wrote about them, but so too did others. Patrick received a pamphlet containing several errors. Worried such misinformation might find its way into Mrs Gaskell's book, he wrote to the biographer.

My Dear Mrs Gaskell
Knowing how careful you are to record the truth, I enclose a pamphlet
which contains certain errors. The truth is as follows. I met my wife in
Yorkshire and have never set foot in Cornwall. Her parents could not
have objected to our marriage because they died before I met my wife.
If you wish to know my character, I believe I can be likened to
Margaret's father in your novel, North and South. He is a thoughtful,
well-meaning gentleman, a lover of peace.
We are not alike in every way because I enjoy analysing people and this
has given rise to some calling me eccentric, a description I quite enjoy.
I hope you will receive my humble declarations and use them to correct
any falsehoods which are in circulation.
Yours sincerely
Patrick Brontë

Mrs Gaskell didn't correct the errors. Instead her book listed many lies about the "dreadful" Haworth curate. She had the testimony of the nurse who cared for Mrs Brontë, and hundreds of letters describing intimate Brontë activities. Mrs Gaskell chose to publish and be damned.

But then disaster struck and damned she was.

A publisher told Elizabeth Gaskell that quoting remarks made by a deceased person was risky. The biographer needed approval from the executor of the deceased person's estate.

If true, this wasn't disastrous; it was catastrophic.

The biography contained many direct quotations. Charlotte's words dominated because they gave the book life—they were its raison d'être. Remove the quotes and the book would die. But publish as is, without the executor's permission, and anything might happen—court action, damages, even destruction of the book. Help!

Mrs Gaskell begged for advice from her publisher, George Smith. He suggested a simple blanket approval form to be signed by Arthur. That would remove any threat of legal action. Smith posted the form.

The executor, Arthur Bell Nicholls, exploded. He regarded the request as insulting. He never gave permission for his wife's personal remarks to be used. He never wanted to hand over his wife's letters and papers in the first place. And he most certainly wanted them returned.

To survive this incident, George Smith needed all his people-handling skills, and got lucky as Patrick indirectly saved the publisher's and biographer's bacon.

Arthur and Patrick discussed the form.

'I ask you, Mr Brontë, what is this latest missive from George Smith? It is a trick to allow him and Mrs Gaskell to publish whatever they choose.'

'Let us have no more fuss,' said the older curate. 'I'm sure Charlotte would want us to be proud of her biography.'

Rather than upset his father-in-law, Arthur agreed to sign the form, but in returning same gave George Smith a blistering response.

Dear Sir,
I want nothing more to do with your wretched project which I regard as a desecration. It is only because my late wife's dear father wishes the book to be published that I have signed your form. Kindly desist from ever contacting me again.
Arthur Nicholls

Arthur was another Irishman using the Yorkshire characteristic of plain speaking. George Smith shuddered when he thought about having to receive Arthur's opinions in person; thank God for the mail.

And so the biographer and publisher cleared the final hurdle and almost two years to the day after Charlotte died, Elizabeth Gaskell's, *The Life of Charlotte Brontë* appeared. It did well; it did very well.

"Patrick Brontë is a monster" was the gist of one review. Arthur's dire prediction and grave fears came true. The book sold as well, if not better than *Jane Eyre,* and generated some ruthless comments.

Mrs Gaskell achieved her goal. Critics inferred that the female novelist wrote such wild and unrefined novels because of her wild and unrefined upbringing. In short, "it was the father wot done it".

Perhaps the most remarkable response to the book came from Patrick. The one person who had most to complain about, even rage about, was positively mild in his response. Elizabeth Gaskell sent copies of the book to Patrick who wrote to thank her.

My Dear Mrs Gaskell
When I considered having my daughter's life set out in a book, the first person I thought of was you. I wanted the best biographer. I am sure there are many people better qualified to comment on your work but, with your indulgence, I will share my thoughts. Your book has given me many happy memories of my dear wife and children. You have handled difficult events in the life of my family in a truthful and sensitive way. There are a few trifling mistakes which can be corrected in a second edition. Thank you for your kindness and your magnificent book.
Yours sincerely
Patrick Brontë

Talk about the patience of Job. What sort of man reads harsh and untrue comments about himself and barely mentions them? Others did. Was Patrick too polite? Was he just grateful that a book about his daughter had finally appeared?

Mrs Gaskell worried. She wrote and asked what Patrick meant by "a few trifling mistakes". His reply surprised her. The claim about his children being denied meat was false. Unless corrected, it might give weight to a wrongful claim about the death of his daughters, Maria and Elizabeth. A story circulated that the appalling situation at Cowan Bridge didn't cause or contribute to their deaths. Rather, it was the frail condition of the Brontë sisters because of their poor diet at home. Wrong. At Haworth the children ate well, whereas at Cowan Bridge the food was sometimes rancid, insufficient and badly cooked.

Patrick wanted the vegetarian myth destroyed and added a sting in the tail of his response. His blunt postscript gave Mrs Gaskell a serious fright.

The facts about me on pages 51 and 52 are lies.

Anyone cheering for Patrick rejoiced that at last he spoke up for himself and the truth. But his was the voice of one crying in the wild moors. The press ran with Mrs Gaskell's "facts". A local Yorkshire reporter wrote that, "if the poor old man is sad and lonely, he brought it upon himself". The clear inference being that Patrick's children died because of the harsh, even brutal regime, perpetrated by their cruel father.

Thank you, Mrs Gaskell.

But she too was unhappy. Many challenged her description of Patrick. One letter, in a newspaper, stated it was outrageous to attack such a well-respected, elderly clergyman. Mrs Gaskell's anger increased.

'I wrote what I believe is the truth,' she told her husband.

'And whose version of the truth would that be, my dear?'

'The nurse from Burnley remembers total silence in the parsonage. The children cowered in fear of their father.'

'Or, alternatively, such quiet behaviour reflected their love and respect for a dying mother.' Elizabeth bristled.

'I quoted the words of a nurse employed by the curate.'

'A sacked nurse who may have borne a grudge.'

A frustrated Mrs Gaskell delivered her knockout punch.

'Do you remember Mr Brontë's instructions? "No quailing Mrs Gaskell! No holding back!" Well I did exactly that.'

'So in a book about Miss Brontë, why bother with Mr Brontë?'

Elizabeth raised her voice. 'Because he's the key. He's responsible for the content of the novels. His brutal behaviour led Charlotte and her sisters to write what they did.'

Mr Gaskell went back to his newspaper as his wife clenched her teeth. Her displeasure would soon become fury.

Patrick's mild response contrasted with the reaction of others. The book claimed Branwell had been seduced by Mrs Robinson. The alleged seductress, now Lady Scott, cultivated apoplexy.

The remarried society lady threatened legal action, forcing George Smith to publish a retraction in *The Times*, and recall all unsold copies of the book. And in attacking the book, Lady Scott found an unusual ally.

The book infuriated the family of William Carus Wilson. The implication that Lowood School and its headmaster in *Jane Eyre* were based on a real school and a real headmaster, caused outrage, with the family demanding a retraction. Patrick strongly disagreed. He believed Jane Eyre was Charlotte Brontë and Jane's friend, Helen Burns, was Charlotte's sister, Maria.

So controversy raged, sales soared, and the name and work of Charlotte Brontë became even more famous. And with the book's success, came a new development in the town of Haworth—tourism.

Chapter 19

TOURISTS SPEND MONEY and naturally Haworth's shopkeepers and publicans welcomed an increase in trade. But in Victorian England, in the late 1850s, why on earth would tourists flock to a non-descript, industrial town on some windswept moor in West Yorkshire?

Ah, because this was now Brontë country. Three sisters writing novels was interesting, but when a memoir, written by Elizabeth Gaskell, revealed intimate details of the most famous sister and her father, the reading population took notice.

Were they interested in the books or the people who wrote the books? They couldn't meet the novelists, but their father was still alive—just. And what a father. According to *The Life of Charlotte Brontë*, the old man was a cross between an eccentric lunatic and a malevolent madman. He chopped up his children's boots, slashed his wife's clothes, wrecked furniture and half-starved his offspring. Put it down to him being Irish.

But not only did curious tourists venture to Haworth, so too did the fourth estate. One journalist, keen for the good oil on the parson, toured the graveyard. Surely the rumours about the wild priest were invented. The reporter chatted with a local.

'I can't believe the stories I've heard about old Brontë, the father of the novelists.'

'Oh,' said the local. 'What stories be they?'

'Well, one ridiculous tale has him taking pot-shots at the graves here in the churchyard. I mean, did you ever hear him fire a pistol from his bedroom window?'

The local stared at the reporter as if the man was stupid. 'Only about a thousand times,' he said and walked away. The reporter had a sudden re-think about his story angle.

Other journalists arrived and, armed with Mrs Gaskell's tome, asked questions about Patrick. He'd been a major part of the life of Haworth for decades. The locals knew him as their curate, the advocate for proper sanitation and fresh water for the town, and the crusader for removing their children from factories and having them educated. To them he was a tireless worker for the sick and the poor. People who loved, admired or respected Patrick, gave short shrift to any criticism from Elizabeth Gaskell. Who the hell was she? What would she know? The curate might be an incomer and even Irish, but he's *our* curate, and we picked him so "tha can bugger off!"

Patrick and Arthur avoided the tourists, although some received a welcome. The Duke of Devonshire and the Revd Arthur Benson, a future Archbishop of Canterbury, popped in. Both men could not reconcile the curate, his ministry and Haworth itself, with Mrs Gaskell's writing. Her version of the truth seemed vastly removed from what they saw.

The same response came from influential American visitors, including a former editor of the *New York Times*. The elderly, white-haired gent residing in the Haworth parsonage appeared nothing like the wild, even dangerous man described by Mrs Gaskell.

Going to a church service became the best way for tourists to see and hear Patrick. Despite his age and deteriorating eyesight, health permitting he preached every Sunday. But tourists had to be early with services invariably packed.

All his life, Patrick preached without notes. In his eighties, wearing his large white cravat and black clothes, the tall but frail curate spoke clearly using simple hand gestures and short sentences. He was a people's parson with a faith both basic and sound.

The partnership between Patrick and Arthur grew ever more solid. The younger curate would conduct the service then step aside for his father-in-law to deliver the sermon.

Patrick continued to outlive people he knew. William Morgan died, the Welshman who married Patrick and Maria and who was married by Patrick in the same service. So when would Patrick die?

He ordered the tablet in the church, bearing the names of his family, be removed and destroyed. It listed so many names, Charlotte's details wouldn't fit. Patrick ordered a new tablet with new details inscribed, leaving room at the bottom for one more name—his.

The old tablet was smashed and the pieces buried to foil souvenir hunters. Patrick received requests from Americans wanting a sample of Charlotte's handwriting.

For years he campaigned to get Haworth a new and improved water supply. It gave him particular delight, in his dotage, to see a reservoir constructed above the town and, finally, to operate. He even lived long enough to see gas-lit streets in Haworth.

But death drew closer and nobody knew more about death than Patrick. Mind you, he teased the obit writers on many occasions.

'How is old Mr Brontë?' asked a concerned parishioner.

'He has bronchitis and is poorly,' said Arthur.

A week or three later the same people met in the street.

'How is old Mr Brontë?' asked the concerned parishioner.

'His bronchitis is gone and he is much better, thank you,' said Arthur.

Another example of Patrick's character came with his final act as a clergyman. The Haworth stationer, John Greenwood, had a son he wanted to name Brontë. Because of Patrick's health, Arthur performed all parish tasks, but refused to baptise the child with that name.

With the infant seriously ill, Greenwood sent word to Patrick who summoned the family to the parsonage, meaning Patrick's final religious service was to baptise a baby named Brontë, in his study.

That in itself was remarkable, but when you consider John Greenwood operated as a snitch for Mrs Gaskell, providing her with Brontë family gossip, it revealed Patrick to be someone who found it easy to forgive. Arthur was furious.

Both curates enjoyed more happiness when Charlotte's unfinished novel, *Emma*, was published, with a foreword by Thackeray. Even Patrick's poetry collection, *The Cottage in the Wood* was reprinted.

But the Grim Reaper was heard sharpening his scythe on one of the headstones in the Haworth graveyard, and being Irish, Patrick knew all about leipreacháns and ghosts.

Haworth turned on one of its bitter winters where the frost had teeth. Patrick succumbed to colds and bronchitis and, if not bedridden, remained indoors. Yet still he lived.

The Bishop of Ripon conducted a service in Haworth with the curate absent. Word spread that the grand old man lay at death's door. Not so. He recovered sufficiently to "take the air" in the grounds of the parsonage on the arm of his faithful son-in-law.

Patrick's fame became such that the *Bradford Observer* published details on the health of the Haworth curate. They published the weather report, and the Patrick Brontë report.

Out of the blue he received a letter from a certain Mrs Elizabeth Gaskell, asking if she might pay him a visit. Patrick was now constantly ill, and a visit from the one person who did so much to blacken his name seemed like an insult too far. He wrote in his now scrawling hand.

Whatever bones Patrick had in his body, the one labelled *Don't forgive* had gone missing.

Mrs Gaskell arrived with her daughter Meta. Martha showed the women into the dining-room and asked them to wait. When would Patrick appear? He wouldn't. The women climbed the stairs and entered the elderly cleric's bedroom to greet the bedridden curate.

There he was, sitting pretty, bespectacled, ancient and wrinkly and yet, all smiles. The ladies sat for a chat. Patrick was amazingly alert, and the pleasantries proceeded before the conversation turned to "that book".

'There is only one thing to which I object,' he said.

The mood darkened and both women believed he would raise the issue of Branwell and Mrs Robinson. He didn't.

'I am concerned, Mrs Gaskell, about the statement you made regarding my children being denied meat. The fact that it's not true is important, but more so because Mr Carus Wilson and his family have claimed it was the reason my daughters fell ill and died.'

Mrs Gaskell remained silent. Her daughter looked at her.

'Mama, you said the nurse told you the children were vegetarian.'

'She may have done,' replied the unhappy novelist. Patrick continued.

'My children regularly ate meat, Mrs Gaskell, but I decided not to complain because I didn't want to help people who wished to denigrate your outstanding biography.'

Whack! Take that, madam. Patrick copied his son-in-law's tactic of fighting ignorance and wrongdoing with kindness and respect.

Some might call it a back-handed compliment, whereas others may see it as typical of Patrick's humility. He was, certainly in this case, able to forgive those who trespassed against him.

Mrs Gaskell couldn't wait to get out of the parsonage and Haworth.

'We've taken up too much of your time, sir,' she said.

'Thank you again for your kind visit,' said Patrick. 'And it might be a propitious moment as Mr Nicholls is due back directly.'

Enough said, and the Gaskells departed. They endured an unpleasant trip to the Keighley station.

'Oh Mama,' said Meta. 'How could you write such things about Mr Brontë? He is a kind, wise and forgiving gentleman. He even forgives you for all that nonsense you wrote about him.'

Mrs Gaskell looked at her daughter and, for once, was lost for words.

Another winter came and went and still the old codger survived. His 84th birthday came and went and still he survived. But Patrick would not see another St Patrick's Day. He was bedridden and fading slowly, although his brain remained in excellent condition.

He died in the summer on a sunny Saturday on June 7, 1861, in his 85th year. Early that morning he suffered convulsions and fell into a coma. Arthur and Martha sat with him until the end. He died peacefully in the early afternoon, in his bed, in his parsonage, in his Yorkshire.

Patrick wanted a simple funeral and his wish was granted. The day of the funeral proved remarkable. The county, country and world went about their business, but Haworth stopped. Every shop shut. Clergymen became pallbearers. Clerics came from Keighley, Skipton, Bradford, Oxenhope, Cullingworth, Newsholme, Oakworth and Morton.

People travelled miles. The packed church left hundreds standing outside. Many openly wept. The short and solemn service had no singing or sermons. It was basic and traditional. The graveyard had long closed, but they opened the crypt yet again, and Patrick was finally reunited with his family. His patient wife had been waiting almost four decades.

He served the people of Haworth for more than forty years. He served them well. To those who didn't know him, he was the eccentric ogre who mistreated his children. To those who did know him, he was the curate who loved and inspired children, including and especially his own, suffered unbelievable grief, and did all he could and more for the people he served. He and Job were due a good yarn.

The spirit of Yorkshire lived on after Patrick's death. A new perpetual curate was required and, unsurprisingly, Arthur applied for the post. But his sixteen years as assistant curate counted for nowt as the trustees, to demonstrate again their contrary nature and proud independence, appointed an outsider. It must have been those sheets in the cemetery.

The no-longer-required Arthur gathered the Brontë memorabilia and his dog, left Haworth, the priesthood, the county and country. He returned to Ireland, re-married and became a gentleman farmer dying in 1906. The final Brontë connection with Haworth was no more.

*****

Saucy Pat

THE NOVEL *Cassocked Savage* is based on the play *Saucy Pat,* by Cenarth Fox, a one-person drama in which a modern-day Anglican vicar describes a biography he (or she) has written. The book is the life of the father of the famous Brontë novelists. Towards the end of the play, the vicar receives an invitation to deliver the inaugural Patrick Brontë lecture. The occasion is the 500th anniversary of Cambridge University, Patrick's alma mater. The play's setting switches to St John's College, Cambridge, and the vicar approaches the lectern.

VICAR

Master, Fellows, students and friends, as part of your 500th anniversary celebrations, I am delighted to deliver the inaugural Patrick Brontë Oration.
What a privilege to stand in St John's College, Cambridge where once the young Irishman stood and speak of his great but unknown achievements.
I have entitled my speech, *Mrs. Gaskell Goofed.*
Elizabeth Gaskell is highly regarded as a writer and she it was who gave us the term that something unique to Charles Dickens was 'Dickensy'.
But today I will not discuss her novels or Dickensy donation, but rather her Brontë biography, and while I applaud Mrs. Gaskell for her insights into the Brontës, I challenge her comments about the family patriarch.
I believe the biographer:

- used falsehoods and selective research, and
- ignored the clergyman's finer points

The falsehoods are easily exposed. To claim the children were not allowed meat is nonsense. The parsonage was overrun with dogs, the children clearly described their carnivorous diet, and staff spoke often of regular meat dishes.

Was Patrick aloof? The fact at times he ate alone is well known, but why? Mrs. Gaskell should have known of Patrick's lifelong digestive problems beginning with his childhood diet of buttermilk and potatoes. His absence from meals may simply have shown his wish not to offend fellow diners.

In addition, at meal times, his young children often spoke about their deceased mother, and these conversations tugged at Patrick's heartstrings.

Then we consider her selective research.
When Mrs. Brontë was dying, Patrick employed a local woman to care for his wife. With death close, he dismissed the carer not wanting a stranger involved in so private a matter. The sacked carer clearly bore a grudge.
But what of the women who worked for Patrick for years? Nancy Garrs lived with the Brontës at Thornton *and* Haworth and described Patrick as 'the kindest man who ever drew breath'. Mrs. Gaskell rejected positive comments from staff who knew Patrick well, yet repeated unproven tittle-tattle by a part-time, disgruntled employee. Selective research.
Did Mrs. Gaskell verify her claims? Her prejudice was alive and well, and the impact of her description of Patrick prompted reviewers to state that Patrick was a 'cassocked savage' and 'a dog who should be shot'. Did her Unitarian beliefs include incitement to murder?

Finally Mrs. Gaskell says little positive about the Cambridge graduate; nothing about the heroic Patrick Brontë who rescued a boy drowning in the River Calder.
Nothing about Detective Brontë who uncovered evidence to set free a young man wrongly imprisoned for desertion.
Nothing about reformer Brontë, who improved the deadly Haworth water supply, started a new school and helped reduce poverty, unemployment and disease.
We search her book for truth and balance. We search in vain. He was a good man, Mrs. Gaskell, a good man done wrong. The truth, if you please, madam, the whole truth.

(The setting returns to its original location and *Saucy Pat* reaches its conclusion. The vicar sums up his feelings towards the Irish curate)

VICAR

Patrick Brontë remained at Haworth and died in his 85th year. On the day of his funeral, all the Haworth shops were shut and the church filled to overflowing.

I've enjoyed researching and writing about Patrick. I'm proud to talk about a humble clergyman who served so many, so well for so long.

I'm proud of his unshakeable faith despite constant, heart-breaking grief.
I'm inspired by his passion for education and his campaigns to eradicate poverty and disease.
I'm inspired by his boundless love for his family.

And what a family. From Patrick and Maria came children who gave ... who *give* us joy, knowledge and inspiration.
Patrick was unusual, eccentric and strong-willed. He was a doer, a quiet achiever with a legacy to enrich us all.
I salute you, Paddy Brunty. I thank you Patrick Brontë. And while Mrs. Gaskell believed you should never have had children, I say, "Thank God you did!"

Cenarth Fox in *Saucy Pat*

The script of *Saucy Pat* can be read at <u>www.foxplays.com</u> under Plays then Two-act plays

The novels of Cenarth Fox are listed at <u>www.cenfoxbooks.com</u>